LADY, BEHAVE!

By the Same Author

LADY, BEHAVE!

A NOVEL

by

PETER CHEYNEY

THE BOOK CLUB
121, CHARING CROSS ROAD
LONDON, W.C.2.

100713974

CHEY

COPYRIGHT
PRINTED IN GREAT BRITAIN
FOR COLLINS CLEAR-TYPE PRESS: LONDON AND GLASGOW
BY WILLMER BROS. AND CO. LTD , CHESTER STREET, BIRKENHEAD
1950

TO
WINARETTA, SUSAN
AND
DAVID

CONTENTS

CHAPTER ONE

SIERRA MADRE

FIFTY YARDS from the spot where the by-pass curved into the main Winchester road, Vallon braked the Jaguar to a standstill on the grass verge. He lighted a cigarette and sat, resting his arms on the wheel, looking through the wind-screen.

He was tired and lazy and bored. Bored or worried. He was not quite certain which. Somewhere in the vicinity someone was burning dry leaves, and the acrid, not unattractive smell came through the open windows of the car.

The smell reminded him of something. Maybe, he thought, at some other time, in some other place where dry leaves were being burned, he had been tired or worried about something else.

He was not quite certain what he wanted to think about. Whether to think about Madeleine and make up his mind just what he wanted to do about her attitude, or whether to think about Allard—an interesting if not a particularly attractive subject.

Women, Vallon decided, could be hell. Not for any other reason but that they were never satisfied with anything. If they failed to understand a situation they seldom brought any logical processes to bear on the problem. They preferred to use the thing they called instinct. After which anything could happen—any goddam thing—and it usually did! He thought that on occasion it must be tough to be a woman and depend on instinct.

Vallon reflected that the easiest thing for him to do would be to return to London ; take a cold shower, telephone Madeleine and tell her not to be silly, too imaginative, too suspicious. That would be the easiest thing. Then she could put on a pretty frock and dine with him somewhere and he could talk her out of her present frame of mind. . . .

He could do that. Or he could go on to the Sierra Madre and find out what the Allard business was all about.

He threw the cigarette stub out of the window ; took her letter from his jacket pocket ; read it.

" *Dear Johnny,*

" *There are moments, my sweet, when I am inclined to wonder, just a little tiny bit, about you and me. Please don't think that I am filled with doubts about you, because I believe, in your own peculiar way, you are as faithful to me as you know how to be. But recently the idea has forced itself on me that you are going off on one of your peculiar angles—mainly because I haven't seen very much of you lately and because when I have seen you I've had a weird impression that you are keeping something from me.*

" *I often wish that you hadn't decided to continue running Chennault Investigations after Joe Chennault died. I know you've made a success of the business, but it is a weird business, isn't it? I suppose that's what makes it so attractive to you.*

" *It isn't another woman, is it, Johnny? That can happen, you know. Especially to a man like you who is very attractive to women—even if, like you, he doesn't know it or care a lot about being like that. Probably it's because you are like that and don't care that they are attracted.*

" *However, my instinct tells me that I ought to do something about things. Especially when I remember that you once told me that if one was in doubt the thing to do was to do something definite about it. So I'm doing it, Johnny. I'm telling you that I'm not going to marry you next month as we'd arranged. I'm going to give you more time to think—so that you are quite certain of yourself and me.*

" *I'm going for a holiday—to France—for two or three months. Then I'll return to England and get in touch with you. In the meantime I won't telephone you or write you or worry you at all. This will enable you to make up your mind; to discover for yourself if you feel the same way about me as you did six months ago. In any event it won't do either of us any harm and it might do a lot of good. . . .*

" *Be nice and think a lot about me.*

" *Madeleine.*"

Vallon shrugged his shoulders. He tore up the letter; threw the pieces out of the window. He thought Madeleine was unhappily revelling in one of those instinctive pipe-dreams in which charming and beautiful and romantic women—such as she was—liked to indulge. Just to start things moving.

10

He got out of the car ; began to walk slowly up and down the grass verge. He was thinking that the easiest thing to do would be to go back and talk Madeleine out of her frame of mind. That would be the easiest thing to do. Or would it . . .?

Vallon was just under six feet ; slender. Most of the time his triangular-shaped face was in repose. He seldom showed what he thought or felt. But sometimes the light in his sombre eyes changed and he looked sardonic and mischievously humorous.

He seemed to be a quiet man. He moved slowly ; talked softly ; endeavoured to side-step trouble with women. The process was too often difficult. Women liked him and even if he tried to avoid them he had always experienced a certain difficulty in evading feminine "situations."

He got back into the car ; started up the engine ; drove slowly off the by-pass on to the main road.

He began to think about Allard—a very slick person. Vallon wondered what the hell he was playing at. The idea of Allard being in any sort of spot that he couldn't get out of, one way or another, was amusing. Vallon thought that Allard was damned tough and very clever. Certainly not the sort of person who would go about squealing if he got himself in a jam. He shrugged his shoulders.

A short distance ahead Vallon could see where the road forked—the main road curving off to the left ; the right-hand fork rising and disappearing over a hill. In the apex of the fork was a little wood—a thick clump of trees standing in long grass and bracken. A romantic-looking spot. Somewhere in the vicinity was the Sierra Madre. He looked for a directional sign on the roadside indicating its whereabouts.

There was a man standing on the edge of the apex between the two roads. He was waving his hands in the air, looking over his shoulder. Vallon grinned. Some country swain waving good-bye to his girl friend, he thought.

He swung the car on to the left fork ; slowed down as he saw the notice : " *Sierra Madre Café. One hundred yards.*" He came to the side road—little more than a gravel path, wide enough for two cars to pass, which had been cut into the wood. A clearing had been made and the café, a poor imitation of a one-storied Spanish *estancia*, stood in the clearing. On the other side of the café Vallon could see the path leading to the right fork road. Not a bad idea to have such a place at the apex of the two roads; cars had access from both of them.

He swung in ; stopped the car in the courtyard in front of the Sierra Madre ; pushed open the door ; went in. The place consisted of one large room, dotted with tables set with check-coloured cloths and bowls of flowers. It was not unattractive. On the right were the kitchen and service doors ; on the left doors leading elsewhere.

There was nobody in the place. It had a peculiar, lonely, almost deserted atmosphere. Vallon sat down at a table. After a moment one of the service doors opened and a girl came in. She came over to Vallon and stood at his side, a menu in her hand.

He said : " I'd like a cup of coffee, please."

She nodded ; went away.

He sat there, smoking, still wondering about Allard. The girl came back with the coffee. She put it on the table.

Vallon said : " I've an appointment with a Mr. Allard." He looked at his strap-watch. " I see I'm a little late. I suppose he hasn't left a message for me?"

She shook her head. " Nobody's been in for the last half-hour. We don't do a lot of business in the evening, you know. We close in an hour's time."

She went back through the service door.

He began to think about Madeleine. He thought it might be a good thing if she went away for a little while, not for any other reason but because he felt he would like to get the Allard business—whatever it was—finished before he was married. Madeleine was a wonderful girl but there were some things that women wouldn't understand. The Allard thing *might* be one of them. He realised suddenly that he felt tired.

He began to sip the coffee.

The door opened and a man came in. He was sweating. He walked to the service door at the end, knocked on it, opened it and went in. Vallon heard him say :

"There's been a hell of a smash on the Mulbury road—one hell of a smash. A truck's hit a car ; knocked it right over. Can I use the telephone ? "

Vallon finished his cigarette. Then he got up ; went into the courtyard ; turned left ; walked along the gravel path. In a minute he was on the Mulbury road—the road forming the right-hand side of the fork. He began to walk up the hill.

He thought it must have been a hell of a smash. A heavy truck was standing across the road. Both the front wings of the truck were badly smashed, the radiator battered inwards. Over on the left-hand side of the road, capsized in a ditch, was an open touring car. The near-side door was smashed inwards on to the driving seat; the wind-shield was shattered. Almost opposite the rear end of the truck was a small side road ; little more than a path.

The cause of the smash was obvious. The touring car had been driving towards the fork and the truck had run straight out of the side road and hit it amidships with such force that the tourer had cannoned across the road into the ditch. A stupid accident, Vallon thought.

A motor-cycle policeman was sitting sideways on the saddle of his machine writing in his notebook.

Vallon said to the policeman : "Good evening. Not a very nice business."

The policeman said: "No... not the usual sort of accident this."

" Why not ? " asked Vallon.

" Well, the truck comes out of the side road and hits the car. The man who was driving it is in a proper mess. But you'd think the truck driver would have stopped, wouldn't you ? He wasn't even here when I arrived."

Vallon said : " Perhaps he didn't like it. Perhaps he was feeling a little nervous. What's happened to the driver of the car ? "

" We got him away," said the police officer. " I stopped another car. It would have been some time before an ambulance could get here. I did what I could for him. But he was in a mess."

Vallon asked : " Did anybody see it—the smash I mean ? "

The policeman shook his head.

" Would you mind if I took a look at the car ? " said Vallon. " I was expecting a friend." He jerked his head towards the car. " That might have been him."

" That's all right, sir. But don't touch anything. What was his name ? "

"His name was Allard," said Vallon.

"That was him. He had a card case in his pocket. His identity card was in it. You'll find him at the Dudleigh Hospital. That's about six miles from here."

Vallon said : " Thanks." He walked over to the wrecked car ; looked at the gear lever. It was in top gear. There was nothing in the car except bloodstains. He thought it was a little tough that this should happen to Allard just at this time.

He said good night to the police officer ; walked back to the Sierra Madre. When he went in the waitress was standing by his table.

She asked : " Was it a bad smash, sir ? "

Vallon nodded. " I should think so by the look of the car. I'd like some fresh coffee."

She picked up the half-finished cup ; went away.

In the opposite corner, against the wall, were two people. One was a man—tall, broad-shouldered. He was wearing rough country clothes. He looked like the sort of person who might be a regular customer at the Sierra Madre. But not the girl. Vallon thought she was something. He could not see her face but her figure was superb. Her clothes were well-cut, fashionable. He thought they were an incongruous pair.

The waitress brought his coffee. Vallon drank it slowly. He put half a crown on the table ; got up ; went out. He drove along the gravel path towards the main road. He thought: So that was that ! Allard wouldn't feel like talking at the moment.

He swung the car left. He began to drive towards London. He thought perhaps he would go and see Madeleine, that is if she had not already left. Then he metaphorically shrugged his shoulders. It really wasn't any good arguing with women— not if they had a bee in their bonnet, and it was obvious that she had one about him. He grinned. Perhaps she was justified. There had been a lot of women in his life, and how was she to know that as individuals they no longer interested him—at least he *thought* they didn't.

Out of the blue an idea came to Vallon. He pulled the car into the side of the road ; sat there, leaning over the wheel, smoking. He thought it was a funny idea—one of those things! But you never knew.

He turned the car ; drove back to the Sierra Madre. Although it was still early evening the tall trees that surrounded the clearing threw dark shadows—a peculiar effect of light which was almost eerie.

He pushed open the door and went in. As he did so the waitress came out of the service-room. She had on a light coat

14

and a summery hat. He thought she was quite a good-looking girl.

She said : " We're closed now, sir. I'm just going home."

" That's all right," said Vallon. " I don't want anything. I just wanted to ask you one or two questions. I wonder would you mind answering them ? "

She looked at him. She thought there was something very attractive about the shape of his long face with the quiet, deep-set, blue eyes.

She asked defensively : " What is it you want to know ? "

Vallon said : " You remember when I came in here this evening there was no one here ? I sat down at a table and ordered some coffee, didn't I ? "

She nodded.

He went on : " Then a man came in and said there'd been an accident down the road, so after a while I went down to have a look at it. Then I came back and had some more coffee. Remember ? "

" Yes, I remember." She wondered what he was getting at.

"When I came back," said Vallon, "there were two people sitting at that table in the corner over there—a man and a young and very well-dressed woman with him."

" That's right. They both had coffee."

Vallon said : " Tell me something. Did you know either of them ? And did they come in together ? "

" I know the man," she answered. " He's got a farm not far from here. He often comes in in the evening."

Vallon asked : " And the woman ? "

" She came in by herself. She looked round the room and saw that Mr. Brownlow—that's the farmer—was the only person here ; then she sat down at a table and ordered some coffee. When I brought it she asked me if there'd been anyone else in during the evening. I thought maybe she'd an appointment with someone and he'd stood her up. Then I went back to the service-room. When I brought you that second cup of coffee I noticed she'd gone over ; that she was sitting with Mr. Brownlow. I thought perhaps she hadn't seen who it was when she first came in."

Vallon said : " Thanks a lot." He took a pound note from his waistcoat pocket. " Have a little drink with me some time. Good night."

He went out of the room ; got back into his car. She stood in the centre of the floor holding the pound note in her fingers. She wondered what it was all about.

.　　　.　　　.　　　.　　　.　　　.　　　.

At half-past ten Vallon parked the car in Lower Regent Street ; began to walk slowly towards the offices of Chennault Investigations. He took the lift to the first floor ; walked down the corridor, past the lighted night staff-room to his own room.

He decided to telephone Madeleine. She was obviously disturbed and worried about him. He smiled. Women in love were never completely happy unless they worried occasionally. Just in case they forgot what it felt like. He sat down at his desk ; called through to the night telephone operator ; asked for the number.

When the call came through Vallon asked to be put through to Miss Thorne's apartment. After a moment the girl at the other end said : " I'm sorry, Mr. Vallon, but Miss Thorne's out. She's leaving to-night for France, but she'll return here first. She'll be here in half an hour. She said I was to give you that message if you called."

He said thanks and hung up. He lighted a cigarette and sat, slumped back in his big office chair.

He thought Madeleine was probably right. Being a private detective was a weird business, when you came to think about it—or even if you didn't. But it *was* an attractive busi- ness—if you liked that sort of business.

He picked up the telephone ; spoke to the night operator.

" Look up the number of the Allard Detective Agency and ring them. I want to talk to anyone who's there, if there *is* anyone there at this time of night."

The girl said : " Very good, Mr. Vallon."

Vallon hung up the receiver ; put his feet on the desk. A minute later the telephone rang. He picked it up.

A voice said : " Hullo . . . this is the Allard Agency."

Vallon asked: "Are you expecting Mr. Allard back to-night?"

" No, I'm not. He's not coming back. He's had a car smash. He's in hospital in the country somewhere."

" This is Chennault Investigations—John Vallon speaking. Do you know how badly Mr. Allard's injured ? Who is that ? "

The voice said : " This is Allard's partner—Inskip. And I don't know about Allard. They're not through with the examination. He's not conscious yet. It looks as if he's smashed up pretty bad. They told me to ring to-morrow morning."

Vallon said : " All right. I'm coming round to see you. It's urgent and important. I'll be round in ten minutes."

" I'll wait for you," said Inskip.

Vallon went out of his office. He locked the door ; put his head in the night-room ; said good night to the operative on duty ; went downstairs.

He wandered across the street thinking about Inskip. He wondered what sort of a person Inskip would be. He thought he could guess. There was not a great deal of doubt about the type of partner that Allard would have. Unless of course the partner was merely a stooge—a "front" to be used in some of the more peculiar operations in which Allard was known to indulge.

He parked the car near the St. Martin's Lane end of Long Acre ; walked slowly down the street until he came to the dilapidated door that bore a plate announcing that the Allard Detective Agency was situated on the second floor. Vallon went up the dusty wooden stairs, that smelt vaguely of tired fruit, along the second-floor dimly-lit corridor. At the end was a frosted glass door with " *Allard Detective Agency* " painted on it. The place looked like one of those places. The sort of dump that you would expect Allard to operate from— cheap and nasty.

Vallon grinned. He shrugged his shoulders. If you wanted a private detective you wanted one. You paid your money and you took your choice. And the choice you made depended on what your business was . . . if it was *your* business.

He pushed open the door ; went in. The outer office in which he found himself smelt even more offensively than the stairway. The single window was dirty. There were a couple of old filing cabinets against one wall and a typist's table with a typewriter with an old oilcloth cover in the centre of the room. In the left wall was another door—the door to the private office.

Vallon walked across the room ; pushed open the door ; went in. He stood just inside the doorway, looking at the man seated behind the desk facing him.

17

He said : " You're Inskip, aren't you ? "

The man nodded. " That's me—Arthur Inskip—very much at your service." He grinned cynically. " Take a chair, Mr. Vallon," he went on ; " but I'd dust it first if I was you."

Vallon said : " I'll stand up. I came up here because I thought you might like to answer a few questions. And I might as well tell you that if Allard was here I think he'd like you to answer them."

Inskip nodded. He fumbled in his pocket ; produced a packet of Player's cigarettes ; lighted one. Vallon noticed that his hand was trembling.

Inskip, he thought, might be an interesting type—or not. Just as easily *not*. He was short, broad-shouldered, paunchy. Heavy jowls hung over his too-tight, soft, creased and soiled collar. His hands were pudgy and restless and the fingernails were grimy. His thinning hair was plastered down across his head with a thick pomade which gave off a perfume strong enough to assail—even at that distance—Vallon's nostrils.

But there were humour lines at the ends of his lips and about his eyes. Inskip might have a sense of humour. Vallon thought that a sense of humour would probably be necessary with a partner like Allard.

Vallon said : " Did you know that I'd gone down to the country to-night to see Allard? Did you know that we had an appointment at a place called the Sierra Madre—a café near the Winchester by-pass ? "

The man shook his head. " Allard does a hell of a lot of things he never tells me about. He's clever, you know. He never lets his left hand know what his right hand's doing."

" Maybe," said Vallon. " You probably know there was a little trouble between Chennault Investigations and this Agency three or four months ago ? "

Inskip said : " I knew something about it, but I didn't know exactly what it was."

" If you're curious," said Vallon, " I'll tell you. This Agency was doing some work on a commercial investigation. Because he'd been on it at the time about three or four months Allard had charged some pretty high fees and a hell of an expense account."

Inskip said: " The dirty So-and-so. He told me he got out of that job because it wasn't paying off enough."

"He was lying," said Vallon. "He got out of the job because the firm he was working for weren't very pleased with his methods. They asked Chennault Investigations to keep an eye on him and see what he was doing." He grinned. "He was doing practically everything. What he wasn't doing you could have stuck under a postage stamp and never even missed. He was bribing and taking bribes. He was giving himself a good time. The firm didn't want any publicity so they asked me to see him and tell him where he got off. In other words they employed me to kick him out."

Inskip nodded. "That could happen."

Vallon said: "It *did* happen. So Allard can't like me very much."

The other man grinned. "It looks as if he wouldn't have cause to like you. But then Allard never liked anybody much, especially you."

Vallon asked: "Why?"

Inskip shrugged his shoulders. "You know how it is in a business like this. Things aren't so good. We've been suffering from a sort of depression. Most of the work we get these days isn't so good either—divorce investigations, most of them collusive. We get along as best as we can. Allard often talks about you and Chennault Investigations. He wouldn't like you because I believe you run your business straight. He never liked anybody who was straight."

Vallon grinned. "Does he like you?"

Inskip grinned back. "I don't think he does—not *too* much."

Vallon went on: "You can imagine that I was surprised when Allard sent me a personal note three days ago. He said he wanted to see me on very important business—a matter in which he was certain I'd be very interested. He said he thought it would be a good thing if we met somewhere where we couldn't possibly be seen by anybody who knew either of us. He suggested a meeting at this café—the Sierra Madre. He said he'd be coming back from somewhere in that part of the world and it would be a good place to meet."

"And so you didn't meet?" said Inskip. "He had to have a car smash instead?"

Vallon said: "That's the point. When I was driving to this place—the café stands in a clearing in a wood in a triangle

19

formed by the fork of two roads ; there's the main road curving off to the left, and the right fork running uphill—I came in sight of the apex of the fork just about the time that Allard would be due to arrive there. There was a man standing by the side of the road. He was waving his arm. From where I was," Vallon went on, " I thought he was waving good night to a girl or something like that. But he wasn't. He was waving Allard on. He was telling him the cross-roads at the fork, which Allard couldn't see, were all clear. He was doing that so that Allard, approaching the fork, wouldn't put his car into low gear and slow down to a few miles an hour as he normally would have done because of the danger of approaching traffic."

Inskip said uneasily : " What the hell's the idea ? What are you trying to say ?"

" There was a truck pulled up in a side road near the apex of the fork, about a hundred yards from the cross-roads. As Allard went sailing by, the truck drove out and hit him hard. It cannoned the car into the ditch—a terrific crash. The driver of the truck then disappeared. No one's seen him. When the motor-cycle cop arrived the truck was standing there empty."

Inskip whistled. " Not so good. . . ."

Vallon said : " It looks as if somebody knew that he was going to meet me at the Sierra Madre to-night to talk to me about this important business whatever it was, and somebody had made up their mind that he wasn't going to talk, so they laid it on for him. An accident can happen to anybody, and lots of drivers of stolen trucks disappear after they get involved in an accident, don't they ? "

Inskip said : " I wonder what the hell he wanted to see you about ?"

" So do I. But he was pretty scared about something because—work it out for yourself—Allard didn't like me." Vallon smiled reminiscently. " I'll go further and say that he disliked me very much indeed. If he wanted assistance from me about something or other it had to be something that was pretty tough—something that scared him—because you know he was no push-over. He didn't frighten easily."

Inskip nodded. " You're telling me ! . . ."

Vallon said : " You wouldn't know a very good-looking girl of about twenty-one or two, would you ? Dark-brown hair, a very white, oval face with deep-set eyes. Very good legs and ankles. And she knows all about clothes. You wouldn't remember anybody who looked like that, would you ? "

The other shook his head. " It rings no bell with me."

Vallon said : " Fine. If I ring you up some time to-morrow afternoon and ask you where Allard is and how he is, do you think you'll know ? "

" I'll make a point of finding out," said Inskip. " Come through and I'll let you know. I suppose you'll go down and see him ? "

Vallon shrugged his shoulders. " Who knows ? I might. Good night to you."

He went out of the office.

Allard's junior partner heard the outer door close. He scratched his head; shrugged his shoulders. He thought sometimes life was damned funny. He reached out for the telephone.

* * * * *

It was nearly half-past eleven when Vallon got back to his office.

He began to walk about the room, smoking, thinking about Inskip. It would be like Allard to have a stooge for a partner and keep him in the dark about what was going on. To collect on expense accounts and profits on the good cases and say nothing, and hand the dud work to his partner.

Or would it ? It might be pretty difficult—even for someone as smart as Allard—to run a business and succeed in keeping his partner in the dark about everything that mattered. Vallon shrugged his shoulders.

Then he remembered Madeleine. He picked up the telephone; told the switch-board girl to call Miss Thorne. When the call came through the girl at the other end said : " I'm sorry, Mr. Vallon, Miss Thorne's been back and gone. She didn't leave any address. I told her you'd telephoned through ; that you'd said you'd call again. She waited for a quarter of an hour and then left."

Vallon said thanks and hung up. He thought it was tough about Madeleine. He thought he ought to have remembered to telephone earlier. He thought women could be hell when they became mixed up with business.

He rang through to the switch-board ; told the operator to put him through to the night staff-room.

When Harding—the night man—answered, Vallon said:

" Go down to the record room and get me anything we've got on the Allard Agency, or the proprietor Vine Allard. One time he was a bankrupt. His partner's a man called Arthur Inskip. You'd better check on him, too. Let me know what you dig out in the morning."

Then he put his feet up on the desk and thought about Madeleine. He thought she was a hell of a girl. He thought she was right when she said as she often had said—half-playfully—that he was a heel. Well, what the hell . . . everybody was a heel sometimes. The trouble with him was that he was inclined to become too interested in things—things that did not seem to interest other people. . . .

He wondered where she was going for a holiday.

CHAPTER TWO

VALASEY BAY

THE NIGHT-DUTY girl on the switch-board at Chennault Investigations said to her day colleague when she handed over the switch-board : " I wonder how he's going to take it. When he came in last night he telephoned through to Miss Thorne at her apartment. The girl on the switch-board there said she'd gone out but she was coming back before she went away. He said he'd ring later, but when he did ring—and it was pretty late, too, I'm telling you—she'd gone."

The other girl said : " What does that mean ? Is it all off ? Is she giving him the air or is he ducking ? "

The night girl shook her head. " You know how he is . . . casual . . . ! You know what he's like when he's got something on his mind—some case or other." She sighed. "I think he's terrific."

The day girl put her head on one side. " Ye-es," she agreed. " But I go more for the Clark Gable type."

The night girl said : " Johnny Vallon's got something. Ever taken a look at those eyes of his ? They sort of look through you. Suddenly they light up and you find they're laughing at you. Look at the way he walks ; the way he wears his clothes. What a personality ! " She sighed heavily. She got up ; took off her headphones ; handed them over. She went on : " Me—I'm tired. One thing about this night work . . . you've got a lot of time to think."

The day girl sat down at the switch-board. She grinned at her friend. " It looks to me as if you found plenty of time to think last night. I believe you're another Johnny Vallon fan."

The night girl took her coat and hat from the locker. "Why not—even if I am at the end of a queue ? So long, Tutz ! "

She went out.

.   .   .   .

Vallon came in at eleven o'clock. He went into his own office through the door leading from the corridor. Then he rang through to the switch-board and said he wanted to see Marvin—the manager of the office.

23

Marvin came in. He was a short, spare man with a lined face and grey hair.

He said : " Good morning, Mr. Vallon."

Vallon asked : " What did Harding dig up on the Allard Agency ? "

" Nothing that matters. You know that Allard was made bankrupt about two years ago. He was discharged last year. While he was bankrupt Inskip, his partner, was the official head of the agency. Their business is pretty bad, you know. They handle all sorts of peculiar things that nobody else would touch."

Vallon nodded. " I know. Is there anything on Inskip ? "

Marvin shrugged his shoulders. " Not a thing. We can't even find out where Allard found him." He went on : " You know, Mr. Vallon, this isn't information ; it's just a few ideas of my own. If you'd care to hear——"

Vallon grinned. " Ideas are very good sometimes, Marvin. Get them off your chest."

Marvin said : " I met Allard over a job in the old days when Mr. Chennault was running the firm—before your time here. Just one of those commercial cases, and I can't quite remember how Allard came into it, but he only played a very unimportant part. I talked to him once. He was a rather extraordinary man, Mr. Vallon. He seemed clever and intelligent ; had a forceful sort of personality.

"I believe in those days the type of work he was handling was much better than it is now. I'm surprised that he's come down in the world and that he's running an agency with a reputation like the Allard Agency's got for itself."

Vallon said: "What are you trying to say, hey? That you think Allard's a better type than most people imagine him to be ? "

" Something like that," said Marvin. " You remember when we had this trouble with him over that commercial agency business three or four months ago ; when I was making inquiries on that case for you, I had a talk with Allard just before you told him that he'd finished for the firm he was working for. He didn't seem to care about anything very much. I thought that was funny."

Vallon said : " You mean he didn't mind getting a bad reputation ; even knowing that his firm was going to lose a lot of business by getting that reputation. You mean that you think Allard had something up his sleeve—something that was good ; that he wasn't worrying about what his agency did or what reputation it got."

" That's what I wanted to say, Mr. Vallon. You found the words for me."

Vallon said : " Maybe he was on something good. But I don't think he's on a very good wicket at the moment." He went on : " You didn't know about it because I didn't tell you, but Allard made an appointment to meet me last night out in the country. He never arrived. He got involved in a car smash and is in hospital at Dudleigh. I've an idea he wanted to ask my assistance about something."

Marvin said : " That's a little strange, isn't it ? "

Vallon nodded. " I think so. And I don't think the accident was an accident either. He was run into by a truck while he was driving at high speed. The truck driver disappeared. He just got out of the truck and cleared off. He was well away before the country policeman arrived. The number of the truck was *PXY* 76421. Check who the truck belongs to ; find out what it was doing out yesterday. See if you can find out the name of the driver. You can put one of the men on that."

" Anything else ? " asked Marvin.

" Yes. The police officer said that Allard was pretty well smashed up—so badly they didn't even wait for the ambulance. The policeman rendered first aid ; did what he could for him. They put him in a passing car to get him to the hospital as quickly as they could. He might die. If he does I want you to send a man there somehow. I don't know or care how he does it, but he's got to get at Allard's clothes. They'll probably be in the hospital store. He must go through them ; go through his pocket-case—he had one because the policeman found his identity card in it ; read anything that's in his case—any letters he had. It might be difficult but "—he smiled—"there are ways and means, you know, Marvin."

Marvin said : " Very well, Mr. Vallon. I'll send one of our best men."

He went out. Vallon looked through the mail ; took out a fat foolscap envelope. Printed on the outside of the envelope was " *Dyce, Grant & Dyce, Solicitors, Valasey Bay. Urgent. By hand.*"

Vallon slit the envelope ; took out the pages of closely typed notepaper. He read :

"*Dear Sir,*

"*We have to inform you that our client Mr. Augustus Jones Clavering of Valasey Bay, Dorsetshire, who has recently died, was at the time of his death interested in tracing the whereabouts of his stepdaughter—a young lady of 21 or 22 years of age, who was the daughter of Mrs. Paula Clavering by a previous marriage, and who was taken away from her mother at a very early age and has since been lost sight of.*

"*Our client, soon after his marriage, when he was very desirous of his stepdaughter being traced, more especially as he knew how very much his wife desired her to be found, had decided to employ a firm of investigators to endeavour to find the missing young lady. And in the course of our conversations the name of your agency, Chennault Investigations, came before Mr. Clavering and me. However, we did not then utilise your services because another firm was suggested to our client and the investigation was handed over to them.*

"*However, the writer was advised on the telephone at ten o'clock this evening at his private house that the investigator has met with an accident and that it may be some time before he has sufficiently recovered from his severe injuries to be able to conduct his business.*

"*The name of this investigator is Mr. Vine Allard of the Allard Detective Agency of Long Acre. In the circumstances we feel it is our duty as trustees and executors, more especially as the name of your firm was originally suggested by no less a person than Mr. Clavering, to ask if you will contact the Allard Detective Agency and take over this matter. We have no doubt they will be in a position to supply you with all the information which you require.*

"*We enclose herewith a cheque for £250 to cover your immediate expenses in anticipation of your acceptance, and we have no doubt that further financial terms, mutually satisfactory, will be arranged when we have the pleasure of meeting you.*

"*We shall be grateful if you will inform us whether you are prepared to carry out this work.*

"*John Dyce.*
"*For Dyce, Grant & Dyce.*"

Vallon threw the letter on the desk. He lighted a cigarette; leaned back in his chair smoking, looking at the ceiling. He thought that when all was said and done the world was a very small place. He picked up the telephone; spoke to the girl on the switch-board.

He said: " Send a telegram to Dyce, Grant & Dyce, Valasey Bay, Dorset. ' I have received your letter confirm that Chennault Investigations are handling the matter referred to. Will report personally or in writing in due course. John Vallon.' "

Then he asked the switch-board girl to put him through to the Allard Detective Agency.

After a minute Inskip's voice came on the line.

Vallon said: " Well, have you heard anything about Allard ? "

" Yes, I've heard plenty. They called through half an hour ago. He died early this morning."

" So that's that," said Vallon. " Would you like to come and see me ? "

" Why not ? I can't lose anything by it, can I ? "

" Not very much," said Vallon. " You might even make something out of it."

Inskip said: " I'll come right away."

"All right," said Vallon. "There's a bar in Jermyn Street. Do you know the place just round the corner out of Regent Street ? "

" I know it. I know every bar in London."

Vallon said: " Very well. I'll meet you there in a quarter of an hour."

He rang the bell. When his secretary came in he said: " You can open the rest of the mail. Sort it out; deal with the things you can deal with, and I'll fix the rest later. I'll be back in an hour."

Walking slowly up Regent Street, Vallon concentrated his mind on Allard. For some unknown reason he found himself very interested in Allard. He wondered why. Maybe, he thought, it was because Allard was an odd character—a mixture of this and that. Vallon, who had always believed that the most important thing in life was motive, wondered exactly what events or happenings had motivated Allard's life during the past six or seven months. The facts at his disposal were few. He summarised them.

Allard, working on the case over which he had first come in contact with Vallon, had in effect defrauded the commercial agency for whom he was working. So Vallon had been put in to kick him out of the job, which he had done. And, however much the process had made Allard dislike him, at the same time Vallon considered that Allard had not seemed fearfully concerned about the business. This rather matched up with what Marvin had said about him ; that it was almost as if he didn't care ; as if he weren't really concerned with what the Allard Agency did or didn't do, or its reputation ; almost as if he had something up his sleeve which was much more important, on which he was prepared to rely much more than on his own business activities.

And his attitude towards his partner Inskip—if you could call him a partner—confirmed this.

Vallon thought it was all very mysterious and intriguing— or was it ? Maybe his guess was wrong and the accident had been just an accident. And maybe it hadn't. *If* it hadn't, there was a woman somewhere ; there had to be, because nothing ever really went wrong unless there was a woman in the vicinity.

He thought that the brown-haired girl who had arrived at the Sierra Madre after he had left it to go to the scene of the accident might easily be the woman. Why not ? She had everything it takes to make trouble. Maybe she had turned up to see Allard, just as Allard had intended to see Vallon, and, possibly having heard of the accident from the waitress, had got into conversation, at *his* table, with the farmer Brownlow, so that she should not attract the attention which a beautiful and well-dressed girl with no companion would receive at a place like the Sierra Madre.

He shrugged his shoulders. It didn't really matter. You followed your nose and began to dig. If you dug deep enough something turned up. And if the something was the brown-haired girl—so much the better.

He turned into the Jermyn Street cocktail bar. Inskip was leaning on the counter at the far end. There was a glass of ginger ale in front of him.

When Vallon looked at him, Inskip grinned ruefully. He said : " No, I don't like it. That's just economy. From now on I shall be living on a shoe string."

"As bad as that, eh?" said Vallon. "Do you like rye whisky?"

Inskip said: "Do I?"

Vallon ordered two large rye whiskies and a jug of water. When the drinks were brought Inskip said: "Don't tell me if you don't want to, but it looks to me as if you were taking a great deal of interest in Allard. Should I know or shouldn't I?"

Vallon shrugged his shoulders. "Why shouldn't you? There's nothing to know. I told you when I first came into contact with Allard. Well, he wanted to see me. He wanted to talk to me and someone stopped him doing it. I'm interested. Wouldn't you be?"

Inskip nodded. "I suppose I should. If I hadn't something more important to think about. But I can understand you being curious."

Vallon asked: "Why?"

Inskip shrugged his shoulders. "Well, everybody thinks you work in a very funny way. Certainly not on the usual lines. You've made a success of it. Chennault Investigations are a damn' sight bigger firm now than they ever were when Joe Chennault ran it. Perhaps that's because of your ' curiosity.' " He grinned at Vallon.

Vallon said: "Maybe. When they rang you through from the hospital this morning what did they tell you?"

"They didn't know Allard's next of kin. I didn't know either. I didn't know very much about him. There's going to be an inquest and they want to find out this or that."

Vallon asked: "Do they want you to go to the inquest?"

Inskip nodded. "I've got to go. I'm the only person who knows anything about him."

There was a silence. Then Vallon said: "What do you propose to do? Do you propose to go down to this inquest and give them that idea I gave you when I saw you yesterday— the idea that somebody deliberately crashed Allard so that he shouldn't meet me at the Sierra Madre? Are you going to tell them that?"

Inskip said: "I don't have to say that. It's your idea. It's not mine. I suppose "—he looked at Vallon sideways—" if I was to do my duty as a good citizen I would tell them. Then maybe the coroner would want to talk to *you* too." He grinned.

"Maybe," said Vallon. "But supposing I hadn't come round

to see you last night and told you what I thought. Supposing you'd merely received the telephone call from the hospital authorities this morning. What would you have had to tell them then ? "

Inskip said : " Nothing, because I didn't know anything. All I know is that I hadn't seen Allard for three days. He didn't tell me where he was going or what he was going to do. All he did was to phone me from somewhere in the country— I don't even know where it was ; he was phoning from a call-box. He said he'd be back in three or four days' time. He asked if anything had turned up in the office. I told him no. He said O.K. ; he'd be seeing me. I believe he was on his way back."

" That's what I think," said Vallon.

There was another pause. Vallon finished the rye whisky ; ordered two more. He asked : " How are you fixed ? "

Inskip grinned wryly. " I'm not fixed. The agency's got a routine job working for a couple of firms of bookmakers—not a very hot job either ; but it is bringing in a few pounds a week and I live on it. But it's not enough to keep the office going. The thing for me to do is to close down."

Vallon said : " And what do you do when you close down ? "

" God knows. I don't. I suppose something will turn up. It usually does."

" It might," said Vallon. " Have you any money ? "

" Yes . . . about one pound seventeen and fourpence, and I'm owing a month's rent at my rooms." He smiled.

Vallon thought it was almost a benign smile. He said : " Do you know what I think ? I think I'm going to give you a fifty-pound note, and I think you're going to keep the Allard Detective Agency running for a while. Don't worry about taking on any new business. Just stick around. When you go down to this inquest forget what I told you about the smash. Forget that you ever saw me last night. Just tell them the same story as you would have done if you hadn't seen me ; that you didn't know where Allard was ; that he was in the country somewhere ; that he had telephoned you and told you he'd be back in three or four days' time. How would you like to do that ? "

" I'd like to do it a lot. Fifty pounds looks good to me."

Vallon said : " You'd better find out if there's any office rent owing. Tell your landlord that you're going to try and carry the business on. If there's any back rent owing get through to Chennault Investigations and tell my office manager, Mr. Marvin. He'll fix it for you." He smiled at Inskip. " There's only one thing," he went on. " Don't try any funny business, will you ? "

Inskip shuffled a little uneasily on his feet. He picked up his glass ; drank some rye whisky ; put the glass back on the bar. He looked at Vallon.

He said : " Look, I've heard about you. You don't think I'm mug enough to try something with *you*, do you ? "

Vallon said casually : " That's fine. So that's all arranged. If I want to see you I'll get in touch with you on the telephone and we can meet somewhere. I'll send you round the fifty pounds this afternoon. That'll keep you going for a bit. In a week's time we can review the situation."

" I won't let you down, Mr. Vallon," Inskip grinned. " I'm not in a position to let anybody down except myself. But if it's all the same to you, I'd like to know what all this is in aid of." He smiled wryly. " Like you, I get a little curious sometimes."

Vallon said : " Use your common sense. If my guess was right about Allard being deliberately killed, whoever's responsible for this is going to start worrying a little bit in a minute, aren't they ? If my guess is right these people or this person was scared because they thought Allard was going to talk to me. Then you appear at the inquest and you tell your story ; which in effect is practically the truth. You say you don't know what Allard was doing ; that you didn't even know where he was. All you knew about him was that he telephoned you and said he was coming back in three or four days' time. Now at first this person is going to like that, but after a minute he's going to doubt it. Figure it out for yourself. This person's going to think it's damned funny for a man to be in a detective agency business with a partner and for his partner not to know anything about him ; where he was or what he was doing ; where his relations are. Put yourself in the place of that person. Wouldn't you get a little suspicious ? "

Inskip said : " You bet I would."

" All right. So what's the next thing that's going to worry them ? They're going to worry about you, aren't they ? They might even make themselves believe that you know all about Allard ; that you knew what he was doing in the country ;

in a corrugated tin roof. Vallon wondered how these three came to Valasey Bay and, being there, what they were doing.

He shrugged his shoulders. Maybe he was becoming a trifle old fashioned. He grinned to himself. In this year of grace anything could happen anywhere, and did. The ordered respectability of places like this was no longer certain. People no longer conformed to any sort of rules and regulations.

He asked a passer-by to direct him to the street where the lawyers' offices were situated. Ten minutes later he went into the offices of Dyce, Grant & Dyce. When he was shown into the inner office, Dyce said :

" I didn't expect to see you so soon, Mr. Vallon. But I'm very glad you have come."

Vallon sat down. He thought Dyce was a rather distinctive and attractive person—one of those lawyers, of about fifty years of age, whose life and looks are improved by the practise of their profession.

He said : " When I got your letter this morning I sent you a telegram. You've probably had it by now. I didn't intend to come and see you at the moment, but I changed my mind. I thought I'd like to ask you some questions. Or would you rather talk to me first of all ? "

Dyce said : " I think I'd like to talk to you ; then you can ask anything you wish to know. I wrote to you because, to tell you the truth, Mr. Vallon, as executor and trustee for Mr. Clavering, who died recently, I'm a trifle worried—just a little perturbed about the situation as regards Mrs. Clavering's daughter."

Vallon asked : " What is the situation ? "

Dyce pushed a silver cigarette box across the desk. He said : " Really, in order to understand the atmosphere of this story, Mr. Vallon, you should have met Mrs. Clavering. I suppose you haven't met her ? "

Vallon shook his head.

Dyce went on : " Mrs. Clavering is one of those extraordinary women whom you meet once in a lifetime. I imagine she is somewhere in the region of forty-five years of age. She looks at least twelve or fifteen years younger than that. She is very beautiful. And she has a peculiar quality. . . ."

Vallon grinned. "Allure ? " he suggested.

Dyce nodded. " Exactly . . . allure ! . . . As I have said, she is beautiful. She has an excellent sense of dress. She posses-ses a sympathetic and charming personality. She is the sort of person to whom any man could lose his head and heart."

Vallon said : " You sound as if you've rather lost your head about her yourself. . . ."

Dyce said quietly: " Mr. Vallon, you're quite right. In point of fact, if my client Clavering hadn't married her I should have liked to have done so myself."

Vallon said nothing. He thought that Mrs. Clavering must be quite a person.

Dyce continued : " Augustus Clavering came back from the East some years ago. He'd lived out there all his life. He was a unique person. He was sixty-six years of age but, as it seemed then, full of energy, both mental and physical. He was a fine-looking man and, if I may say so, a very astute one. He decided to stay here and did so. A few months ago he met Mrs. Clavering, who was also resident here and living on a small income from a previous marriage. He asked her to marry him.

" He was utterly fascinated by her. Well—", Dyce shrugged his shoulders—" she married him, although there were two or three people in the vicinity, who could not be described as poor men, and who were much younger than Clavering was, who would willingly have married her.

" She was perfectly honest about this marriage. Actually, I think she was very fond of Clavering who, as I have told you, in spite of his age was quite an attractive personality, but her main reason for consenting to his proposal was her daughter. It seems that Mrs. Clavering married when she was nineteen years of age a man called del Erest, in South America, and a daughter was born of this marriage. Apparently the husband was a peculiar character—not a very pleasant type from what Clavering told me—inclined to be a sadist. The marriage was a failure from the start. Anyhow, after the birth of the daughter he suddenly disappeared, leaving his wife penniless. He took the daughter with him.

" Mrs. del Erest, as she then was, carried on as best she could for two or three years. She worked, doing all sorts of things, and managed to make a living. Then, in 1929, she received news of her husband's death. Del Erest—strange as it may seem—left her a sum of money, on which she lived until she met Clavering. But she heard nothing of her daughter. What del Erest had done with the child ; where he'd left her, nobody knew, and Mrs. Clavering has apparently been worrying herself sick about this girl for years. All she had been able to find out was that the girl was last heard of, when she was four or five years of age, in Santiago, where she was living with del Erest's old nurse.

" However, she told Clavering that she would marry him if he would institute an investigation to try and find the girl, and if she were found consent to make some sort of settlement on her, so that she would be secure for the rest of her life. Clavering immediately agreed to this. As I have told you, he was a rich man. He told her he was so overjoyed at her acceptance of his proposal that he thought the condition she made a very small one. He told her that he would make a marriage settlement under which she would herself receive a sum of four thousand pounds a year, tax free, as from the date of her marriage, and that, in the event of her daughter being found and proof being forthcoming that she actually was the missing girl, a like sum would be settled on her for the rest of her life.

" He came to me and asked me to draw up this settlement but, after thinking the matter over, I advised against it. I explained to him that the four thousand a year—free of tax— which he intended the girl to have if and when she was found was a conditional settlement. Conditional on the girl *being* found ; and that if he were to die, this firm, as his executors, would have to tie up a very large capital sum in order to provide the four thousand a year for the girl—*who might never be found*.

" He asked my advice, and I made this suggestion : I suggested that he instruct me to pay the sum of eight thousand a year to Mrs. Clavering—this sum consisting of her allowance of four thousand plus the girl's four thousand, which Mrs. Clavering would utilise in the search for the girl, which process is, as you can imagine, a very expensive business. This, I told him, would take care of the immediate present, and he could vary it at any time he liked merely by giving me further instructions.

" I also suggested that he made a new Will at once ; that under this Will—if he agreed to my idea—he should leave the sum of eight thousand a year tax free to Mrs. Clavering with the proviso that if her daughter should be found she, Mrs. Clavering, would renounce four thousand a year of the bequest to her child ; thereby ensuring that mother and daughter had each her own separate income."

Vallon asked : " Did Mrs. Clavering approve of this ? "

Dyce shrugged his shoulders. " Actually, I don't think she was asked about it. She was away on a visit to friends at the time I saw Clavering about this business, and in any event, it made no difference to her. She would receive exactly the same amount of money as under the settlement and, in the event of Clavering's death, she would know that she had the girl's money to use in tracing her, which she could hand over if and when the girl was found."

Vallon nodded.

" Also," Dyce went on, " I had another idea. Mrs. Clavering had not seen the daughter since she was a baby. I thought it better to leave a loop-hole for Clavering to exercise his discretion if the girl were found as to whether he wished to allow her such a large income. I thought he should have a chance to see her first. Anyhow, Clavering agreed with my ideas and he gave me an instruction in writing to pay a yearly allowance to Mrs. Clavering of eight thousand pounds until such time as the daughter was found, when he would vary it as he wished. He also made a Will—which is in this office—under which, in the event of his death, and the daughter being not then found, Mrs. Clavering would receive the same sum per annum, but would renounce half of it—four thousand a year tax free—to her daughter if she were found. You understand ? "

Vallon asked : " What are the chances of finding the daughter ? "

Dyce shrugged his shoulders. " I haven't the remotest idea. And I should like to explain to you the position about that. Immediately after the marriage Clavering came to see me. He suggested that the time had arrived when we got busy instituting a search for the girl, and he suggested that a good firm to employ for such a purpose was your own—Chennault Investigations. I was on the point of getting in touch with you when he stopped me."

Vallon asked : " Why ? "

" Apparently Mrs. Clavering had been talking with some friends of hers who had required to use the services of an agency which had apparently worked very successfully for them. It was called the Allard Detective Agency. Mrs. Clavering suggested to her husband that this firm might try to find her daughter. He instructed me to that effect, and I wrote to Mr. Vine Allard, outlining the case and, on his acceptance by letter, I sent him a sum of money on account of his expenses."

Vallon said : " You heard nothing from him ? "

Dyce shook his head. " Nothing at all. Lately, during the last few days, I had become rather perturbed about the Allard Detective Agency. My London agent heard one or two rumours about this firm which weren't very satisfactory. I telephoned Mr. Allard and asked him whether he'd made a successful start. He said that not only had he made a successful start but he had news for me—news which he preferred to give me personally. He was coming down to see me, but unfortunately," said Dyce ruefully, " he has died as a result of the automobile accident which took place yesterday."

Vallon said : " That's too bad." He stubbed out his cigarette. " What do you want me to do exactly ? "

" Vine Allard said he had some news for me," said Dyce. " That could only mean that he had a line on where the girl was, or that he'd actually found her. I want you to find out exactly what has happened and what he knew. His partner— a man called Inskip—may be able to give you some information."

Vallon said : " You were rather doubtful about Allard ? "

Dyce nodded. " I think so. I'd heard rumours about the firm. I heard that Allard was an undischarged bankrupt."

" You didn't check on the people who suggested the agency to Mrs. Clavering ? "

" Oh, yes," said Dyce. " I talked to them. They're well-known people here. They'd used Allard on some investigation four years ago, and apparently he'd been very forthright and straight and successful."

" That was a year before he went bankrupt," said Vallon. He went on : " Mr. Dyce, supposing for the sake of argument, I go and see this man Inskip and he doesn't know anything about it. Supposing this Vine Allard was one of those men who prefer to work entirely on his own. Many detectives do, you know. I think it isn't very good sometimes for an investigator to let *anyone* know what he's doing."

Dyce said : " I find that very difficult to believe in a case like this, Mr. Vallon. Surely his partner would know roughly what he was doing. He must know something about it."

" Anyway, I can ask him, can't I ? " said Vallon. " But supposing he doesn't know anything ? "

Dyce said : " Then all I can suggest is that you start this investigation again from the beginning ; that you try and find out as best you can what Allard had discovered ; that you carry on where he left off."

" Very well," said Vallon. " I'll do that. Tell me about Clavering's death. How did he die ? "

Dyce said : "A most unfortunate business. He died suddenly. Mrs. Clavering had gone off to spend a few days with some friends. He was alone in the house, except for the housekeeper who was sick. The two servants were on holiday. The house is a large, comfortable place just outside the town, and it seemed that Clavering was in his usual robust health. However, after Mrs. Clavering had been away for two days, the housekeeper went into the library one morning and found Clavering dead on the floor. He'd evidently been walking towards the door when he dropped dead. He had heart disease, which no one had ever suspected."

Vallon asked : " Was he dressed ? Had he been to bed ? "

" He was in a dressing-gown," said Dyce. "Apparently, he'd gone to his room and undressed, put on a dressing-gown and gone down to the library—that was a habit of his—to read for twenty minutes or so before turning in. The book he'd been reading was on the table. He'd closed it and, it seems, was walking to the door when his heart gave out."

Vallon got up. "Thank you, Mr. Dyce. I've got the general outline. Where is Mrs. Clavering at the moment ? "

" She's gone to Montreuil in France," said Dyce. " I advised her to go away. I expect you'd like to talk to her ? "

Vallon said : " I don't know." He smiled at Dyce. " I don't know what I think yet. But I'll let you know. When I've got something to tell you I'll get in touch with you."

Dyce said : " I shall be impatient to hear from you, Mr. Vallon. Don't let anything stand in your way. If you want more money let me know."

Vallon walked to the door. He said : " Of course. . . . Goodbye, Mr. Dyce."

He went out.

He returned to the spot where he had left the car ; sat in the passenger seat ; watched the afternoon sun gleaming on the white caps of the waves as they broke on the shore. He thought that there was a certain air of peace about Valasey Bay. It was a small, remote, peculiarly attractive place. Peculiar because to Vallon it possessed an atmosphere that seemed full of interesting potentialities. Certainly the place had had potentialities for Mrs. Clavering, who had once been Mrs. del Erest ; and for her husband, Augustus Jones Clavering, who had decided at sixty-six years of age to marry a woman over twenty years his junior, and who was now dead. It was a pity, Vallon thought, that it had been necessary for Clavering to die when he did. This game old man who had, apparently, loved life and beauty.

He started up the car ; drove it into the forecourt of an attractive looking hotel at the end of the front. He went into the hotel ; found a telephone call-box : dialled trunk inquiries ; asked for the number of the Mungo Detective Agency. Two minutes afterwards he was speaking to Mungo himself.

Vallon said : " Mungo, I'm in a spot and I'm too busy at the moment to do anything about it. You can help. My fiancée, Miss Madeleine Thorne, has gone to France on holiday. She gave me the address where she will stay but I've mislaid it. I'm pretty certain that she left by air and her luggage will probably be registered to follow her. I'm supposed to telephone her but I can't, because I haven't her address or number. Will you check with the air offices that ran a service to France last night. And check with the charter offices. She may have hired a plane to fly her. If you succeed in finding where she's gone to, telephone my office and they'll tell you where I am. Then you can ring me."

Mungo said : " O.K., Johnny. Give me a day."

Vallon said so long and hung up.

He came out of the call-box ; went to the reception on the other side of the hall-way ; booked a room for the night. Then he went out ; walked along the front ; went into the town ; bought some pyjamas, a toothbrush and shaving kit. He went

40

back to the hotel ; took the lift to his room ; lay on the bed, smoking cigarettes, wondering about Allard.

.　　.　　.　　.　　.　　.　　.

At seven o'clock Vallon went down to the cocktail bar. It was an "L" shaped room, with the bar following the shape of the room. Vallon sat on a stool near the apex of the bar ; ordered a large whisky and soda. He sat there, sipping it. He thought the idea of spending a night in Valasey Bay, for no particular reason that he could think of except that he felt tired, was incongruous. Just as the sight of the three pansies walking down the main street earlier in the afternoon had been incongruous.

There were two or three people standing up against the bar drinking. One of them began to snigger. Vallon looked over his shoulder and saw the reason. The bar door leading to a side street had opened and one of the three pansies came in. He was the auburn hair type—the one who had worn the evening trousers with the yellow shirt and blue tie. Now he was correctly dressed in a dinner-jacket, except that the points of his soft silk collar were too long and his black satin bow too flowing. He minced along the bar ; turned into the top of the "L" ; sat on a stool three or four removed from where Vallon sat. He ordered a dry Martini in a precise, rather high-pitched voice.

Vallon finished his drink ; ordered another. When the bar-tender went away to mix it, the pansy said precisely :

" Good evening. I hope you like Valasey Bay."

Vallon asked : "Are you talking to me ? "

The pansy smiled whimsically. " Yes, I'm talking to you. I'm a mine of information. There's practically nothing I don't know about Valasey Bay. I ought to be a licensed guide."

Vallon said : " That's very interesting."

" I expect it is. I find life *very* interesting. I hope you had a successful interview with Mr. Dyce this afternoon."

" Not too bad," said Vallon. " How did you know ? "

The man got up ; picked up his glass. He moved to the stool beside Vallon. He looked at him sideways.

He said : " I assure you there isn't a thing can happen in this town but *everybody* knows about it. A friend of mine saw you

41

go into the office this afternoon. I thought I knew what you might be doing. I thought perhaps you might have come down about that business of Mrs. Clavering's."

Vallon said : " That's not bad guesswork. It was a very good guess."

The pansy said : " Believe it or not, my name's Friday—Julius Friday. I think it's a *scream* of a name, don't you ? "

" I think so too. But it's as good as any other. My name's Vallon. I'm a private detective."

" You don't say." Friday produced a thin, imitation gold cigarette case ; helped himself to a cigarette. When he had lighted it he went on : " I wonder what's happened to the other one ?"

Vallon asked : " Do you mean Allard ? "

Friday said : " I don't know what his name is, but I expect that's it. I mean the one who was looking for Mrs. Clavering's daughter."

" That was Allard," said Vallon. " He's dead."

Friday raised his eyebrows. " That's *too* bad. . . . Do you know what he died of ? "

Vallon nodded. " He has died as the result of a car smash which took place yesterday afternoon. I should have thought you'd have known that too."

Friday smiled deprecatingly. " No, I didn't. I must be losing my form. I suppose you're going to do the job that Allard was doing?"

Vallon said : " I'm trying to."

"I wish you luck. Everybody knows about it of course, but then everybody knows everything. I hope you find the girl."

Vallon asked : " Why ? "

" I don't know . . . except that I like to see everybody happy. And I'd certainly like to have Mrs. Clavering find her daughter."

" Would you ? " said Vallon. " Why ? "

" Why not ? I'd like you to find her and I'd like her to turn out to be a most fearful bitch, just so that she'd annoy Mrs. Clavering. She might easily be a bitch, you know, if she was lost sight of all those years ago in a place like South America, where I understand the most peculiar things happen at any moment. She might easily have turned out a thoroughly *bad* type, don't you think—the sort of girl of whom Mrs. Clavering,

42

who's so lovely and good and sweet, might be thoroughly ashamed ? "

Vallon grinned. " Quite obviously Mrs. Clavering isn't a great friend of yours. But I think your point of view is refreshing."

" I think so too *sometimes*. What are you going to do to-night ? "

" What the hell's that got to do with you ? " asked Vallon.

Friday smiled. " Nothing at all. Except that I wondered why you were staying on here. You've seen Dyce. You can't see old Clavering because he's dead . . . the damned old fool. . . ."

Vallon asked : " Why was he a damned old fool ? I thought he was rather cute."

" He was cute enough," said Friday. He stubbed out his cigarette end daintily in an ash-tray. " But I think an old man who marries a woman a lot younger than he is a damned fool. It's a stupid thing to do. I think maybe it's *very* lucky for him that he died."

" Meaning what ? " asked Vallon.

The other shrugged his shoulders. " Meaning anything you like." He got off the stool. " But if you're not doing anything in particular, and if you're staying on, you could do much worse than come round to the theatre and see our repertory. I'm the stage director. And there's a very good play on to-night. I think it's an amazing play. It starts at eight o'clock. Good night to you, Mr. Vallon."

Vallon said good night.

Friday went away, leaving the vaguest suggestion of Channel No. 5 on the air.

.   .   .   .

The repertory theatre—a large converted barn—stood a mile from the centre of the town. Vallon, who had parked his car off the main road, walked into the theatre at half-past nine, bought himself a stall and went in.

He was interested in the man Friday. Friday, who seemed to know about everything that went on in Valasey Bay, including the story of Mrs. Clavering's missing daughter.

They were playing act two. Vallon, relaxed in his comfortable stall, thought that the play was bad and the acting worse. He changed his opinion—about the acting—when the girl playing the principal part came on to the stage. When she arrived, the atmosphere of the play changed. She had a certain quality which came over the footlights. Her performance was finished. She spoke delightfully ; looked charming. Her clothes were almost too fashionable, too well cut, for the rest of the cast. When she went off the stage Vallon got up.

He went back to the hotel ; sat in the bar. He sat there drinking rye whisky until half-past ten. Then he drove back to the theatre. He found the stage entrance ; went in. There was no stage-door keeper.

Vallon walked along the short corridor, up a curving flight of stairs ; found himself in a passage. There were three or four doors on the left and right of the passage with cards attached to them. He knocked at the end one. A voice told him to come in. He went in.

She was sitting in front of her make-up table. She wore a black velvet wrap with a ruffle at the throat, and in spite of the fact that she was engaged in taking off her make-up she still looked very attractive.

He said : " I'm sorry to burst in on you like this, Miss Mannering. My name's John Vallon. I had an appointment last night with a Mr. Vine Allard of the Allard Detective Agency at a café called the Sierra Madre just off the Winchester road. Remember ? . . ."

She said : " Ye-es. . . ." She swung round ; turned towards him. " Can you tell me what you went to see Mr. Allard about, Mr. Vallon ? "

He shook his head. " I'm a private detective. My agency is called Chennault Investigations. I had a letter from Allard asking me to meet him there on the most important business. I've known him for some time. I decided to go. When I arrived you weren't there, but when I came back from the scene of the accident in which Allard was injured—by the way, he's since died—you were talking to a Mr. Brownlow. I wonder if you'd like to tell me why you went there ? "

" Why shouldn't I, Mr. Vallon ? So far as I'm concerned it is all very mysterious. Two or three days earlier I received a telephone call from Mr. Allard at my rooms here. How he got the telephone number I don't know, but I think I can guess. He told me that he wished to see me very urgently. He said he was a private detective. He said a situation had arisen

44

which might be extremely important from my point of view."
She shrugged her shoulders prettily. " He went so far as to
suggest," she went on, " that this appointment might have
quite a lot to do with my happiness or otherwise. He suggested
that I got a day off from the Repertory Company here and
meet him at the Sierra Madre."

Vallon nodded. " You were intrigued, I expect ? "

" Very intrigued," she said. " The more I thought about
it the more mysterious and—shall I say, attractive—the idea
seemed. Being an actress, I suppose I have a romantic streak in
my nature. Being a woman I was very curious, so I went. When
I arrived there I sat down by myself. He wasn't there. He'd
told me what he looked like but there was nobody else in the
place except a Mr. Brownlow, who looked like a farmer. Then
I heard the waitress talking about an accident down the road.
I wondered if it could be the mysterious Mr. Allard. So I went
over to Mr. Brownlow, who seemed to know the place well, and
asked him if he knew anything about the accident. I talked
to him for a little while ; then I left."

Vallon asked : " So you have no idea what Allard wanted
to say to you ? "

She shook her head.

He went on : " You don't even know how he got your
telephone number—the number of your rooms here ? "

She said : " Well, I have an idea about that. I had to ask
permission to get the day off to meet Mr. Allard, so I went to
the stage director here—rather a peculiar type, but very nice
in some ways."

" A Mr. Julius Friday ? " said Vallon.

She nodded. " I don't know why, but I had an idea that he
knew something about it. I had an idea that this Mr. Allard
had got my telephone number through him. I don't know why
I should think this except that when I asked him if I could
have the day off—which meant a great deal of inconvenience
here in the theatre because my understudy wasn't really ready
to go on for me, and normally I would have expected Friday
to do everything he could to stop me going—he gave me permission, and he was smiling when he did so in an odd manner.
He gave me the impression that he knew much more than he
cared to say." She shrugged her shoulders again. " It was just
an idea, but——"

45

Vallon finished the sentence : " Ideas can be right sometimes." He took a card from his pocket ; put it on the dressing-
table. " Here's my address in London. If you get any other odd
deas perhaps you'd like to telephone me."

She said : " I will. Naturally I'm most intrigued. I shall go
on worrying and being curious about what I was to be told ;
what was the purpose of this meeting which was never held."

" So shall I." Vallon smiled at her. " You never know, we
might even find out one day. Good night, Miss Mannering."

She got up ; held out her hand. She wrinkled her nose very
attractively. " Do try and find out, Mr. Vallon. It would be
such fun knowing, wouldn't it ? "

Vallon nodded. He went out of the room. As he was passing
through the stage door a voice said :

" Well, Mr. Vallon, I hope you had a *nice* interview."

He turned. Friday was standing in the passage-way.

Vallon said : " Not so bad. You know, Friday, one of these
fine days I'm going to get around to you."

" Are you ? How exciting. I expect you're one of those
awfully clever detectives—the sort of people one reads about
in books."

Vallon said wryly : " You can take it from me I'm much
worse than that. I expect you'll find out."

" Like *hell* ! " said Friday. " And to hell with *you*, Mr.
Clever Dick. You're one of those people who find out only what
they're supposed to know." He stood in the half-darkness of
the passage, his white face working with rage.

Vallon grinned at him. He walked back to where he had
parked the car ; drove back to the hotel. He went to his room ;
drank a final whisky and soda ; went to bed.

He lay there in the darkness, thinking. He was so busy in
his mind with the charming Miss Mannering, and the angry
Mr. Julius Friday, that he forgot to think about Madeleine.

CHAPTER THREE

VALLON ARRIVED in London at eleven o'clock ; went straight to his office. He went directly to his own room ; sat at his desk —the morning's mail pushed to one side. He was relaxed and interested.

He amused himself by trying to come to conclusions about the personalities in the Clavering case, wondered how the traditional detective of fiction, the stage or the films would deal with the absence of cohesion or coherence in the personalities and events of the last few days.

Most interesting, Vallon thought, was Vine Allard. In his mind he was certain that the case revolved round that one. He wondered why Allard hadn't trusted his partner Inskip. After all, when you work with a man you've got to let him know *something* of what you are doing—or have you ? But perhaps Allard was mean. Maybe he liked—as Inskip had suggested—taking the profitable business that came along himself and leaving the not-so-good jobs to Inskip who had to handle them whether he liked it or not.

An intriguing set of personalities. Vallon considered that they would form a very good caste for a drama or perhaps a comedy—except that it hadn't been very much of a comedy for Vine Allard. Everybody was intriguing. Everybody he had encountered, or heard of, seemed to be very definite about what they wanted ; what they didn't want. And as definite in their likes and dislikes.

Clavering had been very definite in his desire to marry Mrs. del Erest, who had been just as definite, and quite properly so, in her desire first to find her missing daughter and, secondly, to see that she would be well looked after for the rest of her life. Vallon thought, with a half-smile, that he wasn't quite certain what Vine Allard had tried to be definite about, but in the circumstances in which he was placed Vallon guessed that whatever it was, it had been quite definite enough to scare Allard—who did not scare easily.

Julius Friday's almost livid rage against everybody and

everything, including Mrs. Clavering and, for that matter, Vallon himself, was probably the most definite business up to the moment.

The girl whom Allard had wanted so much to meet—the girl who had waited for him at the Sierra Madre—presented the one indefinite picture in the story. She wasn't certain about anything. Or so she said. She didn't know why Allard had wanted to see her. She had seemed surprised that Julius Friday was prepared to give her the day off. But she didn't know why. She was just a rather nice and very good-looking bundle of not knowing anything. Or she gave that impression. Maybe she was lying, or covering up for somebody. She could be doing that. She was a very good actress with a hell of a personality. She was not, thought Vallon, the type of girl who would allow herself to be pushed around by events. Not without doing something about it.

He picked up the telephone ; asked for Marvin. When he came into the room, Vallon said :

" What did you find out . . . anything ? "

Marvin nodded. " I sent Toler down to the hospital. He got into the store-room attached to the hospital mortuary where they keep the clothes and effects of people who die there. He went through Allard's pocket-book. There was nothing in it, except some money, one or two unimportant accounts and Allard's identity card."

Vallon asked : " What was the address on the identity card —his office address ? "

" No," said Marvin, " not his office address. His private address—11a Fitzroy Crescent—that's in the west central district. I checked up on that. Allard had a bed-sitting-room there. He'd been there for some time."

Vallon made a note of the address on his blotter.

Marvin went on : " The number-plate thing is interesting. The plate you saw on the truck was a trade plate. We had a bit of luck over that."

" Did you ? Did you find out where it came from ? "

Marvin nodded. " A set of trade plates was stolen some days ago from the Excelsior Garage at Valasey Bay. They reported the loss to the local police, and under a new system the police are operating about stolen plates the report automatically went to the Yard."

Vallon said : " Very interesting." A picture of Mr. Julius Friday came into his mind. Julius, who didn't like anybody very much ; who lived at Valasey Bay. Vallon thought it might be interesting to find out just what Julius was doing on the day of the crash.

Marvin said : " I don't think I've seen you so interested for a long time, Mr. Vallon. Is it that sort of case ? "

" I don't know what sort of case it is, Marvin, but it's interesting enough." Vallon pushed the mail across the desk. " You deal with this. I've an idea I'm going to be busy for a few days."

Marvin picked up the packet of letters ; left the office.

Vallon leaned back in his chair ; put his feet on the desk ; lighted a fresh cigarette. Marvin's discovery of the address on the identity card might mean something. Then again it might not. But the interesting thing was the telephone call. Somebody had been able to telephone Dyce at Valasey Bay fairly soon after the accident, informing him that there had been a crash. Vallon wondered who that person could be. It was either somebody who knew the Dyce firm's connection with the case ; knew their telephone number, or else the answer was that Allard had been carrying some sort of letter or a note of the address and telephone number in his pocket-book and somebody had had an opportunity to go through the case, get the number, and telephone through to Dyce that night.

Vallon got up from his chair. He shrugged his shoulders ; began to walk about the office. He thought that this was one of those things ! He had an idea in his head that this was going to be one of the highlights in the case—the person who had telephoned through to Dyce.

And it might easily be Friday. Why not ? It was through him that Leila Mannering had received permission to take the day off and go to the Sierra Madre. Well, Friday would have an assistant stage manager—wouldn't he ? Supposing for the sake of argument that Friday for some reason best known to himself had decided that the girl was *not* to meet Allard, which meant that he knew that she was going to meet him, it would be fairly easy for him on some pretext or other to obtain the trade plates from the Excelsior Garage. If he knew the Sierra Madre district he would know that the side roads were deserted. He would know that Allard must take the right fork road to reach the place from Valasey Bay. Vallon thought

49

it might easily be that Friday, filled with the extraordinary rage which seemed to take hold of him at any moment, had decided to finish Allard.

Vallon realised suddenly that this reasoning pre-supposed *that Allard had been at Valasey Bay*. Why? And if he had been there why had he not seen Leila Mannering and explained his reasons for wanting her to meet him? And how had he obtained her telephone number at her rented apartment? It rather looked, thought Vallon, as if Allard had been doing a little under-cover work at Valasey Bay and, for reasons best known to himself, had decided that he did not want to be seen there more than was absolutely necessary.

The telephone rang. Vallon walked to the desk; picked up the instrument. The girl on the switchboard said: "It's the Mungo Agency, Mr. Vallon. They want you personally."

Mungo came on the line. He said: "Johnny, I got it for you. Miss Thorne chartered a plane. She flew to Boulogne. It was a night trip. She took some luggage with her. My man at Boulogne who covered this said she hired a car which collected her and her luggage at the airport. She was going through to Paris. He's checking. He says he thinks he can let me have her Paris address either to-day or to-morrow. When I've got it I'll ring you through."

Vallon said: "Thanks a lot, Mungo. That'll be a great help to me." He hung up.

He opened the bottom drawer of his desk; took out the whisky bottle and glass; gave himself a long swig. He wondered what the next thing was going to be. He could do one of two things, he thought—sit down and wait till something else happened—and it might easily be that nothing else would —or do something about it.

He called through on the office telephone to Marvin's room. He said: "I'm going to France for a couple of days—maybe longer. I don't know. I'll take the afternoon boat. If you want me I'll be at the hotel in Montreuil-sur-Mer—the Château Montreuil. Don't ring unless it's something important. But if Mungo comes through with Miss Thorne's address in Paris, call me and let me know."

Marvin said: "O.K."

Vallon picked up his hat; walked out of the office; went down to the car. He remembered what Dyce had said about

Mrs. Clavering. He thought it must be tough to be Mrs. Clavering. To be so beautiful, so alluring and so unhappy. He shrugged his shoulders. Usually, beautiful women were unhappy—more unhappy than homely ones. Because beauty and allure were potent weapons, and if a woman was armed with such weapons it was not unusual for them to come back on her—whether she liked it or not.

As he got into the car he thought about Madeleine. He hoped Mungo would get her address in Paris. He thought it might be a good thing to telephone her. Or would it ? You never knew with women.

Vallon thought he wasn't sure about that.

.   .   .   .   .   .

It was eight-thirty when Vallon arrived at the Château Montreuil. He realised that he had been driving about the coast roads for a long time. Not because he was interested in the countryside—which he knew well—but because he was experiencing the relaxation of mind that he always associated with France. Most of the time he had been thinking vaguely of Allard and Julius Friday.

He checked in at the office ; went into the long, ground-floor room that looked out on to the gardens and lawns on three sides. He went to the bar at the far end ; ordered a double brandy and soda.

He said to the barman : " Do you know where Mrs. Clavering is ? Is she in ? "

The man shrugged his shoulders. " I don't know, M'sieu, I think she ees dressing. Usually at this time. . . ."

Vallon nodded. He finished his drink ; went out through the side door on to the lawn. The evening light was just beginning to fade. He stood just outside the door admiring the long sweep of the flower-bordered lawn, a hundred yards long, down to the old bridge that ran over the sunken road ; led to the smaller château which formed an annexe to the hotel.

He began to walk slowly across the lawn towards the bridge. He had almost arrived when he saw her, standing beneath the ancient oak-tree on the far edge of the lawn, in the shadow of the ivy-covered wall.

He whistled softly under his breath. So this was Paula

Clavering ! . . . Vallon thought he understood a lot—a hell of a lot. He thought that Dyce had been right when he had said that Mrs. Clavering had an amazing personality.

She wore a sea-green chiffon dinner-frock over a primrose yellow silk foundation. Her high-heeled green sandals almost twinkled against the darker green of the lawn. As she came towards him Vallon could see the thick red-gold snake with ruby eyes about her white throat, the matching bracelet on her wrist. A short sable cape was thrown carelessly about her shoulders.

Her face was white and oval, framed in dark hair that was drawn loosely back.

He thought with an inward grin that old Clavering had certainly known what he wanted in the evening of his life ; that he had been damned lucky to be able to get what he wanted—no matter what it had cost. He thought that Mrs. Clavering was definitely *something*.

Now she was near him. He smiled at her. He said : " Mrs. Clavering, I *believe* ? "

She nodded. She said in a low, soft voice : " Mr. Vallon . . . isn't it Mr. Vallon ? "

Vallon said : " Right first time. It's a lovely evening, isn't it ? "

She nodded her head again. In some strange way she managed, Vallon thought, to imbue this very ordinary gesture with a peculiar charm.

" I've always believed that Fate works sometimes in the most mysterious manner, Mr. Vallon." Now she was standing quite close to him. A suggestion of an attractive perfume came to his nostrils. " I came out here to try and think about things. Just as you arrived I was thinking that somehow everything might have been very different if, in the first place, I had come to you for help instead of going to Mr. Allard ; that everything might have been so different, so much more happy.   To-day I was speaking to Mr. Dyce on the telephone, and he told me that he had seen you and that your personality filled him with confidence ; that he hoped you would be able to clear up all this unhappy trouble. I was thinking that it would be rather nice if I could see you and talk to you and— at that very moment—you appear." She smiled at him. "And there are some people who do not believe in Fate."

Vallon grinned at her. " Mrs. Clavering, too many people believe in Fate and the rest of them believe in Santa Claus and the fairies. I don't."

" I expect your profession is inclined to make you cynical, Mr. Vallon. I don't wonder at that."

Vallon took out his cigarette case, offered it to her and, when she refused, lighted a cigarette. He drew the tobacco smoke down into his lungs. He stood there looking towards the bridge and the twinkling lights in the windows on the château on the other side.

The silence went on for a long time ; then she said : " What are we going to do, Mr. Vallon ? " She shrugged her shoulders hopelessly. " What are *you* going to do ? "

"I don't know," Vallon answered. "But there's a seat just over here that looks comfortable. It's a warm evening. Don't you think that we might sit down and talk about this thing generally ? "

" Why not ? " she said.

They moved over to the seat. Once or twice, as they walked, her sable cape touched him. Vallon found her proximity was disturbing. He thought to himself that Mrs. Clavering had a hell of a personality. They sat down.

Vallon said : " There are quite a lot of murderers wandering about—people who haven't been arrested because the police couldn't find an adequate motive for the murder. That's the first thing they look for. A policeman—or a private detective for that matter—without a motive is like a lost soul. So I'm looking for a motive at the moment, Mrs. Clavering."

She asked softly : "A motive for what ? "

" You said to-day you'd spoken to Dyce. I expect he told you about my visit to Valasey Bay ; that he'd given me a broad outline of what all this was about. But I'm not concerned so much with all that at the moment. I'm concerned with Vine Allard. I expect Dyce told you about the accident, didn't he ? "

She nodded. " A terribly unfortunate thing."

Vallon said : " It wasn't an accident. Allard was murdered. Somebody drove a truck into his car. My guess is that it was done deliberately."

She said tensely : " Oh, my God ! . . . That can't be true. Why should someone want to do that ? . . . It isn't possible."

" You'd be surprised," said Vallon, " at what is and isn't

53

possible. I'm telling you that the accident wasn't an accident. It was a planned job and damned well planned. At the moment the police think it was just a hit-and-run driver—some stupid fellow who was joy-riding with a pair of trade plates, and who smashed into a motorist and cleared out, leaving the truck, knowing that it couldn't be traced and even if it was *he* wouldn't be picked up for the job."

She said unhappily : " But why—why ? "

He shrugged his shoulders. " This is a new angle for you. Before Dyce wrote to me and asked me to take over this job, Allard got into touch with me. He wanted to see me about something. He made an appointment at a roadside café called the Sierra Madre. I went down there and waited for him. He was on his way when the smash happened."

She said quickly : " So you don't know what he wanted to see you about ? "

" No, I don't. I can't even guess. Perhaps you could help me ? "

She shook her head slowly. " I'm afraid I can't."

Vallon went on : " Mrs. Clavering, when I came here this evening you said you were very glad to see me arrive because you'd been thinking about me. That means to say that you wanted me to do something. Were you going to ask me to continue the search to find your daughter, or was it something else ? "

She said : " I don't know. I'm not quite certain."

There was a long silence ; then Vallon said : " Supposing we start from the beginning, and I'll make certain that I've got my facts right. Dyce told me that your husband—Augustus Clavering—met you in Valasey Bay ; that he fell in love with you." He smiled at her. " I think he was a very wise and a very clever man. And I can understand his point of view. He was rich. He thought he was fit and the idea of spending the remaining years of his life with a woman as beautiful as you are must have appealed to him very much. I envy him." He looked at her sideways. "So did Mr. Dyce." He grinned. " He's got an awful lean on you, you know."

She smiled. " Has he ? I think he's a very nice man—a good friend."

" So do I," said Vallon. " Well, to get on with this business. You were very honest with Clavering. You told him you

54

didn't love him, but you admired and respected him ; that you'd marry him if he'd agree to try and find your daughter by your first marriage to del Erest—the man who lived with you for two years and then disappeared, taking your daughter with him. Is that right ? "

She nodded.

" Clavering was keen to do what you wanted and he suggested that my firm—Chennault Investigations—might handle the job. But you saw some people—some friends of yours for whom Allard had done a good job of work some years previously—and, quite understandably, having had such a good recommendation, you suggested to your husband that you went to see Allard about this. Is that right ? "

She said slowly : " Yes, that's right. How I wish I hadn't. How I wish, Mr. Vallon, that we'd gone to you instead."

Vallon went on : " Before you went to see Allard you had a talk with your husband about the financial angles. I believe that he intended to allow you a personal income of four thousand a year ; that he was prepared to spend a like sum on looking for the girl, and that when she was found he proposed to settle the four thousand a year on her for the rest of her life. And then you went to see Allard ? "

She nodded. " Yes, I went to see Allard—or rather he came to see me. I went up to town. I stayed at the Hotel Splendide. My friends down at Valasey Bay telephoned him and he came to see me."

Vallon asked : " What did you think of him ? "

She shrugged her shoulders. " I didn't think a lot about it. . . ." She gave him a quick smile. " I'm not used to private detectives, Mr. Vallon. He seemed quite a nice businesslike sort of man. I told him the exact situation. I told him that I wanted no trouble or expense spared in finding my daughter.

" Did you tell him about the financial arrangements between yourself and your husband—about your allowance of four thousand a year and the four thousand a year to be settled on the girl when they found her ? "

" I told him everything," she said.

Vallon asked : " Mrs. Clavering, have you any reason to believe that he knew that those financial arrangements had been altered ? "

" No . . . how should he know ? "

"After you'd seen him," said Vallon, "and given him his instructions, and you went back to Valasey Bay, I expect your husband told you that Mr. Dyce had advised him to alter the financial arrangements?"

"Oh, yes . . . Augustus told me that he'd seen Mr. Dyce who'd said that the idea of tying up the four thousand a year for a settlement on my daughter wasn't practicable because it would take an awful lot of capital to secure that allowance and it might be years before she was found. And as I was to be responsible for the search for her, Augustus said that he was allowing me four thousand a year which would be paid by Mr. Dyce; that he was paying for the search whatever it might cost, and that he'd made a Will saying that in the event of his death I received eight thousand a year with a proviso that, if and when my daughter was found, of that eight thousand I should settle four thousand a year on her."

Vallon nodded. "That's what Dyce told me. But Allard never knew about the different financial arrangements which had been made?"

"No, why should he? It made no difference to him. His charges would have been paid in any event either by my husband or Mr. Dyce."

"Precisely," said Vallon. "You never went to Allard's office?"

She shook her head.

"You never met his partner Inskip?" queried Vallon. "Or did Allard ever mention Inskip to you?"

"He spoke of him," she said, "and I asked what sort of person he was. Allard said I wasn't to worry . . . he was going to handle this business on his own; that Mr. Inskip only dealt with the rather small cases that came into the office. Mr. Allard said he personally was looking after the search for my daughter."

Vallon said: "Mrs. Clavering, when you were in Valasey Bay, did you ever meet a rather peculiar young man called Julius Friday?"

She smiled reminiscently. "Yes, I did. He's extraordinary, isn't he? He came to Valasey Bay with a theatrical company not very long ago. I met him at a party. For some reason which I cannot explain he didn't seem to like me very much."

"I can understand that," said Vallon. "He's a peculiar

type. I don't suppose he'd be awfully keen on any very attractive woman like you, Mrs. Clavering."

Vallon dropped his cigarette stub on to the grass; put his foot on it. He went on : " It seems that Allard got into touch with Dyce not long before the accident and told him he had some news for him. He didn't say what the news was. Have you any idea what it was ? "

" I think I can guess. At the time I was staying with some friends near Valasey Bay, but I'd sent my address and telephone number to Mr. Allard's office in case he wanted to get in touch with me. He telephoned me that he had the most exciting news. He said he thought he'd found my daughter. Then a few minutes afterwards he said he was *fairly* certain he'd found her; that he thought it would only be a matter of days."

" I see," said Vallon. " Did you tell anybody about that ? "

She shook her head. " I didn't, because——" She turned towards him ; put her fingers on his arm. " That's what I meant when I met you this evening when I said that I was thinking about you ; that I hoped I should meet you. For some reason which I can't tell you, I had begun to distrust Allard. Don't ask me why. Call it woman's instinct . . . call it anything you like. Whilst I was staying with my friends I'd come to the conclusion that when I went back to Valasey Bay I was going to have a talk with Mr. Dyce. I was going to ask him to terminate the arrangement with Allard. I was going to ask him to go to Chennault Investigations and instruct them to carry on with this business."

" But you didn't know why you wanted to do that ? It was just an instinct—an urge ? "

She nodded.

" And that feeling of mistrust persisted ? " said Vallon. " Even after you'd had that call from Allard—the call in which he said he was practically certain that he'd found your daughter."

" It persisted more strongly than ever," she said. " But my mind began to crystalise. After that telephone call I knew what I thought."

Vallon asked : " What did you think ? "

"An awful idea came to me," she said. "An idea came to me that Allard had found some girl that he was going to produce—someone who was not my daughter."

Vallon said: "Well . . . isn't that rather peculiar? What would Allard gain by that, Mrs. Clavering? It would be common sense for him to make that search extend as long as possible. By producing a daughter he was going to cut off his nice income."

"My ideas were possibly stupid and illogical, Mr. Vallon, but that's what I thought."

"And that's why you wanted to see me?" asked Vallon. "The idea in your head was that if Allard hadn't had this smash you were going to ask me to check on him?"

She nodded. "That's what I was going to ask you to do."

There was another silence; then Vallon asked: "Mrs. Clavering, did you know that Allard had gone down to Valasey Bay? Did you know what he was doing there?"

She said: "I didn't even know that he'd gone there."

Vallon lighted a fresh cigarette. He went on: "When Allard last spoke to you on the telephone; when he told you that he thought he'd found your daughter, did he tell you anything? Did he tell you how he'd achieved this success so quickly?"

"Yes, I asked him how he'd found her. Already I was doubting every word he said. He said he'd been very lucky; that he'd met a man over in France—at the Casino in Le Touquet; that this man had known my first husband—del Erest; that he was able to give Allard information which led him directly to my daughter. That he'd spoken to her on the telephone; that she'd been able to answer all his questions; that there was practically no doubt that she was my daughter."

Vallon said: "Is that why you came over here, Mrs. Clavering? To try and talk to this man—to find out if what Allard said was true?"

"That's what I came over here for. First of all I was terribly shaken by my husband's death. I expect you know all about that?"

Vallon nodded.

"I wanted to get away," she said. "I wanted to be by myself. But I knew I should want to try and check on what Allard had told me."

Vallon asked: "Have you seen this man?"

"No, I have been into Le Touquet, and I went to the Casino twice. They say he's gone away. His name is Bizard—

Rene Bizard. They said he'd been there. He'd stayed there for a few days ; then gone. They thought that he'd gone to Italy or Spain. No one knew if he was coming back. No one knew where he'd gone to."

Vallon said : " There's one more question I want to ask you, Mrs. Clavering, although I doubt if you'll be able to help me. After the smash, Allard was taken to a hospital at Dudleigh. When he reached the hospital he was alive. He died early next morning. But before he died somebody rang through to Dyce at Valasey Bay—I think about ten o'clock that night— and told him about the accident. The caller didn't give his name. You wouldn't have any idea as to who that might have been ? "

She shrugged her shoulders. " Why should I ? " she asked.

There was another silence ; then : " Mr. Vallon, have you any idea what you're going to do—how you're going to proceed ? "

" Not the slightest. All I can do is to hang around until something happens." He smiled at her. " Mark you, I'm going to try and make something happen if I can. I want to find out who was responsible for Allard's death. I think that's the main thing at the moment."

" You think you'll be able to do that ? " she queried.

" I don't know. I can try. How long are you staying here, Mrs. Clavering ? "

" I feel I should go back to-morrow," she said. " I shall take the afternoon boat from Calais. I expect Mr. Dyce will want to see me. There are all sorts of things to be done—things I omitted to do before I came here. I was so distressed that I just let everything go."

Vallon said: " I understand that. I'm probably going to Paris to-morrow. I'll be there for a day or two ; then I'll go back to England. I'll get in touch with you, Mrs. Clavering."

She got up. She said : " It's getting a little cold. I think I'll go in."

They began to walk across the lawn towards the château. They were half-way there when she put her hand on his arm. Her voice was trembling. " Mr. Vallon, I'm so distressed . . . so unhappy. I don't know what to do. I seem to have brought bad luck to everybody . . . to my dear, kind husband. Everything I've done has failed." She began to sob bitterly.

Almost instinctively Vallon put his arm round her shoulder. He said: "There are times when everything looks pretty bad. This is one of them. But things happen and we can't help them happening. Why don't you take a pull at yourself?"

She said: "I'll try."

"In the meantime," said Vallon, "on these occasions there is nothing like a cocktail. Supposing we go and drink one or two?"

She asked: "Do you think that will help? I don't."

Vallon said: "You never know until you try. So let's try . . . let's see if it helps."

.   .   .   .

The waiter put the brandy bottle, the siphon and the tumbler on the bed-table. Vallon told him: "I shan't be dining to-night. But you can leave some sandwiches up here in case I need them later."

When the man had gone, Vallon took off his coat, poured a drink; switched off the light; lay in the half-darkness, drinking brandy, thinking about Mrs. Clavering.

He thought the whole business was a hell of a rap for Mrs. Clavering. He thought he could easily understand the scene in the garden, and her tears. Things hadn't gone too well for her, and she didn't know a thing about anything. She was only certain that she didn't trust anyone in particular—especially the late Vine Allard; that she wanted someone to lean on and to do something—but she wasn't quite certain what.

Vallon wondered why she hadn't married someone *before* she met Augustus Clavering. Then he thought he knew the answer to that one. Dozens of men would have been glad to marry her, thought Vallon, but they didn't size up to what she wanted. A younger man—more suited to her by age and temperament than her husband—would have been bored with the idea of starting a wide-world search for a missing daughter in whom he had not the slightest interest. In any event, that sort of business needed money— lots of it. Looking for Miss del Erest would be rather like looking for a needle in a haystack and before she was found—if ever she was found—a great deal of money could be spent. Too much money, maybe.

Vallon drank some more brandy and thought about Allard.

60

From the motive angle Allard's conduct was inexplicable to say the least of it. Allard who was hard up, who needed money badly and to whom the commission to find the missing girl must have seemed like a gift from heaven, decided that he had found her so quickly that it seemed unbelievable. So unbelievable that Paula Clavering was certain in her own mind that Allard had produced an impostor.

Why should he do that ? To hang out the search for the missing girl would be the thing for him to do. To run it at least for a year or two, fake the expenses and charge the highest fees. That would be the normal thing for Allard to do. Unless...

Vallon got up and sat on the edge of the bed, the brandy glass in one hand, looking at the carpet and not seeing it.

Supposing, he thought, that Allard, who was inclined to look after himself, *had* been looking after himself in saying that he had found the girl. Supposing, for the sake of argument, Allard, having examined the situation in all its aspects, had decided that the search would be useless in any event. *Supposing he had discovered somehow that the girl was dead.* Then he would be wise to find a substitute as quickly as possible. This was logical. Probably, at her first interview, Mrs. Clavering had told him that the girl was to have four thousand a year. What would be easier than to find a young woman who sized up roughly to a possible Miss del Erest, tell her the whole story and make an arrangement with her that when she received the money he, Allard, was to have half.

Paula Clavering was definite in her mind that Allard had pulled a fast one ; that the girl he proposed to produce was an impostor. She had no specific reason for this idea except the speed with which Allard had run the missing girl to earth and her own instinct. Vallon grinned in the darkness. A hell of a lot of people were inclined to disbelieve in woman's instinct but, Vallon thought, very often a woman's instinct was right.

And then, just at the wrong moment—certainly the wrong moment for Mrs. Clavering when circumstances had already been made tough for her by the sudden death of her husband at a time when she needed counsel and advice—Allard gets himself killed, and she is left holding the bag, wondering just what she is going to do about it.

All she can do is to come to Montreuil, hoping that the one person who may know something can help her—the mysterious Rene Bizard who, just at the time when he is most needed, disappears into thin air.

Vallon yawned. He drank some more brandy and began to think about Allard. He began to think that one part of Allard's conduct was, at least, logical.

It was possible, he thought, that at the meeting between Allard and Mrs. Clavering she had told him that her husband's original idea was that they should consult Chennault Investigations; commission that agency to search for the missing girl, but that she had been specially urged by her friends to use Allard's services. This would be a normal thing for her to do, and Allard had remembered it. He had remembered it when he had talked to her on the telephone; told her that he had found the girl. Maybe he sensed her doubts at the news, had conceived it a good idea to get quickly into touch with Vallon and get him on *his*, Allard's, side. So he had made the appointment at the Sierra Madre and he had arranged that Miss Leila Mannering of the Valasey Bay Repertory Company should also be there. Miss Mannering, who didn't know why she had been asked. . . .

Vallon thought his guess might easily be right; that Miss Mannering might be the impostor whom Allard had found. And she was to be brought in to meet Vallon who, Allard hoped, might be talked into believing in the girl and talking Mrs. Clavering into believing in her.

That guess might easily be right—and just as easily wrong.

He lighted a cigarette; smoked it slowly; drank a little more brandy.

Then he lay down on the bed; went to sleep.

.   .   .   .

It was midnight when Vallon woke up. He stretched; put his hands behind his head; lay looking up into the darkness, wondering what it was he was going to do now.

After a while he gave it up. He got off the bed; switched on the light; began to walk about the bedroom. His tongue was dry from cigarettes and brandy. He poured himself another glass; drank it slowly. He began to think about Rene Bizard. He thought there was something attractive, something euphonious, in the name Rene Bizard.

Vallon went into the bathroom; washed his face in cold water. He re-tied his tie; put on his coat. He went downstairs to the lounge. It was deserted except for the barman who, behind the bar at the end of the long low-ceilinged room, leaned against the wall, yawning.

Vallon went over to the bar. He said: "I've decided to leave. I'll send somebody over for my bags within the next day or two. They'll pay my bill at the same time. Good night."

The barman said: "But of course, M'sieu . . ." He thought that the English had not changed since before the war; that they were as mad as ever; that you never knew what they were going to do next.

For want of something better to do he began to polish a glass.

. . . .

Vallon stopped the car in a side turning off the main street in Le Touquet. He lighted a cigarette; began to walk to the Casino. When he arrived he went into the office at the end of the foyer. The man in the black coat behind the desk said:

"Good evening, M'sieu."

Vallon said: "Good evening. I wonder if you can help me. I'm looking for a Mr. Rene Bizard. I was told that perhaps I could find him here."

The other shrugged his shoulders. "He was here, but I think he's gone. He comes and goes, you know, like a bird of passage . . . especially when he wins a little money." He turned to the clerk sitting behind him. He said in French: "Do you know anything of M'sieu Bizard?"

The man said: "Yes . . . when I passed the Chatham half an hour ago he was just going in."

"Excellent," said the other. He turned to Vallon. "You see, M'sieu, you are lucky. Apparently M'sieu Bizard is at the Chatham."

"Thank you. . . ." Vallon went out of the Casino; began to walk to the Hotel Chatham in the main street. He thought that it was a very good thing always to check; that it was lucky he had tried to find Bizard for himself.

He went into the Chatham; ordered a drink. When the waiter brought it he asked: "Do you recognise a Monsieur Rene Bizard here?"

" But yes, M'sieu, over in the corner on the right of the orchestra."

Vallon got up ; walked across the dance floor. Seated on the right of the orchestra, at a table by himself, was an individual who seemed very pleased with life. He was about forty-five years of age, immaculately dressed. He wore a gardenia in his button-hole ; had a pencil-line moustache, a round, tanned face. He looked as if he had been spending weeks on a Mediterranean beach.

Vallon said : " M'sieu Bizard——?"

The man smiled. " Rene Bizard, at your service, M'sieu," he said pleasantly. " Can I help you ? "

" You might be able to. My name's Vallon—John Vallon. I'm a private detective. Not long ago I had a conversation with Mrs. Clavering. I expect you know her."

Bizard said : " No, I don't know her, M'sieu . . . but I have heard of her. Won't you sit down ? A drink ? "

Vallon sat down. " Thanks . . . I'll drink some brandy." He went on : " I expect you heard of Mrs. Clavering through a colleague of mine—a Mr. Vine Allard ? "

Bizard nodded. He took out a red and white striped gold cigarette case ; extracted a fat Turkish cigarette ; lighted it. His hands were well kept, manicured, the nails polished. He seemed a very happy, contented individual, Vallon thought.

Bizard said : " Yes, I was very interested. Mr. Allard got in touch with me originally from England. He spoke to me on the telephone." He leaned back in his chair ; exuded a mouthful of tobacco smoke. He went on : " You will understand, M'sieu, that I am a theatrical and film producer. I have what you call touring companies that visit the most important towns in France.

" I was very interested when M'sieu Allard told me on the telephone that he had been employed by some wealthy and important English people—a Mr. and Mrs. Clavering—to endeavour to find a daughter of hers who had been missing for a long time. He asked me about a young woman who was playing a leading part in one of my touring shows. I told him about her. Naturally, I was very intrigued about this. You will understand, M'sieu, I am of a romantic and possibly dramatic disposition. The idea that, concealed in one of my theatrical productions, was a missing heiress was superb.

I liked it. I became even more interested when, after I had told him about this young woman, M'sieu Allard said this was the girl; that he would very much like to come over to meet her; that he wished to talk to her. He told me that I was not to worry, if his surmise was correct and she was the girl, about losing her; that in any event I should be well recompensed."

Vallon nodded.

Bizard went on : " He flew over the next day. I met him here and we went to Abbeville. There I introduced him to the young woman in question, and after half an hour's conversation with her, which took place in my presence, he told me that he was perfectly satisfied that this was the person he was looking for."

Vallon asked : " She was a young Englishwoman, wasn't she ? Would her name by any chance be Leila Mannering ? "

" Precisely," said Bizard. " She was Miss Leila Mannering. It was amusing having her in one of my companies because first of all she was an English woman and, secondly, she spoke French perfectly."

Vallon said : " So Allard was satisfied that this was the girl. He asked her a lot of questions, I suppose ? "

" Yes. . . ." Bizard shrugged his shoulders—a gesture which might have meant anything. " You should know, M'sieu Vallon, I am a disinterested party. I am not concerned in any event. I was not concerned because even if it was necessary that Miss Mannering should leave me—well, that was quite all right . . . I can always get another actress in France. We have many good actresses here. But, if you will forgive my saying so, it seemed that he was not so much asking her questions as telling her the answers. That was the impression I got."

The waiter brought the drinks. Vallon drank some brandy. He said : " Exactly what do you mean by that ? "

Bizard said : " You know what your lawyers call a leading question, M'sieu ? For instance, it struck me that never did M'sieu Allard say : ' I want you to tell me where you came from ; where you were before you came to France.' Always he said : ' Isn't it right that you came from so-and-so to France ? ' ' Isn't it correct that you have done so-and-so ? ' ' Am I not right in believing that for such and such a time you were in such and such a place ? ' One might almost have thought he was making the answers easy for her, because you will understand all she had to say was, ' Yes, that is right.' ''

65

Vallon said : " I see. . . . You definitely had the impression that Allard was possibly making it easy for the girl to pretend she was the missing young woman even if she weren't ? "

Bizard said : " I would hate to say that, but that is how it seemed."

Vallon asked : " What was Miss Mannering's attitude ? "

Bizard shrugged his shoulders again. " Actually, I don't think she seemed very interested. You know, Miss Mannering is a very happy person. She liked her work very much. I don't think she would be very excited about anything. I must say she was a little interested when M'sieu Allard told her that she would probably have a great deal of money. But that would interest anybody, would it not ? " He smiled benignly at Vallon.

Vallon said : " Miss Mannering didn't know anything about her own background, and what was suggested to her by Allard appeared to have fitted in with her own ideas of her earlier life and troubles."

Bizard nodded. " That is the impression I got." He finished his drink. Vallon signalled to the waiter ; ordered more drinks.

He said : " Tell me something. In what circumstances did Miss Mannering join your comapny ? Do you remember ? "

" But of course," said Bizard. " From time to time it is necessary that I recruit fresh personnel for my companies, so I am in touch with different theatrical agents. Her name was brought to me by a man I've known for some time. He is a man of the theatre—an agent. I was sending out a play and he said he knew of a young woman who would be ideal for a certain part. He said it was all the more attractive because she was English. He thought that would be rather a novelty. So I saw her. It was Miss Mannering and she read the part, and liked it very much. So I engaged her."

Vallon asked : " What was the name of this gentleman, M'sieu Bizard ? "

Bizard said : " I cannot forget his name because, although I don't know him very well, it is an odd name. His name was Friday—Julius Friday. He was in the company with her. I should tell you that as well as being a theatrical agent he did stage management. He went out with the company."

" Did he know that subsequently Allard had seen the girl ; talked to her ? " asked Vallon.

" Oh, yes. She told him all about it. Because after M'sieu had gone, an arrangement was made under which she was to go over to England. It was Julius Friday who came to me a few days afterwards and said that it was necessary that they both left as she had to go to England and he was going with her. He said it would not inconvenience me a great deal because he had already rehearsed an understudy for her part, and had arranged for someone else to take over his duties as stage manager. It made no difference to me."

" So they went off together ? " said Vallon. " Miss Mannering and Friday. And you've heard nothing from either of them since ? "

" Nothing at all," Bizard answered. " I was a little disappointed because this is some time ago, and I expected that at least Friday would have written to me and told me something about this business. But, no, I have heard nothing."

Vallon finished his drink. " Thank you very much, M'sieu Bizard. I am obliged to you."

Bizard said : " It has been a pleasure. I am sorry you must go. Another drink ? "

Vallon said : " No, thanks." He got up. " By the way, did you know that Mrs. Clavering was trying to find you ? She wanted to speak to you about all this."

Bizard shook his head. " I didn't know that, but you see, I went away and I have only just returned. So this Mrs. Clavering wished to speak to me. . . ." His face brightened a little. " I understand, M'sieu Vallon, that she is a very beautiful woman. Mr. Allard told me that."

Vallon said : " I'm telling you she is ! "

Bizard shrugged his shoulders. " What a pity that I was not here." He leaned forward. " Tell me, in confidence, what do you think she wanted to see me about, M'sieu Vallon."

Vallon said : " I'm not certain, but I have an idea in my head that she wasn't very pleased with Mr. Allard ; that she has a decided feeling against Miss Mannering being her daughter. She felt that possibly Allard was playing a game of his own ; that he wanted to find her a daughter, so he looked round and found one quickly."

There was a silence. Bizard looked at the table. He said : " You know, that's rather peculiar, M'sieu Vallon, because if Mrs. Clavering had seen me and told me all this I would have agreed with her. I don't know why, but I received the impression that M'sieu Allard was very, very keen on Miss Mannering being the right girl, you understand ? "

" Yes . . . you're suggesting that he practically told her what to do ? "

Bizard said : " Yes. Like that . . . without of course making it *too* obvious."

" You've been very kind," said Vallon. " Perhaps we'll meet again."

" Why not ? " said Bizard. " I'm always here. I come and I go, but I always come back here—in the season, anyway. *Au 'voir*, M'sieu. . . ."

Vallon went out ; went back to his car ; started the engine. He drove out of Le Touquet ; took the main road for Calais.

CHAPTER FOUR

INSKIP

I

VALLON PAID off the cab outside the cocktail bar in Jermyn Street ; went inside ; ordered a double Bacardi ; leaned up against the bar and thought about Mrs. Clavering.

He thought that it was quite difficult *not* to think about Mrs. Clavering—however much you didn't want to do that, and however dangerous you thought the process might be. Because thinking about her could be dangerous. She possessed an extraordinary allure—a peculiar fascination. It would not be difficult for any man—almost in spite of himself—to *want* to agree with Mrs. Clavering.

Half her charm, Vallon considered, was due to the fact that she was unaware of what she had. She was entirely unconscious of her beauty, personality and allure— a process which made these attributes worth double, and when a woman who looked, talked and moved as she did was also unhappy, it might easily be difficult for a man who was temperamental about women not to fall hard and go on falling.

Vallon wondered if he was a man who was temperamental about women. The idea made him grin. He didn't think he was—well, not so that you would notice it—even if Madeleine believed he was ! She believed that he attracted most women with whom he came in contact—a not unusual belief for a woman who loves a man and is naturally a little jealous.

He wondered if Mrs. Clavering found him attractive. He thought that maybe, one of these days, he would find out about that.

He ordered another Bacardi, drank it, paid his bill ; walked slowly to his office.

He called through to the switch-board ; asked for Marvin. When he came into the room, Vallon asked : " Has anything happened ? Anything I ought to know—about the Clavering business, I mean ? "

Marvin shook his head. " Not a thing. I'm glad you let me

69

know you were here. I'd just put in a personal call to you at Montreuil." He grinned. "I didn't expect you to be back so soon."

Vallon said : " Neither did I. What did you want me for ? "

" Mungo came through," said Marvin. " He said he'd been wrong about Miss Thorne being in Paris. Apparently she intended to go there but didn't make it. They had a breakdown, after midnight, near Montreuil. So she stopped off there at the Château. I expected you to meet her there, but I was going to call you and tell you just in case she'd left to go on to Paris or somewhere before you arrived."

" I was only there an hour or two," said Vallon. He thought it was damned funny that Madeleine should have been staying at the Château. Or was it ? Because if you had a breakdown anywhere near Montreuil it was the obvious place to stop.

He said : " I've left my car at the Municipal Garage, just off the quay, at Calais. Get Toler or someone to get on the afternoon boat ; pick up the car ; drive over to Montreuil ; pay my bill and pick up my bag and then bring the car back. He ought to be able to catch the night boat back here. He's to leave the car in the garage at Kensington. I'll want it to-morrow, I expect."

Marvin said : " O.K." He went out of the office.

Vallon opened the lower drawer of his desk ; took out the whisky bottle and the glass ; gave himself a drink. He looked at his strap-watch. It was five o'clock. In the right-hand corner of the blotter in front of him he could see the piece of paper on which he had written Allard's address—11a Fitzroy Crescent. He put the piece of paper in his pocket ; put on his hat ; went out.

Fitzroy Crescent was one of those antique neighbourhoods which had been fashionable in the Victorian era. Now it was dismal. The fronts of the houses that formed the crescent were dilapidated, many of them not yet repaired from the effects of war-time bombs. But No. 11A had an air. The front of the house was clean and there were window-boxes in front of two or three of the windows.

Vallon rang the bell ; stood, leaning against the portico, smoking a cigarette. The door was opened by a plump and motherly woman.

Vallon said : " Good afternoon. My name's Vallon—

John Vallon. I wanted to ask one or two questions about Mr. Allard who used to live here."

The woman said : " Oh, yes, sir." She was obviously interested. " Wouldn't you like to come in ? I'm Mrs. Brown. I own the house."

Vallon said : " Thanks." He followed her into the hall-way ; through a door on the right that led to her sitting-room. The room was clean and bright, rich in antimacassars.

She said : " Please sit down. There's some tea coming in a minute if you'd like a cup."

Vallon smiled at her. " I'd like that very much." He went on : " I came here because this was the address that Mr. Vine Allard had on his identity card. We are trying to trace any near relatives, but we're not having much luck. Was he living here for long, Mrs. Brown ? "

She nodded. " Over two years. . . . I liked Mr. Allard. His rent was always paid on time—well, most weeks. Just once or twice he was a little bit behind, but never for very long. And he always had a kind word for everybody. It's a shocking thing about his being killed like that."

Vallon said : " Yes. It was hard luck. Used he to have many visitors here, Mrs. Brown ? "

She shook her head. " He wasn't here very much—just in the evenings, you know, and when he came in at night. He always used to have his breakfast in bed." She smiled. " I think he had a lot of lady friends," she went on. " I've seen him meet them at the other end of the crescent."

Vallon said, with a smile : " He was the sort of man whom women like, I suppose ? "

" Yes, I should think so. I always thought he was a nice man."

Vallon said : " I suppose the Dudleigh Hospital, where they took him after the smash, telephoned through here ? And that would be quite early in the evening ? "

She nodded.

" Yes, they said the accident had only happened half an hour before."

A maid almost as plump as her mistress brought in the tea-tray. Mrs. Brown began to pour out the tea.

Vallon asked : " What did the hospital people want to know ? Did they ask any questions ? "

" Well, they were looking for what you're looking for, sir . . . any near relatives . . . because I think then that they thought that there wasn't very much chance for Mr. Allard. They said that he'd been examined and he was in the operating theatre then ; that the doctors thought it was a serious business. I believe he was pretty badly smashed up."

" Yes." Vallon took the cup of tea she handed him. He asked : "And were you able to give them the address of any relative, Mrs. Brown ? "

She shook her head. " I didn't know anybody. I never knew any relatives of Mr. Allard's. It was the sort of thing I never thought about. He never had anybody here."

" So you told them that you didn't know of any ? " Vallon asked.

" That's right. I said I didn't know of any. And then I told them that his partner Mr. Inskip might be able to help them. I said I'd telephone through to Mr. Inskip at the office —I had the number, because Mr. Allard gave it to me in case he was wanted at any time. I said I'd ask Mr. Inskip to get in touch with them."

"And I suppose you 'phoned Mr. Inskip immediately ? "

She said : " Yes, sir. Directly I hung up I got through to him. He was shocked. He said he'd get in touch with the people at the hospital."

Vallon asked : " Have you let Mr. Allard's room yet, Mrs. Brown ? "

" No, I haven't. I haven't tried to and I've been busy. It'll be let soon, though ; we're never empty very long."

Vallon said glibly : " I shouldn't think you would be with such an attractive house, Mrs. Brown. I wonder if you'd be very kind and let me look at Mr. Allard's room."

" Of course. He never kept very much up there, but what he left is still there. I have been waiting to hear from somebody about what I should do with his things. It's on the first floor."

Vallon put down his cup. He followed her portly figure up the thinly carpeted stairs ; went into the room on the first landing. It was plainly furnished, meticulously clean. There was an old writing-desk in one corner with some papers on it. One or two books of reference and a Kelly's Directory were on a shelf behind the desk.

Downstairs, the bell rang.

Mrs. Brown said : " That'll be the front door, if you'll excuse me for a minute, sir." She went out of the room.

Vallon went over to the desk. He looked at the papers. They were not very important—one or two reports on cases that Allard had apparently handled. A list of names and addresses with notes against each name as to the credit of the people concerned. Vallon guessed that these would be inquiries that Allard had carried out for the bookmakers Inskip had talked about.

As he moved the papers from the blotter, Vallon could see that one of the leather corners was bulging a little. He took out the blotting paper ; put his finger into the triangle formed by the leather corner. There was a piece of paper which had been doubled into a small square. He opened it. On it, written in pencil, was a number—136a. He put it back ; replaced the blotting paper.

He looked round the room. In a cupboard at the side of the bed were a couple of suits of clothes. He shut the door of the cupboard as Mrs. Brown came into the room.

He said : " I suppose you looked through Mr. Allard's things, Mrs. Brown, to see if you could find anything that night lead you to some relative."

She said : " We did that late that night. Mr. Inskip came round. He said he'd been in touch with the hospital and told them he would try to give them the name and address of a relative. When he came round we went through all Mr. Allard's things—through his clothes and things—but we couldn't find anything."

Vallon nodded. " That wasn't a very pleasant process, I expect, Mrs. Brown."

She shook her head. " I didn't like it, Mr. Vallon, and I don't think Mr. Inskip did. It was sort of funny, you know, going through Mr. Allard's things at that time of night. It was one o'clock in the morning before I got to bed. I couldn't sleep all night for thinking of Mr. Allard."

Vallon said : " Yes, that must have been tough for you Mrs. Brown. Well, I must be on my way. Thank you for your help."

He went down the stairs, out into the street. Somewhere at the back of his mind was an idea—an idea he liked quite a lot. He wondered how much Inskip would like it.

.   .   .   .

73

Vallon, who was seated on a high stool at the cocktail bar in Jermyn Street, looked at his strapwatch. It was a quarter to eleven.

He thought it was a hot night. He ordered another large Bacardi ; sat there in the almost empty bar, sipping the drink, thinking about Leila Mannering. He thought that the process of following one's nose was often very useful. He had followed his nose when he had gone to Montreuil because he wanted to talk to Mrs. Clavering. Through meeting her he had seen Rene Bizard—the benevolent and smiling Mr. Bizard who, in a few words, had given Miss Mannering away.

It would be interesting to find out why she had decided to lie to him. Apparently she was as definite as all the other people. He remembered the conversation he had had with her in her dressing-room. She didn't know how Allard had got the telephone number of her apartment at Valasey Bay. She didn't know what he wanted to talk to her about. She was awfully pleased because Julius Friday had given her the day off. Vallon thought that Miss Leila Mannering should go far in her profession. She was a damned good actress and a very enterprising liar. But why ?

She knew perfectly well what Allard wanted to see her about. He wanted to see her because he wanted to continue the conversation he had had with her in France, when he had asked her a number of leading questions—a process which, as Bizard had said, enabled him to give her a certain amount of information about herself. She knew perfectly well that she was supposed to be the missing daughter—the daughter of del Erest and the lady who was now Mrs. Clavering. And it was a stone certainty that Julius Friday knew that too. It was also certain that Friday knew that she wanted the day off because Allard had asked to see her.

Vallon thought it would be interesting to know exactly what Friday was doing on the day of Allard's death. He yawned ; got off the stool ; said good night to the barman ; went out into Jermyn Street. It was a nice night. Vaguely, or perhaps not so vaguely, he found himself walking in the direction of Long Acre. He thought it might be a good idea to have a further conversation with Inskip. Finding out things, he thought, was more or less a process of talking to people ; remembering what they said and what they didn't say.

Whether they were definite, indefinite, crystal clear or ambiguous. There was usually something to be deduced.

The street in Long Acre was dark; deserted. The old-fashioned street lamps made pools of light on the asphalt pavements.

Vallon went into a doorway opposite the offices of the Allard Detective Agency. The light was on in the second floor front room. So Inskip or somebody was there. Vallon guessed that the street door would be open. He walked across the road; tried it. The door opened. He went inside; closed the street door carefully behind him; began to walk up the stairs. He went along the passage-way; pushed the door open. There was no light in the outer office except that which came through the unwashed window. There was the same vague smell. But the door of Inskip's room was open and the light was on.

Vallon walked across; pushed the door open; closed it behind him. He said : " Good evening, Inskip."

Inskip looked up. He was sitting at his desk, his head resting on one hand. He looked at Vallon vaguely. Vallon saw that he was half-drunk.

" Good evening, Mr. Vallon." said Inskip. " I'm very glad to see you." He hiccoughed loudly.

Vallon said : " I'm glad to see you. I thought it was time that you and I had a little talk." He smiled almost benevolently. " I don't think I'm very pleased with you."

" That's too bad," said Inskip. " Because you've been a very good friend to me, Mr. Vallon—a damned good friend. Except for you, I wouldn't have known anything at all. Like hell I wouldn't ! . . ." He produced a not-too-clean handkerchief from the breast pocket of his jacket ; wiped his wet lips. " I was only thinking about it tonight, so I went out and had a few drinks just to sort of put myself on top of the world."

Vallon said : " Why not ? An occasional drink hurts nobody."

" You're telling me ! " Inskip wiped his mouth again ; dropped the handkerchief on the desk ; put his elbow on the desk and pushed the handkerchief on to the floor. From where he sat Vallon could see it was soiled and crumpled—rather like Inskip. He began to sniff vaguely. He sensed some sort of perfume in the air. He wondered where he had smelled that perfume before. He wondered if it was in Leila Mannering's dressing-room.

He asked: " Have you anything to tell me, Inskip? You remember the idea was that I kept this business going at my expense in case somebody wanted to come and talk to you; in case somebody connected with this business of Allard's came in and talked."

Inskip shook his head. " Nobody's been to see me. I've just stuck around here all the time like you said waiting for somebody to turn up. But nobody's turned up. That's why I went out and had a few tonight. I was fed up with sticking around."

Vallon said: " Yes? You don't look to me like a man who's been drinking because he's bored. You look to me like a man who's been drinking because he's been celebrating. You're not too unhappy about yourself, are you? "

Inskip shrugged his shoulders drunkenly—a process which was too much for him. One elbow slipped off the desk.

Vallon said casually: " Get up and come here. . . . "

Inskip got up. He walked round the desk. He said: " If you've got something to say to me, I bet it's good and important."

Vallon hit him—not too hard—a short right-arm jab to the side of the jaw. Inskip staggered across the office; hit the wall; slithered down on to the floor. Then he sat up, leaning against the wall, holding his jaw, looking at Vallon dully.

Vallon moved over to the desk. He sat on the edge of it. " How do you feel now? " he asked. "A little more sober—a little more inclined to talk? "

Inskip got to his feet. He leaned against the wall. Now his eyes were steady and wary.

Vallon said: "Just listen to me, will you? And don't make any mistake about what I'm saying to you. Just carry your mind back to the night when Allard had his motor smash. Remember? "

Inskip nodded.

Vallon went on: " You remember I came to see you pretty late that evening—I saw you here in this office? I told you that I didn't believe that the smash had been an accident. I told you that I believed that somebody was laying for Allard; that they wanted to kill him before he could talk to me. Remember that? "

" Yes, I remember. . . ." Inskip's voice was steady.

" So he died," Vallon went on. " That makes it murder. The police probably think it was a hit-and-run driver—somebody

76

who had borrowed the truck and stuck a couple of trade plates on it—somebody who got the breeze up when they found they'd smashed into a car, and made a getaway while the road was empty. Well, I think differently. I know it was murder, and eventually the police are going to know that. How would you like to tie up in a murder job, Inskip ? "

Inskip said quickly : " What—me—— ? What the hell had I got to do with it ? "

" I'll tell you," said Vallon. " When I came here you told me that the hospital authorities at Dudleigh had phoned through to you and told you about the smash. That's what you told me, isn't it ? "

Inskip said : " Yes, that's what I told you."

" You told a damned lie. The hospital people at Dudleigh never telephoned through to you. In the early evening they got through to Mrs. Brown—the woman who keeps the place where he lived. And they got through to her because that was the address on his identity card—*not* this address. It was Mrs. Brown who telephoned through to you immediately after she'd finished talking to them. And I'll tell you exactly what you did. You thought this was a good chance for you to get wise to what Allard had been playing at. You got yourself a motor car and you went down to Dudleigh. You went down to the hospital and you identified yourself as Allard's partner. They took you to the store room because at this time they were pretty certain he wasn't going to recover—so that you could go through his effects and if necessary get in touch with his next of kin.

" Inside his pocket-book you found a letter or some document connected with Dyce, Grant & Dyce of Valasey Bay. You removed that document, which bore the address and telephone number of Dyce, the solicitor. And it was you who phoned him up at about ten o'clock that night and told him that Allard had been smashed up. Would you like to know why you did that ? "

" Yes," said Inskip warily. He was watching Vallon closely, fighting to keep his mind clear but not quite succeeding. " Yes . . . you tell me why. . . . You know every goddam thing, don't you ? "

" No," said Vallon cheerfully. " I don't, but I'm a damned good guesser sometimes. You did it because you hoped that,

Allard being out of action, Dyce would employ you to carry on because you were Allard's partner. You thought this way you'd get to know all about this business he was working on. But what you didn't know was that at that time Allard had an appointment with *me*, and you didn't know that Dyce was going to get in touch with me and ask *me* to go on with this investigation."

Inskip said : " So what ! Suppose all this is right. what the hell does it mean to me ? How does it tie me in with a murder job ? "

" That's an easy one," said Vallon. "As I said, my guess is that when you went down to the hospital on the night of the accident and went through Allard's things, you took a document or letter or something of the sort from his pocket-book. That pre-supposes you knew a great deal more about what he was doing than you've let on. That pre-supposes that you might have been in the plot to kill him." He smiled. "Anyway, that's my story and it's a good enough story to take you round to Scotland Yard and suggest that you might like to talk to them. How do you like that idea, Inskip ? "

" I don't like it at all." Inskip moved away from the wall ; walked across the room ; sat down on the chair in front of the window. He said : " You know, I got to hand it to you. I think you're a bloody good detective."

Vallon said : " Maybe I am and maybe I'm not, but I'm good enough for you, and I'm going to be decent enough to try and come to terms with you. I'm going to make you this offer. You get out of here and go wherever it is you sleep and give yourself a good night's rest. To-morrow morning you come round to my office at eleven o'clock and you tell me all about it. You're going to tell me why it was necessary for you to ring up Dyce at ten o'clock on the night of the accident. You're going to tell me why it was you had to get down to that hospital in such a hurry just to see what Allard had in his pocket-book. You're going to tell me what it was he had in his pocket-book that made you ring up Dyce, and if you've got that document—and I bet you have—you're going to produce it at my office at eleven o'clock to-morrow morning." He took out his cigarette case ; lighted a cigarette.

He went on : " If you like to do that I'll lay off you for a bit, anyway. If you don't do it I'm going round to-morrow morning to make a report to the Yard to the effect that I believe Allard was killed ; that I believe you were concerned in the business that led to his murder. And you know what they'll do, don't you ? They'll pick you up. They'll make you talk one way or another. Well, which is it to be ? "

Vallon got up ; moved away from the desk. He went towards the door.

Inskip said : " I think I've been a bloody fool." He grinned vaguely. He moved back to the chair behind the desk. " I ought to know I haven't enough brains to try to play both ends against the middle. You can do it, Mr. Vallon, but I can't. If I had more sense I'd have talked to you in the beginning ; I'd have kept myself out of this mess."

Vallon asked : " What are you going to do ? "

Inskip rested his head on his arm. Now he looked a trifle more bleary. The transitional period towards sobriety induced by the punch was wearing off. He said : " Don't you worry about me ; I'm going to be at your office at eleven o'clock to-morrow morning. I'm going to be dead sober, and I'm going to shoot the book—the whole book too."

" That's fine." said Vallon. He opened the door.

Inskip dropped his hands. His head fell on the desk. Something like a snore came from him. Vallon shrugged his shoulders. He walked to the side of the desk ; picked up the handkerchief. He was about to put it on the desk when he saw the mark. He had another idea. He put the handkerchief in his pocket.

II

Vallon went into the office at half-past ten. He walked down the corridor ; turned into the telephone room.

He said to the girl on the switch-board : "Any calls for me ?"

She looked at him. He was wearing a dark-blue gaberdine, double-breasted suit with a cream silk shirt and blue tie. He wore his soft black hat slightly to the side of his head.

She sighed inwardly. She thought that Johnny Vallon was definitely something.

She said : " Yes, Mr. Vallon. Miss Thorne put a personal call in for you from France. She'll be through at a quarter to eleven."

"All right," said Vallon. "I want to see Mr. Marvin."

He went to his own room. When Marvin came in he said: "Sit down, Marvin, and listen. I'm going to get on to Chauvet International Investigations in Paris. They're going to do a job for me. I want a very thorough check up made on a man I met in France, but I want a really quick job of work done. At the moment it seems rather difficult, but when the thing's started it may be easy. I'll talk to Chauvet on the phone myself. What you have to do is to send a first-class operative—somebody who speaks French—over to work with the Chauvet people—somebody who's going to keep in touch with this office all the time. You understand ? "

Marvin said : " Yes. We'd better send Willy Vowles. He speaks French like a native and he knows France well. You remember he worked with Chauvet a year ago on that Mellidrew case ? "

" I remember," said Vallon. "Will you get him off immediately ? Tell him to go straight to Chauvet in Paris."

Marvin asked : " Is that all ? "

" That's all ; except that I want some tea."

When Marvin had gone, Vallon picked up the telephone ; got through to the girl on the switch-board.

He said : " I want a call as quickly as you can get it to Mr. Chauvet of Chauvet International Research in Paris. Make it snappy, but keep one line clear for Miss Thorne in case she comes through."

The girl said : " Very good." She hung up. She plugged in for the Paris call ; pushed her headphones to one side. She said to the other operator : " He's a lovely man. He came in this morning and stood in the doorway with his hat over one eye. Everything about him is right. His clothes ; the way he looks ; the way he stands ; the way he talks to you."

" You've got it bad," said the other girl. " You'd better watch your step, Mavis."

" What the hell do you mean ? You wouldn't think he's going to look at me, would you ? "

" No, I wouldn't. But you might bounce off him on to something else. I've known it happen. What about that boy you used to know—the one who worked in a vinegar factory?"

Mavis shrugged her shoulders. "Aw, nuts. . . . I never did like vinegar."

When the girl came in with the tea, Vallon poured himself out a cup. He began to think about Madeleine. He thought maybe he had been wrong after all not to try and get in touch with her before. He thought he might have created a difficult situation. Quite obviously Madeleine had been at the Château Montreuil when he had encountered Mrs. Clavering there. For all he knew she might have seen them out of her bedroom window. There were balconies all over the place. She might have been on any one of them. He thought there might be a certain amount of explaining to be done. He shrugged his shoulders. Vallon did not like explanations.

The telephone rang. The switch-board operator said : "Here's your French call, Mr. Vallon. It's Miss Thorne."

Vallon waited. When Madeleine spoke he experienced the same sense of exhilaration that he always got when he heard her voice.

" Is that you, Johnny ? " Her voice was low and soft, almost embracing.

He leaned back in his chair ; put his feet on the desk.

He said : " Yes, honey, it's me."

" You know, you're rather sweet, Johnny. When I wrote you that letter before I went away I wondered what you'd do. You see, I know you so well I thought first of all you'd be angry, in which case you'd just do nothing at all, or you might feel a little guilty about some little thing I don't know about, because women—especially the nice ones—will always make a pass at you, Johnny. You're that sort of man. But I thought the best thing that might possibly happen was that you'd be so worried about me, feeling a little unhappy and just a tiny bit suspicious, you'd find out where I was and come after me. I think that was sweet of you, Johnny."

Vallon said slowly : " Well, you know, I'm like that, honey."

" I know. The night I arrived here we had a bad puncture just outside Montreuil. More than a puncture. It was a blow-out, and there was something wrong with the carburettor too—you know what hired cars are. We weren't near a garage so I went to the Château Montreuil. I meant to go on to Paris the next morning, but I liked the place so much I stayed on, and it just had to be my luck that when you arrived to see me I was over at Le Touquet. I thought I'd try and win a

81

little money at the Casino, so I missed you. I suppose you *had* to leave as quickly as you did."

Vallon breathed a sigh of relief. He said : " Well, Madeleine, I thought I'd better come to Montreuil just to have an hour with you. The Mungo Agency tailed you there. I asked them to. But I couldn't wait longer than I did. I had a phone call from England. I had to come back. It's a pity you weren't in. I suppose they told you I'd been there."

" No, when I came down this morning I saw your registration form in the hotel book." Her voice grew softer and warmer. You can't imagine what a thrill I got out of it. Are you very busy ? "

Vallon said : " I'm right in the middle of a very important case. It's going to tie me up for quite a bit, I think."

"All right. Then you don't want me to come back ? I'll come back immediately if you want me to, Johnny."

Vallon said: " Don't do that. I'm going to be busy getting around quite a lot. Come back in a month's time. And have a good time, honey."

"All right, my sweet." She laughed happily. " I'm sorry you couldn't stay here for another reason. A most beautiful woman has been staying here. Her name's Clavering. I'd have liked you to have had a look at her."

Vallon said easily : " Why should I worry about other women ? I've never seen one as beautiful as you."

" Well, anyway, she's gone now. You're being good, aren't you, Johnny ? "

" What else should I be ? Besides, I'm too busy to think about anything else. So long, baby."

" So long, my sweet," said Madeleine.

He hung up the telephone. He thought there must be some little angel who sits up aloft and looks after private detectives.

He drank some more tea. The telephone bell rang again. This time it was Chauvet.

He said : " Good morning, Johnny. And what can we do for you ? How are zings going, *hein* ? "

" Not too bad, Pierre. There's a job. Will you tie it up as quickly as you can ? And don't mind about the money."

Chauvet said : " I am all yours. I leesten to every word you say mos' carefully."

" There's a man called Rene Bizard. I think at the moment

82

he's at Le Touquet doing a little gambling. Anyway, he won't be difficult to find. He runs theatrical companies in France. Some time during the last six or seven months he's been working with or associated with a man called Julius Friday— an Englishman. I believe that at some time or other this Friday was stage manager to one of Bizard's companies. Have you got all that ? "

Chauvet said : "Just a meenit. I write everyzing down."

Vallon waited ; then he went on. " This Rene Bizard knew a man called del Erest quite a few years ago. This del Erest was a South American. I believe at some time or other he was in the theatre business too. Probably that's how Bizard met him. Del Erest died in South America about twenty years ago. When he died his lawyers wrote and advised his wife Mrs. del Erest, who was in England, that he was dead, and sent her some money that he'd left her. Try and check up on the Bizard/del Erest combination, and Friday. Let me know anything you can about any of them. I'm sending one of my men out who speaks French and knows the country—Vowles. He'll contact you some time this evening. Get cracking, will you, Pierre ? "

Chauvet said : " As always I move quickly. Unfailingly I am what you call it—the eye that never sleeps."

" O.K.," said Vallon. " Don't sleep on this. I'll be seeing you." He hung up.

He poured himself another cup of tea ; looked at his strap-watch. It was nearly ten past eleven. He wondered if Inskip was going to pull a fast one and not turn up. Vallon thought if he didn't appear there could only be two reasons. One was that he was trying to do a little business before he saw Vallon, or that he'd decided to clear out while the going was good. Either of those things would explain his non-appearance. Vallon wondered why Inskip had wanted time to think about things before seeing him ; why he couldn't have talked last night. But he thought he knew the answer to that one. The telephone rang again.

The girl said : "A Mr. Inskip to speak to you, Mr. Vallon— a long distance call."

Vallon said : " Put him through." He waited for the connection ; then Inskip's voice came on the line.

" Good morning, Mr. Vallon. Sorry I didn't turn up."

83

Vallon said: " That's all right for me if it is for you. Did you ring me up to tell me that ? "

" No, Mr. Vallon. It's like I told you last night. I wanted to have a little time to sort things out in my mind. You know I said that. And I wanted to do one or two other things too. And don't you worry about me. I'm not letting you down. I'm not such a mug."

" I'm glad to hear that," said Vallon. " I think it's about time you stopped being one. By the way, where are you ? "

" I'm at a very nice little place called Valasey Bay. It's a lovely place. You ought to come down here some time. I hope you will."

" Why not ? I suppose I'd be curious if I asked what you were doing there."

Inskip said : " Well, just at this moment I wouldn't like to say. But I'm going to have some news for you. Don't worry. You know what I think you ought to do, Mr. Vallon ? And don't think I'm taking a liberty in asking you to do it. You don't know Valasey Bay, I suppose."

Vallon said : " No, I've never been there in my life. Where is it ? "

" It's in Dorset," said Inskip.

Vallon said : " That's easy enough. Well, what is it you wanted ? "

" There's a big place outside the town—an empty house. It lies right behind the town in its own grounds. It's called Valencia House. There's no one there. It used to belong to a Mr. Clavering, but he gave it up because it was too big for him. He took a place on the other side of the town. I'm going to be at Valencia House tonight at half-past ten, and I wish you could be there too. I want to talk to you, but I want to talk to you down here. And I thought it would be a good idea to meet at the Valencia House place because I don't want to be seen down here, Mr. Vallon, and maybe after you've heard what I've got to tell you you won't want to be seen either."

Vallon said : " I see . . . so it's like that, is it ? "

" Yes . . . just like that,"

" All right," said Vallon. " I'll come down some time today—probably this evening. I'll be at Valencia House at ten-thirty. Where do I find you ? "

Inskip said : " Go round to the back of the house. There's a big lawn there. There's a door in the centre of the house. It leads through a conservatory into the front part of the house. I'll see that door's open. I've got the keys. I got 'em from the estate agent. I don't have to return them till to-morrow. You go through the passage-way right through to the front hall. I'll be waiting for you."

"All right," said Vallon. " But you'd better make it sound good ; it'll be good. So long, Mr. Vallon."

Vallon said : " So long." He hung up ; lighted his first cigarette of the day ; drew the smoke into his lungs. He thought it tasted very good. He thought that the Clavering case had begun to crack itself wide open. All it needed now was a little push.

.   .   .   .

Valencia House stood, in its own spacious grounds, at the end of a long, curving carriage drive. The fine Georgian mansion, bathed in the silver moonlight looked romantic ; full of atmosphere. An attractive background, thought Vallon with a grin, for the heart-pourings of the not-so-nice Inskip.

He slowed down ; drove the car off the road on to the grass verge ; got out ; threw his cigarette stub away. He went through the half-open iron gates, up the carriage drive, keeping in the shadows of the trees. To the left and right of him were tangled shrubberies. Here and there a large flowering rhododendron bush threw a patch of colour in the moonlight.

Vallon thought that Clavering must have had a lot of money —buckets of it. To leave a place like this empty without converting it meant that money meant nothing to him. He skirted round to the left of the house. When he arrived at the back he stood looking at the sloping lawn towards the small wood on the other side. Vallon found the conservatory ; pushed open the door. He went in, closing the door softly behind him. On the other side of the conservatory was another door. He went through this. He found himself in complete darkness. He took a flash from his pocket ; switched it on. He was standing in a long oak-wainscoted corridor. A thick carpet was still laid, although when he put the light on it it showed traces of wear. It was thick with dust.

Vallon walked along to the end of the passage-way ; pushed open the door at the far end. He went through. To his right was a circular flight of stairs leading upwards, and in front of him a large hall-way. Under the light of his flash two armoured figures—one on each side of the hall—showed thick with dust. But there was no sign of Inskip. Vallon looked at the illuminated dial of his watch. It was five and twenty to eleven. He dusted off a high back Queen Anne chair with his handkerchief; sat down.

At five minutes to eleven he got up. He went through the big, lonely rooms on the ground floor, up the wide circular staircase, into the rooms on the second, third, floors. They were deserted and empty. The stillness of the place was almost eerie. Here and there in dust-laden rooms, the silver moonlight flooded patches of the floor, casting grotesque shadows.

Vallon came downstairs to the hall. He lighted a cigarette ; found the stairways to the basement in the passage from the back of the house ; went down the stairs. He searched through the kitchens and sculleries, the large store-rooms, coal-cellars. There was no sign of Inskip. He went back to the hallway ; sat down.

Now it was nearly a quarter past eleven. Vallon wondered what had happened to Inskip. The idea that this meeting was a plant on Inskip's part was one that he did not believe for a moment. Inskip was not such a fool as that. He had wanted to talk. Vallon believed he had meant to be there. The only question was had he arrived ? Then Vallon thought of the tank. He thought of the tank, and at the same time the idea occurred to him that Inskip might possibly have walked into the same position as Allard. He had known enough and possibly too much. He put the torch back in his pocket ; dropped his cigarette stub on the floor ; put his foot on it. He went up the stairs again, up past the second floor on to the third floor. He produced his torch, walked through the servants' quarters looking for the trap-door. He found it in the passage-way that ran sideways across the house from which the servants' quarters led. There was a ladder against the wall beneath it.

Vallon put his flashlight on the rungs of the ladder. It had been recently used. Months' old dust was formed on the side of the rungs but was disturbed in the middle. He put the ladder up against the inner ledge of the trap-door ; mounted it ; pushed open the trap-door ; pulled himself up. The smell of ancient dirt and rotting woodwork came to his nostrils. He was under the eaves of the house. He flashed his lamp around. Ten yards to his right, set against the division of the eaves, and again to his left, were two eight-foot-square water tanks.

Vallon went over to the one on his left, picking his way gingerly over the floor joists, listening to rats scurrying as he moved. He put his hand on the side of the tank. He bent his knees ; jumped for the top ; drew himself up. He got one knee across the side of the tank ; put the flash into it. It was empty—empty and unused for years. Old rust had formed on the bottom.

He dropped down on to the wooden joists ; moved across to the other tank ; jumped for the top ; drew himself up. He put the flash on the inside of the tank and saw that Inskip had kept his appointment even if it wasn't in the right place.

He lay face upwards at the bottom of the tank. Obviously he had been pushed over the edge ; had fallen like a sack to the bottom ; turned over on his back. His head and neck were at a strange angle to the rest of his body, but not particularly strange when you considered, thought Vallon, that his neck was broken.

He dropped down inside the tank ; put the flash on Inskip. Inskip, who had tried to be clever and finished up in such a stupid manner. Inskip, whose eyes were wide open looking at Vallon with the peculiar vacant stare of a man who had died suddenly.

Vallon bent down ; unbuttoned Inskip's jacket ; laid it down flat so that he could kneel on it. He began to search the body. There was nothing except a pocket-book. Vallon took it out ; opened it put the flash on it. It was quite empty except for two twopenny-halfpenny stamps tucked away in the stamp compartment, and two one-pound notes in the compartment used for money. Vallon took out the notes ; examined them carefully. He put them back. He closed the case ; was about to put it back in Inskip's pocket. Then he re-opened it ; took out the stamps. He put them under the flash. On one, on the gummed side, was written " 136a."

Vallon put the stamps back into the case ; wiped the case off with his handkerchief ; put it back into Inskip's pocket. He got out of the tank ; straddled the top ; dropped on to the joists. He went to the trap-door ; got on to the ladder.

He shut the trap-door ; put the ladder up against the wall ; cleaned off the sides of it with his handkerchief.

He went down the stairs, through the passage-way, out of the back entrance, down the drive. He walked along the road; got into his car. He thought it had been a not-unpleasant and possibly constructive evening. He started the engine ; turned the car. He by-passed the town of Valasey Bay ; headed back for London.

He felt quite satisfied.

CHAPTER FIVE

FRIDAY

VALLON AWAKENED at four o'clock in the afternoon. He got up ; began to walk about the large carpeted bedroom in his bare feet. He thought, cynically, that the Clavering case was beginning to develop ; to acquire some sort of form ; to become a matter of processes which now shaped themselves towards logical sequences instead of a jumble of contradictions.

Now, having got so far, anything could happen. Mainly because so mush *had* happened. Plenty had happened to Vine Allard ; to Inskip—the sleazy, somewhat stupid and slightly drunken Inskip who had discovered, too late, that he was not an adequate person for the odd business of playing both ends against the middle. Yet he was not alone in that process. He had merely been no more successful than Vine Allard had been—Allard, who was so much quicker in the mind, so much more resourceful, so much more tough.

The telephone bell rang. Vallon went to the side-table ; picked up the receiver. It was Marvin.

He said : " I've been through before, but they said you were asleep. Mrs. Clavering telephoned about twenty minutes ago from Valasey Bay. She asked if you were back from France yet. I told her that you were. She said she'd be very grateful if you could arrange to see her some time or, if it would be more convenient, she'd come up to town."

Vallon thought for a moment ; then he said : " Get through to her. By the way, what's the address ? "

" The house is called Ellerdine Court. It's about a mile from Valasey Bay, just off the main London-Valasey Bay road."

"All right," said Vallon. " Call her and say that I'll come down some time tomorrow ; that I'll see her in the late afternoon or in the evening after dinner. And get through to Valasey Bay on the phone. There's a small hotel there called the Crown Hotel. Tell them I'll be down some time this evening."

Marvin said : " O.K."

Vallon hung up. He began to walk about the bedroom. He thought that the time had come to put the squeeze on Julius Friday. He thought Julius was interesting. Not only interesting but clever. He thought that he wasn't a man who could be frightened easily. He had all the peculiar twisted moral courage of his type. Vallon thought, with a shrug, that all the same you had to weaken some time—even people like Julius.

He began to work out exactly what sort of a fast one he could pull on Friday. After a bit he gave it up; went into the bathroom; took a hot and cold shower; shaved. Then he dressed, packed a handbag and went downstairs. He told the hall porter that he didn't know when he would be back. He walked round to the garage; got out his car. He drove down to Valasey Bay.

. . . .

At half-past nine Vallon parked his car in a small side turning about a hundred yards from the theatre. The evening was just beginning to draw in. He walked down the road; halted under a clump of trees that faced the stage door of the theatre. Ten minutes afterwards Leila Mannering came out. She looked about her; began to walk up the curving road that led towards the town.

Vallon came out of the shadow of the trees. He said: "It's a lovely evening, Miss Mannering, isn't it?"

She stopped for a moment. She was startled. Then she smiled. Vallon thought she looked very charming when she smiled.

She said: "Mr. Vallon . . . what a nice surprise. . . ."

Vallon grinned at her. "Meaning you're really glad to see me?"

She said: "But of course I am. I think you're a very nice person."

"I'm glad. I don't think you're so bad, either," said Vallon. He went on: "My car's parked up the road. I think you and I ought to go for a little drive. I think we have one or two things we ought to say to each other."

She said: "Really? This sounds very thrilling, mysterious; perhaps a little bit startling."

Vallon asked: "Are you interested?"

" I'm curious, Mr. Vallon."

They began to walk towards his car. He said : " I'm glad you're interested. You should be."

" Should I ' Supposing you tell me why. . . ."

Vallon said : "Well, the night I met you previously and we had a conversation in your dressing-room at the theatre, I thought you were a remarkably nice-looking and honest young woman. I still think you're very nice looking—handsome in fact." He smiled. " But I don't think you're quite so honest."

She said : " Oh, dear . . . it makes me feel awful . . . this so pleasant accusation of dishonesty."

Vallon opened the door of the car. She got in. He began to drive slowly up the road into the dusk. He said : ". We'll find some nice, lonely spot where we are not likely to be seen. Then I'm going to ask you a few questions. And take a word of advice from me—tell the truth. If you don't you're going to be in a spot."

" Am I ? " Her voice was almost disinterested.

Vallon nodded.

She said : "A little farther up the road, if you take the turning on the left, the road winds through a little wood. It is deserted, very pretty ; quite charming in fact. You see how I trust you, Mr. Vallon."

Vallon said : " Yes ? . . ." He took the turning to the left ; drove a little way along the winding road ; stopped the car in a clearing by the side of the wood. He said : " I wonder what you think about me. I wonder what Allard told you . . . or perhaps Mr. Friday. It must have been something that made it necessary for you to lie to me."

" Yes ? Go on. . . . Now you *are* beginning to interest me."

Vallon said : " When I saw you last time you told me that Vine Allard had got through to your apartment here in Valasey Bay ; that you didn't know how he got your telephone number ; that he told you some amazing story and said that it was necessary for you to meet him at a place called the Sierra Madre off the Winchester road. You told me that you went to your stage manager Julius Friday and asked him for the day off ; that he gave it to you quite willingly. You said in effect that he seemed not at all surprised at your asking for the day off. Remember ? "

She said : " I remember . . ."

Vallon went on : " To put it plainly all that was damned lies, wasn't it ? You've known Friday for a long time and you'd seen Allard before. I'm going to suggest to you that you saw Vine Allard not so very long ago—when you were playing in Rene Bizard's company in France. I'm going to suggest to you that Allard went over to France and asked you a lot of questions and suggested the answers. I believe he told you that you were the missing daughter of a very rich woman in England, who'd been looking for you for a very long time. Isn't that right ? "

She said : " It might be."

" I'm going to suggest," said Vallon, " that you had a talk with Julius Friday ; that you told him about our conversation, and Friday told you that I was up to some game or other ; probably that I was employed by somebody who was trying to do you out of your inheritance. He told you that the thing for you to do was to tell me nothing. In point of fact, I believe he told you that before I appeared at the theatre. I had a conversation with him at the bar of the hotel here before the evening show. It was he who suggested that I come to see the show. Do you know why he did that ?

She shook her head. " No, Mr. Vallon. Perhaps you'd like to tell me."

" I'll tell you." said Vallon. " Friday wanted me to come to the theatre to see the show because he knew I'd recognise you as the girl who had been waiting at the Sierra Madre, waiting to keep an appointment with Vine Allard, who didn't turn up because he had a car smash." He looked at her sideways. He grinned. " Right ? "

She said: " Oh, yes . . . that's right . . . perfectly right, Mr. Vallon."

He went on : " When I tell you that I'm inclined to be a friend of yours you'll believe me not for anybody's sake but your own. All this business in which you're concerned, Miss Mannering, is very involved and not very nice. You wouldn't like to be mixed up in a first-class scandal, would you ? "

She asked : " What sort of scandal ? "

" Oh, just a little matter of murder, you know."

She looked horrified. " Murder ? . . . What do you mean ? "

"I'll tell you exactly what I mean. For some reason best known to himself Allard wanted you at the Sierra Madre on that night—and me too. Because he wanted us to meet. I think he was in a pretty bad spot and he was trying to find a way out of it. So he wanted to meet me and he wanted me to see you. Well, it didn't come off because somebody hit his car with a truck and he died some hours afterwards."

She said : "You're not by any chance a police officer, are you, Mr. Vallon ? "

He shook his head. "No, I'm a private detective. But you can take it from me that the police are going to be concerned in this business very shortly. I'm going to see to that. If you're a wise girl you're going to come over to my side. You're going to do what I tell you."

"Now I'm beginning to be scared. What are you telling me to do, Mr. Vallon ? " She stopped talking ; then quickly : "I ought to tell you that I don't disbelieve in you."

He smiled cynically. "That's a good thing for you. What I'm telling you *not* to do is to talk to Friday about me or anything else. Don't do anything at all. Don't do anything that Friday or anybody else tells you to do in connection with this business without talking to me about it. In other words, just stay put. That's not very difficult, is it ? "

She said : "No, it sounds easy enough."

Vallon produced his cigarette case. He gave her a cigarette; lighted it and one for himself.

He said : "Tell me something . . . this theatrical company of which you are a member is a repertory company and it uses rather a lot of scenery over the season, doesn't it ? "

She said : "Yes, of course."

"I take it that the scenery is procured from one of the theatrical stores in London as you need it."

"Yes, that's right. Julius Friday looks after that."

"And," said Vallon, "that scenery is sent down from London on the train and picked up by Friday at the station and brought to the theatre in a truck. Is that right ? "

She said : "Yes."

"And," Vallon went on, "I think that on the day you had the appointment to see Allard at the Sierra Madre there were some new sets down at the station waiting to be brought up to the theatre."

She said : " Yes, there were, as a matter of fact. But . . . Mr. Vallon . . . what has all this to do with——? "

Vallon interrupted. "Allard was killed because a truck ran into his car. The truck came out of a side road while he was driving down to the Sierra Madre. It smashed into his car. That truck had Valasey Bay plates on it. They were stolen from the Excelsior Garage down here. That's where Friday hires a truck from, isn't it ? "

She said : "Yes." Then, suddenly : " Good God, Mr. Vallon, you're not suggesting——"

" I'm suggesting just that. I'm suggesting that the truck that finished Allard was the truck hired from the Excelsior Garage Company. Probably the scenery was brought up here in the afternoon and the truck left at the theatre all night. Anybody could have used it any time that day or night. The Excelsior Garage Company wouldn't have known. Whoever used that truck took the number plates off it. They substituted a pair of trade plates which also came from the Excelsior Garage. I wonder if Friday used to drive the truck." He looked at her in the half-darkness.

She said : " Yes, Friday and the stage hands used to go down to the station to bring up new sets. But Friday drove the truck."

" See what I mean ? " he asked.

" Yes, I do see what you mean. . . ."

" One other question," said Vallon. " I wonder whether Friday handed over to his assistant stage manager that night."

She said in a low voice : " Yes, he did. When I came back I heard that he said that as my understudy was playing in my place it would be a good thing for his assistant to have a night on as stage manager. Friday wasn't in the theatre."

Vallon said : " Now you see why I suggest that you don't talk to Friday about anything."

" I see. . . ." She asked anxiously : " What's going to happen, Mr. Vallon ? "

" I wouldn't know," said Vallon. " But you can take it from me that something is going to happen and it's going to happen fairly soon. If you put a pot over a fire it begins to sizzle . . . and it's sizzling now." He smiled. " I think it's going to blow the top off in a minute."

She said : " I think this is awful—awful——! "

Vallon shrugged his shoulders. " Is it ? Well, life's like that, you know. Lots of people think that all strange things that happen are in fiction. Whoever said that truth is stranger than fiction knew what he was talking about." He started the engine. " Now I'm going to drive you back to your rooms. I waited for you because I heard at the hotel that you were on in the last act tonight. I thought I'd like to have an opportunity of talking to you and warning you. Just carry on as usual. Don't let this affect you too much."

She said : " Mr. Vallon, it's not easy *not* to be affected by a thing like this."

He turned the car ; drove on to the main road. She told him the direction to take to her rooms.

They were nearly there when Vallon said : " Just one more question. Were you playing the night before last ? "

" No, I wasn't in that play. It's the one play in which I don't appear."

He said : " You didn't by any chance go up to London, did you ? You didn't by any chance call on a man named Inskip ?"

" No. Why should I ? Who is Inskip ? "

He asked : " What did you do on that night ? "

" I was here in Valasey Bay. I went for a walk ; then I went back to my rooms and read."

" Was there anyone who saw you there ? " asked Vallon.

" But of course—my landlady."

Vallon said : " Good." He stopped the car outside the house; got out. He opened the door for her. " Good night, Miss Mannering. Remember what I told you. Remember the story about the fish."

" What story, Mr. Vallon ? "

Vallon said : " The fish would have been all right if he'd kept his mouth shut. He'd never have swallowed the hook. You be like the fish. Good night, Miss Mannering."

She said : " Good night."

She watched the rear light of the car as it disappeared round the bend.

      .   .   .   .   .

When Vallon arrived back at the theatre the show was over, the audience emerging, chattering, comparing notes, fanning out in the courtyard of the theatre and disappearing into the half-darkness.

He drove up the road, turned and parked the car opposite the stage entrance. He sat there, smoking a cigarette, waiting for Friday.

After ten minutes Friday came out. He stood for a moment in the entrance, lighting a cigarette ; then he looked about him ; began to cross the road.

Vallon called : " Hey . . . Friday . . . ! "

Friday stopped ; turned. He saw Vallon. "So it's you ! " He began to smile—an odd, cynical smile.

" Yes, it's me," said Vallon. " Last time I saw you I told you I'd get around to you some time. Remember ? "

Friday came over to the car. He rested one foot on the running board. He looked down at Vallon. He said with a smirk : " Yes . . . I remember. How could I forget. How could I forget the clever, handsome, attractive Mr. Vallon—God's gift to the detective business—was going to get around to me. I can't tell you how thrilled I am to see you."

He spat theatrically into the gutter.

Vallon grinned at him. " Fine ! Now everyone's happy. Get into the back of the car. I want to talk to you."

" Like hell I'll get into the back of the car," said Friday testily. " Who the hell do you think you are to tell me what I'm to do ? Supposing I tell you to get to hell out of here. What then, Mr. Cleverdick ? "

Vallon was still grinning. " People like you suffer from one or two inhibitions. Sometimes pansies can be tough—very tough. Very often they can be cruel too. But they hate losing their dignity and even more than that they don't like being hurt—physically, I mean. I'm telling you to get into the back of the car and like it. If you don't, I'm going to get out of this car and dust you off. I'm going to smack you around so much—and I said smack—that you won't know whether it's Tuesday or raining."

Friday's eyes were malevolent. He asked : " What do you want to talk to me about ? What have I to do with you ? "

" Plenty," said Vallon. " You'll find that out when we have our talk. We'll go to the Crown. I'm staying there. It's quiet and the lounge is usually empty at this time. If you're very good I'll even buy you a drink. Get in."

Friday got into the back of the car. As Vallon started the engine he said : " I suppose you think you're going to get me to talk. Well, you'll see. . . . You'll find you're wasting your time. And if you try any third-degree rough stuff with me, you bastard, I'll go to the police."

Vallon laughed. " You'll probably find—if you don't talk— that I shall be the one to go to the police. Now relax and give yourself a good time thinking up all the lies you're going to tell me. But they'd better be good ones."

Friday said nothing. He sat back in the corner of the seat, looking out of the window. Vallon could see that he was smiling. He thought that Friday believed that he was on top of the job ; that whatever happened ; whatever Vallon knew or wanted to know, he, Friday, was all right.

Maybe, thought Vallon, he was.

The lounge at the Crown was deserted. Vallon led the way to the far end. They sat down. Vallon said : " What would you like to drink ? "

" Nothing," said Friday. He sneered. " D'you think I want to drink with you—you near copper ? "

" You may not want to," said Vallon. " But you will. And you'll behave yourself. Just for the same reason that you came here. And for the other reason."

" What other reason ? " said Friday. He was almost trembling with rage.

" The other reason is that you're not quite certain how much I know and how much I don't know. But you're damned keen to find out. And why don't you relax ? You're full of hatred, aren't you, Friday ? You hate Mrs. Clavering and you loathed Allard and you don't like me. You didn't even trouble to hide those facts the first time I saw you. And you indicated the rest of it the second time I saw you. When I came to the theatre to see Leila Mannering. You ought to try and take it easy. Otherwise you'll develop nerves."

Friday said : " Mind your own damned business. I can look after my nerves."

" Good," said Vallon. " Now I'm going to tell you something that'll make the rest of the job a little easier for me and a little more difficult for you. Two days or so before Allard had his accident, which you know all about, he wrote me a note. He wanted to see me, to talk to me privately somewhere

where he wouldn't be seen. He made an appointment to meet me in the early evening at a place called the Sierra Madre on the Winchester road. He'd asked Leila Mannering to be there too. Obviously, he wanted her to meet me. She says she doesn't know why he wanted her to go there.

"But I didn't see Allard. He'd had the smash before I arrived, and it wasn't an *accident* either. Or didn't you know that?"

Friday said: "I don't know what the hell you mean. Of course it was an accident. . . ."

"Nuts! . . ." said Vallon. "It was murder. Somebody deliberately ran a heavy truck into his car. They came out of a side road and knocked him into the ditch. Somebody who didn't want him to meet me and talk, somebody who didn't want me to be introduced to the Mannering girl and hear *her* talk—even if she didn't quite know what she meant when she *was* talking. But where you come into this——"

Friday interrupted. He said sarcastically: "Please be nice and tell me where *I* come into this, you snooping fool. . . ."

"It was *your* truck," said Vallon. He lighted a cigarette, watching Friday's face through the flame of his cigarette lighter. "Allard was killed by your truck—the one you hire from the Excelsior Garage to move the new scenery from the station to the theatre. You'd hired the truck for that day. That afternoon it was standing in the courtyard at the back of the theatre, waiting probably to be loaded up with the old sets to take them to the station the next day. Well, somebody drove that truck on to the side road near the Sierra Madre. They stuck a pair of stolen trade plates on the truck. *They* came from the Excelsior Garage too. Remember? . . ."

"Why the hell should *I* remember?" said Friday. "What has all this to do with me. The truck was returned to the Excelsior Garage four days afterwards. The police traced it when the Excelsior people claimed on the insurance company. Somebody took the truck from the theatre yard late in the afternoon when there was no one down at the theatre. Whoever it was abandoned it after the accident. Why should *I* be interested?"

"Why shouldn't you be?" asked Vallon. "You weren't at the theatre that evening, Friday. You missed the performance. You'd given Leila Mannering the day off to keep her appointment with Allard. . . ."

"You're a damned liar," said Friday. His voice was excited. "I gave her the day off. She told me some cock-and-bull story about somebody wanting to see her. I didn't give a damn about that. I didn't even listen. She wanted a day off and so I gave it to her. . . ."

Vallon interrupted. "And you took a day off yourself. Where were you in the late afternoon and evening?"

"Wouldn't you just like to know?" said Friday. "Wouldn't you just like to know, you damned gum-shoeing shyster detective. I suppose the next thing you're going to do is to suggest that I drove the truck down to this place and ran into Allard and killed him. Well—get ahead with it. I don't know anything about it. And I can prove I don't. I was a hell of a long way from that place on that evening. I've got a cast-iron alibi and you'd like to know what it was, and I'm damned well not going to tell you, whatever you threaten; whatever you do. I don't know anything about it, or the truck or Allard. I've never even met Allard. I've——"

Vallon said easily: "You're a damned liar, Friday. You knew all about Allard." He knocked the ash off his cigarette. "The boys aren't doing the right thing by you. I don't wonder you get angry with everyone. They're letting you down left, right and centre, aren't they?"

"What the hell do you mean by that one?" asked Friday. He leaned forward, his bloodshot eyes glaring at the detective.

Vallon said: "You worked with Rene Bizard. You were his stage manager. You knew Leila Mannering in France when she was working with his theatrical company. And you brought her over here. You knew damned well, because if she didn't tell you Bizard did, that Allard went over to France and saw her and asked her a lot of questions for reasons of his own. You knew all that."

Friday sat back in his chair. He ran his tongue over his dry lips.

"The story's going to break some time," said Vallon. "But I want it to break my way. I always try to keep my clients out of anything with a scandal attached."

He signalled to the waiter at the end of the lounge. "Now we'll have that drink, and when we've had it, perhaps we can compare notes."

He ordered the drinks.

There was a long silence. It continued after the drinks had been brought. Friday sat, slumped in his chair, his immaculate, tight-waisted suit wrinkled. He drank his whisky in gulps.

Vallon watched him. He thought that Friday was in a spot : that he was very unhappy about something; that his furious attacks of rage were due to fear and nerves.

He said : " This lounge is going to close down in a minute. The waiter's looking very tired already. I have a bottle up in my room. We'll order some soda water and glasses and we'll go upstairs and continue this seance. Shall we ? "

Friday shrugged his shoulders. " What do I care ? "

Vallon smiled at him—not an unpleasant smile. " Listen to me, Friday. You're not very happy, are you ? You're awfully worried about what I know and what I don't know. You regard everything I say as a trap to make you give something away—something you don't want to give away. All this must be very unpleasant for you. You'd like to tell me to go to hell and you're afraid to do it——"

" Why ? " asked Friday. " Why am I afraid to tell you to go to hell ? "

" Because I might *do* something that would start a hell of a lot. I might, for instance, go to the police about the Allard business and even although you might be entirely innocent of any complicity in that affair yet the investigations which would follow might very easily uncover something you'd like to remain hidden. That's why ! "

Friday shrugged his shoulders again.

Vallon got up from his chair. He said cheerfully ; " We'll go upstairs for another drink. You ought to be pleased at the offer. D'you know why ? You ought to be pleased because I'm going to tell you just what I know ; just what's happened to me since the beginning of this business—isn't that interesting ? It ought to be a lot of fun for you."

He led the way towards the lift.

.   .   .   .   .

Vallon mixed the drinks. He carried the glass over to Friday who sat in the chintz-covered chair by the window. Then he picked up his own glass ; sat on the bed.

100

Friday said with a sneer : " Quite a domestic scene, isn't it ? "

Vallon nodded. " Quite domestic. I like it. And you'd like it, too, if you had any sense."

Friday said, with what was almost a snarl : " You fancy your luck, don't you ? What do you think you're going to get out of me by threatening me ; by pushing me around ? I suppose you think I haven't met people before who've gone in for strong-arm stuff ? "

Vallon said cheerfully : " I should think you've met all sorts of people, Friday—most of them not very pleasant. But, you see, you're in a spot. Either you're implicated in what is after all some very funny business or else you're mixed up with it quite innocently." He drank some whisky. " If you're implicated in it you'll be wise to give me all the assistance you can ; otherwise it won't be so good for you, and if you're mixed up in this thing innocently it's your duty as a decent citizen to say what you know."

Friday said : " I don't have to say anything to any goddam private detective who wants to ask stupid questions. Besides, I thought I was coming up here for you to tell me what you knew." He sneered again. " I don't think you know very much about anything. That's your trouble. You believe, with your snooping little tricks, your threats——" He shrugged his shoulders as if words failed him.

Vallon said: " Don't worry about me. I'm very pleased with my end of the business. When I said I'd bring you here and give you a drink and tell you what I knew, I meant it. That's going to put you in more of a spot than any threat I've made against you."

Friday asked : " What the hell do you mean by that ? "

" Figure it out for yourself," said Vallon. " When I've finished my little story you're going to know everything I know. But I've an idea in my head that you already know plenty *more* than I know, so then you'll be able to put your story and my story together. You'll be able to make one complete sequence in your mind, and I hope you like it. It'll probably scare you a damned sight more than any threats."

" Yes ? " said Friday. " I think I can be the best judge of that."

" That's what I'm saying," said Vallon. " Well, let's start at the beginning. It seems that, originally, the late Mr.

Augustus Jones Clavering decided to employ me as the detective to investigate the whereabouts of Miss del Erest—his wife's missing daughter but for some reason which doesn't matter it was eventually decided to go to Allard. So Allard was brought in on this thing. He saw Mrs. Clavering, and he started his search. One of the coincidences in this case," said Vallon, stretching out to the bed-table for a cigarette and lighting it, " is the speed with which Allard got on the track of Miss del Erest, having regard to the fact that she'd not been seen or heard of for years. But we'll let that pass. It seems that Allard, through some amazing stroke of luck, got in touch with somebody or other who was able to give him some information, as a result of which he went over to France and had a conversation with a young lady. And as a result of this conversation he came back to England and, after having thought things over for quite a time, decided that he didn't like something about it.

Friday said : " What do you mean by that ? Why do you always talk in riddles ? What didn't he like about it ? "

Vallon shrugged his shoulders. " I don't know. I haven't the remotest idea. But he didn't like something about it and I'll tell you why. He wrote me a note. Remember that Allard and I were not very good friends. I worked against him on a case some time ago and through me he had a very bad time. He didn't sit down and write me that note, asking me to meet him, because he liked my face. No there's only one reason why he did that."

Friday asked : " What's that ? "

" It's obvious," said Vallon. " Because he knew that the late Mr. Clavering had decided to use my services in the first place. So Allard thought he was doing *himself* a good turn by coming to me. So he made the appointment. He wrote me and asked me to meet him at the Sierra Madre. He did something else also. I have already told you about that. He got in touch with Miss Mannering and asked her to be present. What do you think he did that for ? "

Friday said : " How the hell do I know ? " He raised his voice. " You're telling me—I'm not telling you. You know everything."

" Well, I know the answer to that one," said Vallon. " He wanted the girl to be there, because in some way or another he

102

intended to get her to substantiate his story. Whatever it was he had to say to me necessitated her being there, and we can make a pretty good guess as to what it was he had to say to me."

Friday grinned evilly. " Aren't you wonderful ? So you're a mind reader too ? "

Vallon said : " I'm a good guesser." He went on : " Allard intended to say to me : ' I know you were supposed to investigate this thing in the first place and then it was given to me. Well, I'm not very happy about it. This is what I have discovered. This is the young woman whom I have questioned because it is believed that she is Miss del Erest—Mrs. Clavering's missing daughter. And because I believe that I want you to meet her and talk to her.' You understand that ? "

Friday said : " I understand what you say. And so what then, Mr. Mind-reader ? What was he going to say then ? "

Vallon said : " My guess is he was going to say : ' I have written a very long and explanatory letter to Dyce the lawyer. I wanted you to see it before I sent it to him or delivered it to him. Here it is. This will tell you all about everything.' And having said that." said Vallon cheerfully, " he was going to take out his pocket-book and show me the letter. He was going to ask me if I thought he'd done his duty by his client and he was going to ask me that question because he was getting good and scared. Are you with me ? "

Friday nodded.

" I'm going to interrupt this little story," Vallon went on, " because here's another coincidence. Allard wasn't very much of a private detective, you know. However decent he might have been at one time or other, his reputation during the last couple of years has not been so good. The other coincidence is this : If Allard was as crooked as he was supposed to be why the hell didn't he go on making this search for the girl last out months or even years ? All the time he was going to be paid, wasn't he ? He was going to be paid big money. But no, within a comparatively short period he throws a spanner in the works. He says : ' I have found the girl.' That's something that's been worrying me a little. I've been wondering why he did that."

Friday said shortly : " Well, go on worrying. I don't know."

Vallon went on : " Let's go back to this meeting of Miss Mannering and Allard at the Sierra Madre—the meeting that never took place—the meeting at which he wanted to show me the letter—the letter which would explain everything to everybody, which he intended sending or delivering to Dyce and which he never sent or delivered because he had a motor smash first of all. And, understand, that wasn't an accident."

Friday said : " Do you mind if I have another drink ? "

" Help yourself," said Vallon. Then, suddenly : " You told me this evening that you had an alibi for that night, Friday. I don't think you're fool enough to lie to me about a thing like that."

Friday said : " Don't be a bloody fool. I was nowhere near the place on that night. That I wasn't at the theatre is true ; where I was is my affair. But I promise you this : If necessary I've got a cast-iron, dyed-in-the-wool alibi. I can prove it. I was with a person who is above suspicion, and whom I do not wish to bring into this nasty business. But I wasn't there."

Vallon said : " Strangely enough, I believe you. My original idea was that two people were concerned in Allard's death. One of them driving the truck which was hidden up the side road ; and another standing at the apex of the fork roads, who signalled Allard—who would naturally slow down at the fork—to come on. I thought that person might have been you. It was just some individual standing at the apex of the fork, who saw Allard's car come round the bend and saw him slow down because he was approaching the fork. This man, as many pedestrians do, signalled to him that the other road was clear. Then he turned away. He didn't even see the smash."

Friday said : " That's very nice of you. I've never been accused yet of indulging in murders. But what's happened, since you're being so candid, to this long explanatory letter which Allard is supposed to have written to Dyce—this letter which explained everything and made his position quite clear ? Surely somebody's got that letter."

" That's the point," said Vallon. " Did you ever meet a man called Inskip—Allard's partner ? "

Friday shook his head.

" On the evening of the smash," Vallon said, " Allard was taken to the hospital at Dudleigh in a very serious condition. The hospital authorities found his identity card in his pocket-book. They phoned to the address on that identity card—the room where he lived. The landlady could give them no information, but she promised that she'd get through to Inskip. She did this. Inskip went down to the hospital. He went through Allard's effects ; through the pocket-book. He found the letter. And how do you like that ? "

He went on : " I don't think Inskip was a very nice guy. At the same time he was a fool. He thought that the investigation Allard had been carrying on would pay off very well. He thought it was the natural thing for Dyce to put him— because he was Allard's partner—on to it now that Allard was out of action. So he wanted Dyce to know that Allard was out of action. So he telephoned through to Dyce at his house—he got the address from the letter which Allard had written—and said that Allard had had a bad smash. Then he rang off. He hoped that next day Dyce would get in touch with him and tell him to go on with the business. But he didn't."

Friday said : " No. He came to you instead ? "

" That's not a bad guess," said Vallon. " He came to me instead. When I saw Inskip the first time, he told me he knew nothing about what Allard was doing about this case— nothing at all. I believed him. I believed he was just a superior sort of office boy. But after he had read that letter he knew plenty about it. And when he found that I was going to continue the investigation he wondered what he was going to do about it. By this time," said Vallon, putting his empty glass down on the bed-table, " I'd come to the conclusion that Inskip was holding out on me, so I put the squeeze on him. I told him that he was to come round to my office and talk. He agreed to do that."

Friday interrupted : " And did he come round and talk ? Did he come and see you and give you this wonderful letter ? "

" No," said Vallon, " he didn't do anything like that. For some reason best known to himself he came down here instead. He phoned me from Valasey Bay about twenty minutes after the time he was supposed to see me in my office. He said he was trying to duck. He said he'd be very glad if I could get down here. He made an appointment to meet me at half-past ten that night at Valencia House. I expect you know it ; it's a big house outside the town. I came down to meet him, but I didn't get anything out of him for a very good reason. He was dead."

Friday sat bolt upright in the chair. He said : " My God ! . . . *That* isn't true, is it ? "

Vallon nodded. " It's true enough. I found him in one of the water storage tanks underneath the roof. He had a broken neck. He was dead enough. There wasn't anything on him." He grinned. " Not even that letter. And here's another coincidence, Friday. Allard, who was a pretty tough egg, got scared and wanted to talk to me before he went any further with this business. Then Inskip took over and Inskip got scared too."

" If he was scared," said Friday, " why didn't he come down to your office and see you like he said ? Why did he have to come down here ? "

Vallon grinned at him. " That's an easy one. Inskip was broke. He was broke and he was hopeless. He wanted some money. But he remembered what had happened to Allard so he thought he'd be clever. My belief is that he got in touch with somebody down here ; told them that he had the letter which Allard had originally written ; told them he was prepared to sell it at his price. My belief is that he made an appointment with somebody to meet them at Valencia House say at about ten o'clock, his idea being this : That if the person whom he met agreed and paid the money over he was going to clear out. The business would only take a few minutes. Inskip was going to clear out and miss his appointment with me."

Friday said : " Do you mean to say that he was fool enough to go to this place ; that he was a blackmailer and he went there taking that letter with him ? "

" No . . . he wasn't as stupid as that. He had the letter somewhere else. He'd hand it over only when he was paid."

Friday said : " Supposing this person had got tough with him ? "

" That was where I came in," said Vallon. " That's why he made the appointment with me for ten-thirty. He thought if they couldn't come to terms, and the other side got a little tough, he was going to hang out the conversation till half-past ten o'clock when I arrived." He smiled ruefully. " Unfortunately for him the other person wasn't having it that way. The conversation must have been very short and sharp. It would be something on these lines :

" These two met at ten o'clock. Inskip told ' X ' how much money he wanted ; ' X ' said he was prepared to pay it ; where was the letter ?

106

" Inskip said he had the letter in a safe place. He'd produce it when he was paid the money. Then ' X ' realised something. ' X ' knew Allard was dead and therefore Inskip would be the only person who knew where the letter was ; that if Inskip were put out of the way quickly enough everything would be in order and he'd save a lot of money. So Inskip was killed very quickly and stuck in the tank. Realise that our friend ' X ' didn't know I was going to arrive. Maybe if I'd been a few minutes early for my appointment I'd have met him on his way out after he'd fixed Inskip."

Friday said : " *He?* . . . Why couldn't it be a ' she ? ' "

Vallon shrugged his shoulders. " I don't know any ' she ' who could have carried Inskip up the stairs ; got him up a ladder to the trap-door in the roof ; pulled or pushed him through and got him into a tank, the top of which was eight feet from the floor. The boy who pulled that one was a strong man." He looked at Friday. " I suppose you've an alibi for that night too ? "

Friday avoided the trap. " I don't even know which night you're talking about, but whichever one it was you'll find I have an alibi all right. My life down here is quite public, you know—a damned sight too public," he finished bitterly.

Vallon got off the bed. He mixed himself another drink ; lighted a cigarette. He began to walk up and down the room.

He said : " Mrs. Clavering's in a very bad way about all this business. She's my client and I've got to do the best I can for her. I went over to Montreuil to see her. She'd gone there because she wanted to see a certain Rene Bizard. She'd learned from Allard that this was the man who'd put him on to the girl. But she was unlucky. Bizard, who'd been at Le Touquet, had disappeared. But after I'd left her I went there myself. I found him—just one of those lucky chances. He told me quite a lot of things. He told me how you produced Mannering originally ; how she joined his company in France. Is there anything you'd like to say about that, or are you still maintaining your very discreet silence ? " He grinned wickedly at Friday.

Friday said : " I've nothing to hide. I worked in France for years. I knew Rene Bizard well. I found Mannering playing a small part in some company. She knew very little about herself. She'd been on the stage ever since she could remember.

I thought she was a good actress. In the ordinary run of business I suggested to Bizard that she'd be good in one of his companies, more especially as she was English. So he took her on. I was with the company myself for some time as stage manager. Then he asked me to come over here. He'd heard of the theatre ; he'd heard that it was going cheap. I reported on it to him and he told me to take the lease. The theatre here was opened as a repertory theatre, and he sent Mannering over to play here. She's a good actress. She behaves herself. Nobody ever has any trouble with her, so I was to have her here."

Vallon said : " And that's all you have to say about that ? "

Friday nodded. " That's all I have to say."

Vallon said : " I hope that's true because you'll find I can be very unpleasant if I have to be, and you'll find that the police are very much more efficacious at checking on alibis than perhaps I should be. They're very thorough, you know."

Friday said : " To hell with you, and to hell with the police ! . . . Thank you for the whisky. And thank you for the story. Do you know what I think ? "

" No . . ." said Vallon. " I wonder what you think."

" I'll tell you. I think it's too damned funny. I think it's a scream, and I hope it keeps fine for you." He got up suddenly ; walked across the room ; opened the door.

He said : " Good night, Mr. Vallon." He closed the door with a slam.

Vallon could hear his quick footsteps going down the passage. He threw his cigarette stub away ; poured himself another drink.

He thought that he liked Julius Friday less than ever.

CHAPTER SIX

PAULA

VALLON GOT UP at ten o'clock ; drank a cup of coffee ; bathed, shaved and dressed. At half-past ten he went down to the hotel garage ; took out his car. He drove along the main road from Valasey Bay to Tor Hill—fifteen miles away. He stopped the car at the side of the cliff road ; began to walk along the wide grass verge that led towards the cliff edge. Presently, the ground in front of him changed. The cliff from a sheer drop to the sea ran into an undulating hill. gorse-covered, that ran down to the sands. Vallon climbed half-way down ; lay on his back ; tilted his hat over his eyes ; lighted a cigarette.

He thought being a detective wasn't a bad sort of business if you liked that sort of business. For himself he wasn't quite certain as to whether he liked it or not. But it was amusing, and it really didn't matter to you what happened. You were concerned with people—people who were engaged in the eternal conflict against other people. You stood on the edge and looked in. You were the onlooker who saw most of the game.

Or were you ? He wondered vaguely how much of the game he was seeing ; how much had slipped past him.

Most of it, he thought. Because there was no outstanding incongruity, and incongruities were the things to look for. But not too many of them. The incongruity in a case was usually what detective stories called " clues." Someone did something incongruous, or wore something incongruous, or said something incongruous. You fastened on one of these incongruities and worked from there. But in this business there were too many incongruities.

The first one was Leila Mannering. She was the king-pin of the whole business. Yet she seemed disinterested. She seemed entirely indifferent to the strangeness of her position. She had gone to meet Allard merely because the idea was " romantic," interesting ; because her curiosity was aroused. She was not at all excited about the fact that she might be an heiress, and she must have known about this. It was all the

109

tea in China that Allard had told her all about it at the first interview.

The second was Allard. Allard had behaved very incongruously. Allard, who was tough and clever and resourceful, had, it seemed, suddenly decided to throw his hand in and talk to Vallon. Had Allard known that someone was out gunning for him? Had he known why? Allard had behaved in the most extraordinary manner.

The third—Julius Friday, who merely became more angry the more he became involved: who seemed to have very little, or no, fear of consequences arising out of his connection with this business which had already produced a couple of murders.

The fourth—Inskip. Inskip, who first of all had said that he knew nothing of what Allard was doing; who must have known what he was doing on the evening when Vallon had first met him. Inskip, who was slightly drunken and stupid and unclever; who, after learning from Vallon that Allard had been deliberately murdered, was still sufficiently courageous to try and go on from the place where Allard had left off. Who believed, for some unknown reason, that he could succeed where Allard had failed.

The fifth—Rene Bizard. Bizard, who had been glad to secure the services of Leila Mannering for his touring companies in France—through Julius Friday—and who had been quite happy to lose both his stage manager and leading lady at a moment's notice. Who could not be found by Paula Clavering when *she* wished to see him but who was more than easily found by Vallon at first try.

And finally Paula Clavering herself. Paula, who desired above all things to find her missing daughter and to have the satisfaction of knowing that she would be well cared for; who was prepared to sacrifice herself by marrying an old man in order that her daughter might be safe and who, hearing from Allard that he thought he had found this daughter, instinctively believed that the girl was a fake—an impostor produced by Allard for his own ends—which could only have been money and more money.

Vallon thought, tipping his hat still further over his eyes, that this case was one of those which suffered from the defects of its virtues. And yet this was the sort of case which any private investigator ought to like, simply because it *was* extraordinary. Because nothing happened in the way it should. All you could do was to get the personalities up against each other, talking to each other ; then talking to you. Occasionally, you could throw a spanner in the works, but you had to be careful about that process. It wasn't at all good to throw a spanner in the works in the way Inskip had tried. Sometimes things might come back on you as they had come back on him.

Vallon began to think about Julius Friday. Friday was obviously a liar. But if he was a liar he was a damned good one. He lied cleverly. Vallon remembered his own conversation with Rene Bizard at Le Touquet. Bizard had suggested that his association with Friday was merely that of a theatrical producer and an agent or stage manager. He had said quite definitely that Leila Mannering had been introduced into his company by Friday who was then an agent ; that after she had joined the company Friday had also joined as stage manager. He had said definitely that after the visit from Allard and after Allard had talked to Leila Mannering, Friday had told him that it was necessary that she went to England ; that he accompanied her. That was the truth all right, but only half the truth. Friday, when told that Vallon had seen Bizard, had talked a little too much because he did not know what Vallon and Bizard had discussed. So he had volunteered the information that he had come to Valasey Bay to take the theatre for Bizard ; that Bizard had taken the theatre because the lease was going cheaply. Vallon concluded they were both lying. Both Bizard and Friday, for some reason best known to themselves, were telling half-truths—maybe not even that. Now Vallon began to see some definite contact between these two.

He threw away his cigarette ; got up. He began to mount the slope of the cliff until he came to the top. He made his way to the main road leading westwards out of Tor Hill. He walked for ten minutes until he found a telephone call-box. He went in. He got on to trunks ; asked for Whitehall 1212.

When the switch-board at Scotland Yard answered, Vallon said : " If he's in I'd like to talk to Detective-Sergeant Maple."

He was told to hold on. After a minute Maple came on the line.

Vallon said : " Hallo, Maple, this is Johnny Vallon. Are you still looking after stolen cars ? "

Maple said : " Yes. Are you interested, Johnny ? "

" I might be," said Vallon. " Do you remember three or four days ago an abandoned truck was found on the Winchester road. There'd been a smash. The driver cleared off. There were two trade plates on the truck stolen from a garage in Valasey Bay. Remember that, Maple ? "

Maple said : " Yes. Somebody picked up the truck from a theatre courtyard at Valasey Bay. A truck with its proper number plates was hired to the theatre for moving scenery. Apparently, it used to stand in the courtyard there when it wasn't actually in transit from one place to another. It looks as if somebody picked it up ; drove it down on the Winchester road with a couple of trade plates stolen from the Excelsior Garage ; had a smash and abandoned it. We're not on to the driver yet. Why should we be ? You might as well look for a needle in a haystack."

Vallon said : " I suppose you handed the Valasey Bay inquiries over to the local police ? "

" That's right. We've learned nothing from them about it up to date."

" Look," said Vallon, " supposing this truck business wasn't just a hit-and-run affair ? You remember there was a smash. Supposing that smash was planned ? I expect you know that the car which the truck drove into was a hired car driven by Vine Allard—a private detective. He died some hours after the accident. Supposing that smash wasn't an accident ? That makes it murder, doesn't it ? "

Maple said : " Yes, Johnny, that makes it murder. I suppose you couldn't tell me what's behind all this ? "

" Just a minute," said Vallon. " Supposing this was a murder rap, do you know who would be likely to handle it ? "

" I don't know, but I think I could make a pretty good guess. I think the job would go to MacIlroy—Detective Inspector."

" All right," said Vallon. " Will you have a word with Detective-Inspector MacIlroy—just a word between you and him. Tell him that the smash wasn't an accident ; it was murder. Maybe he'd like to talk to me some time to-morrow— some time in the afternoon."

" Why not ? Where are you talking from, Johnny ? "

" I'm talking from a box in a place called Tor Hill in Dorsetshire. It's a very nice place and the sun's shining and it looks very good."

" So what ? " said Maple.

Vallon asked : " What sort of an egg is this MacIlroy ? "

" He's all right, Johnny. He's a little short and not very good tempered. And I don't think he likes private detectives. One of them trod on his toes one time."

" No ? " said Vallon.

" Well, he's certain to be interested," said Maple. " He's not very busy at the moment. Maybe he'd like to meet you, Johnny, and hear what you have to say. There's just one snag."

Vallon asked : " What's the snag ? "

" Well, he might want to know why you haven't been in touch before. This smash was some days ago, wasn't it ? "

" Yes," said Vallon. " He might want to know that, but I've a good reason. I've been busy, and if he doesn't like it what's he going to do about it ? You tell him I'll be along about three."

Maple said : " I'll tell him, Johnny. But I think it might be a good idea if he came and saw you. See what I mean ? If you come along here he's going to be very official and all that. He's more or less bound to ask you to make a statement and why you haven't done something about it before. You know . . . withholding information from the police . . . and all that nonsense. Besides which, this sounds to me rather as if you wanted to make some sort of a deal. I know you. If you hadn't had something in the back of your mind you'd have been through before. Right ? "

" Yes-s," said Vallon. " You might be nearly right. All right . . . you ask him to come and see me. I'll be in my office to-morrow."

" O.K., Johnny," said Maple. " Be good now and try and keep your nose clean."

" I will," said Vallon. He hung up.

He went out of the call-box ; lighted a fresh cigarette. He walked back to the car ; drove to Valasey Bay. He put the car in the hotel garage ; began to walk towards the town. It was twelve o'clock when he was shown into Dyce's room.

The lawyer said : " I'm very glad to see you, Mr. Vallon. I expect it's too soon for you to have any news for me." He indicated a chair ; pushed the silver cigarette box towards the detective.

Vallon took a cigarette ; lighted it ; sat down. He said : " I don't know that I have any news, but I've a lot of headaches. This case is beginning to turn into quite something, Mr. Dyce."

Dyce looked over the top of his spectacles. " I wonder what you mean by that, Mr. Vallon. To me the business is quite simple."

Vallon said : " It *seemed* very simple to me. When I came to see you last time the position was as follows : Augustus Clavering and his wife decided to institute a search for her missing daughter. Clavering suggested that I should be employed, but another suggestion was put up that the man for this job was Vine Allard. So he got it. You remember you told me Allard telephoned you that he had or was going to have some news for you. That wasn't very long before his car accident."

Dyce nodded. " That's right."

Vallon said : " I think I can tell you what the news was going to be. He was going to tell you that he had a definite line on the missing girl ; that he thought he'd found her."

Dyce sat back in his chair. " Good heavens ! . . . That was extremely quick work."

" That's what I thought," said Vallon. " It seems that Allard had also been in touch with Mrs. Clavering. She thought as you thought. Apparently, she thought it was pretty quick work. She thought something else too ; she thought it was *too* quick."

Dyce said slowly : " I see. . . . You mean——"

" I mean that Mrs. Clavering thought the obvious thing. Remember it was a long time since she'd seen her daughter. No sort of recognition would be possible, but her instinct told her that somebody was pulling a fast one. She definitely had the idea in her head that Vine Allard was going to produce some fake girl."

Dyce said : " This is serious. I suppose you haven't discovered anything about this peculiar idea, Mr. Vallon ? "

Vallon nodded. " I saw Mrs. Clavering at Montreuil. I talked to her about this. Needless to say, she was very upset about the whole business. She told me that Allard had received the original information which had put him on to this girl from a French theatrical producer called Rene Bizard. She went over to France first of all because she didn't like the idea of living in the empty house here and, secondly, because she hoped to contact Bizard ; to ask him what he knew about this girl. She was unable to do so, but I had a little more luck. I managed to find Bizard very quickly—very easily."

Dyce asked : " What did he have to say ? "

" He told me," said Vallon, " that Allard had been over and had talked to this girl who was then a member of one of Bizard's theatrical companies in France. I gather it was a rather peculiar conversation. Allard apparently was trying to check up on the girl's background and where she'd come from. But Bizard had the impression that he wasn't *asking* her so much as *telling* her. You understand ? Asking her leading questions which practically told her the answers."

Dyce said : " I see what you mean. Putting the girl wise as what her background was supposed to be, after which he was going to produce her as the missing daughter."

" Exactly," said Vallon. " That's how it seemed to Bizard. He was quite definite on that point."

Dyce asked : " Did Bizard know where the girl came from ?"

" Yes. She was apparently introduced to his company by a man called Julius Friday."

Dyce said : " Good God . . . that's the stage manager of the theatre here."

" Yes, that's right. He's the stage manager of the theatre and apparently he took the lease of the place for Bizard. The leading lady of the company is a girl called Leila Mannering. She is the girl whom Allard was going to produce as Mrs. Clavering's missing daughter."

Dyce said : " All this is amazing. It sounds almost like a detective story."

" Of course it sounds like a detective story," said Vallon. " It *is* a detective story."

Dyce said : " Well, it's really not as difficult as all that, is it ? It seems to me that all you have to do is to check on this girl's background. If Allard was going to produce her as the missing daughter he must have had something to substantiate his statements—some sort of evidence—some proof, however vague."

115

" That's perfectly right," said Vallon. " But Allard isn't here to produce it, is he ? "

Dyce said : " This is very unfortunate and it was unfortunate that he had that accident just at the time."

" He didn't have any accident. He was killed. Allard had asked to see me on the night of the accident. He didn't see me. But I'll explain why he wanted to see me before he came to see you. It's my belief that he'd written you a letter—a very important letter that might have made all sorts of things clear, but that letter was stolen, so we're in a rather tough spot, aren't we ? "

Dyce said : " Indeed we are. So we're not merely looking for a missing girl now. *You* are also trying to find a murderer, Mr. Vallon."

" Yes . . . but the two things are bound up. You know, Mr. Dyce, there is one point which, compared with other angles of this story may seem relatively unimportant but to me it's most important. You know as well as I do that Allard was a detective of no particular reputation. You know that it would have been to his advantage to draw out his investigation as long as possible. You certainly wouldn't have been surprised if it'd taken a year, would you ? "

" No, I wouldn't," said Dyce. " I thought it would take at least two years."

" Exactly," said Vallon, " and during those two years Allard, who needed money very badly, would have been very generously paid, both as regards fees and his expenses ; yet almost before anybody can say knife he's found the girl— doing himself out of a good income in the process."

" Not necessarily, Mr. Vallon. Supposing, for the sake of argument, that Allard had found some girl whom he was going to produce as the missing Miss del Erest—although she was no such person—don't you realise that he might have told this girl she was going to receive certain sums of money. Perhaps Allard thought he could make more money by black-mailing the girl after she had been accepted as the missing del Erest girl ; much more easily than by running about the world looking for her."

Vallon said : " I realise that. If that's so, why didn't he produce the girl with such proofs as he had ? He wasn't going to do that, was he ? "

"No?" said Dyce. "What was he going to do?"

"He was going to have this girl and I meet him at a roadside cafe. He made an appointment with her and she was there, and when he drove to meet us he was coming from Valasey Bay. I wonder what he came down here for. He didn't come here to see you, did he, Mr. Dyce, because he *didn't* see you. I wonder who he came to see."

Dyce shrugged his shoulders. "That's an interesting point."

"I've already told you," Vallon went on "that Allard had written a report for you; that that report or letter was in his pocket when he was killed. Isn't it funny that he didn't hand it to you or discuss it with you when he was down here earlier in the day on which he was killed?"

Dyce said: "Most strange. Here he was in Valasey Bay with some report or something for me, yet he did not come to this office. Instead, he makes an appointment to meet you in the evening, and arranges that this girl should be there. I wonder why?"

"I think I can guess the answer to that one," said Vallon. "Allard was uncertain about his own position. Remember he talked to Mrs. Clavering. Remember she suggested to him that her intuition told her that this girl was not her daughter. Maybe Allard thought he was in a difficult situation—so difficult that before he handed in that report to you he wanted to talk to me, and he wanted to meet the girl."

Dyce nodded. "I see what you mean. What are you going to do, Mr. Vallon?"

"I'm going to see Mrs. Clavering this evening. I think it's time she heard what I think about this business, and I'm going to do something else too. To-morrow, I'm going to Scotland Yard. Remember that up to the moment the police quite properly believe that the accident was an *accident*. Naturally, they've been looking for the driver of the truck, but they've not found him." He smiled. "Maybe I know the answer to that one. But now I'm going to give them my story; then they're going to start working from another angle, after which somebody is going to be pushed into doing something that will give their end away."

Dyce said: "Mr. Vallon, I have complete confidence in you. I'm perfectly certain you'll do your duty by your client."

"You can depend on that." Vallon got up. "I want to get

117

one point clear. This point concerns the allowance that the girl was going to have when she was found. Let me repeat what you told me when I came to see you last time. I believe the position was then that after the marriage between Augustus Clavering and Mrs. Clavering he came to see you with reference to making a settlement ; that under the terms of this settlement Mrs. Clavering was to receive four thousand a year and a further four thousand a year was to be tied up so that it was available for the girl when she was found, so that if Clavering had died in the meantime he would know that she would be all right. Is that right ? "

Dyce nodded.

Vallon went on : " But you advised him against that course. You said that the cost of the investigation could be paid in the normal way through this office ; that he could instruct you to pay to Mrs. Clavering four thousand a year ; that if the girl turned up in the meantime he could see her, see what he thought of her and then make her such allowance as he desired. And in order to safeguard both Mrs. Clavering and the girl in the event of his death, he was to make a will in which he left eight thousand a year to his wife until such time as the girl was found, and he directed in that will that when she was found Mrs. Clavering should pay to her four thousand a year through this office. Is that right, Mr. Dyce ? "

" That's perfectly correct. Can it have anything to do with this situation ? "

Vallon said : " I don't know. Maybe one of these days I'll be able to tell you." He went to the door. " Mr. Dyce, when I've something more to report I'll let you know. So long."

He closed the door behind him. Dyce sat down at his desk. He looked a trifle bewildered ; then he shrugged his shoulders ; went on with his work.

* * * * * * *

Vallon sat in the deserted lounge at the Crown Hotel. It was nine o'clock, but the evening was still hot. He ordered another whisky and soda. He thought that maybe it would be a good idea to stop drinking whisky. He had eaten no dinner. He wondered about the efficacy of whisky as an inducement to coherent thinking ; qualified the thought with the idea that sometimes it didn't matter whether you thought coherently or not.

He began to think about Paula Clavering. He thought that life was odd and peculiar—sometimes strangely unkind. He thought it had been unkind to her. He began to think about her life—about her unhappy and unfortunate first marriage to del Erest in South America at a time when she was too young to know what life really meant. Then his disappearance and the twenty-odd years she had spent keeping her head above water until she had met Clavering in Valasey Bay and decided to marry him.

And during all those years she had been wondering about her daughter, maybe putting the blame for everything on to her own shoulders in a way that mothers have. Maybe that's what she had done or maybe not. But in any event, it didn't make very much difference.

Vallon finished his drink ; got up. He asked the hall-porter the way to Ellerdine Court. Then he went outside to his car.

Ellerdine Court, standing behind the town on the east side, was a roomy, comfortable house, surrounded by well-kept lawns, giving out in the evening gloaming a picture of peace. He drove through the entrance gates ; parked his car at the end of the carriage drive. He threw his cigarette stub on the ground ; trod it out ; went up the entrance steps, rang the bell and waited.

When he was shown into the drawing-room, he stood in the doorway, looking at Mrs. Clavering. As the door opened she had got up from a desk ; walked across the room. The room was large ; furnished in exquisite taste. There were flowers everywhere.

She stood in the centre of the room, her arms hanging by her sides, looking at Vallon.

He experienced what was almost a shock on seeing her again. The thought flashed through his mind that each time he saw this woman he would see something different—something more attractive—about her. She was wearing a long, supremely-cut evening skirt of black-corded silk ; above it an exquisite French blouse of black lace over white, covered with tiny black sequins. Beautiful rings glittered on her fingers and one diamond and ruby bracelet sparkled over the long close-fitting black lace sleeve. There were dark circles about her eyes,

Vallon came into the room. He said : " Good evening, Mrs. Clavering. I hoped to see you earlier, but I've been busy."

" I understand. . . ." She held out her hand. " I'm very glad to see you, Mr. Vallon—more glad than I can say. I find that as time goes on this business about my daughter worries me more and more. I find that life seems unreal ; that ever since I heard the news of my husband's death I have been living in some sort of not-very-nice dream." She smiled sadly. " I expect you think I am indulging in a little self-pity. Really, there's no reason why I should. Life hasn't been so kind to me that I can afford such an indulgence."

She motioned him to a chair. " Won't you sit down ? And will you have a drink ? "

Vallon said : " I'd like one. I'd like a whisky and soda."

She moved to the fireplace and rang the bell. When the maid came in she ordered the drinks. Vallon watched her as she moved. Even her walk, he thought, was imbued with an unconscious grace.

When the whisky was brought she mixed the drink for him ; brought it over ; gave it to him. Then she went and stood by the fireplace, one slender arm resting on the mantelpiece. Vallon could see the artistic mould of her long fingers with their beautifully shaped, tinted fingernails.

She said : " Have you any news for me ? "

Vallon nodded. " Yes, I have some news for you, but I'm not thinking very well this evening." He smiled wryly.

She asked smilingly : " Why ? Are you tired ? "

Vallon said : " I haven't such a good reason. I missed my dinner. I didn't want to eat. I drank a little too much whisky. Sometimes it's a help to thought—at least that's my excuse. In any event, sometimes it gives you a lift and sometimes it knocks you flat. And to-night . . ." Vallon grinned. " I think to-night it's inclined to knock me flat. That's one of the reasons I wanted to see you this evening."

She said : " Perhaps you thought that seeing me would give you a lift, as you put it ? "

" Exactly. That's what I believe I thought. I thought that coming to see you would be a sort of rest. Maybe I've been doing a little too much thinking—too much worrying—during the past few days."

She asked: " Have you ? Tell me . . . why should you be worrying ? That isn't your job, is it ? "

He said : " I don't know. I wonder if you've ever thought about being a private detective, Mrs. Clavering ? "

She interrupted : " Mrs. Clavering sounds awfully formal. My name's Paula." She laughed. " Strangely enough," she went on, " I feel I've known you an awfully long time. I like you a lot. Somehow you seem to me to be the only friend I have at the moment."

" I like to hear that, Paula," said Vallon. " My friends usually call me Johnny—though I was christened John."

She laughed again—a low, delicious laugh.

" Johnny's a nice name. I like it. I'm going to call you Johnny. Now tell me about being a private detective. Tell me what's worrying you."

He said : " Well, a private detective is always supposed to be an onlooker who sees most of the game. Somebody comes to him with a case, about this or that—sometimes the most stupid, prosaic case—someone's been stealing the petty cash ; industrial investigations ; insurance investigations ; investigations into people's reputations, their pasts, for some reason so private that the services of the official police aren't necessary or possible. But even if the detective is an onlooker, immediately he comes into the case he becomes part of it, because any investigation must always be a matter of conflict between personalities. He's concerned merely with people : never with things. The fact that a diamond necklace is missing from some house doesn't mean a thing to him. The necklace is just a bauble with a valuation. What does matter to him are the personalities who were in the house the night the necklace disappeared—their lives, their weaknesses and their strengths, their likes and their dislikes." He grinned at her. " A detective would be a pretty poor sort of specimen if he didn't become very interested sometimes, especially when he realises the part he is playing in these people's lives."

She asked : " How does he play a part, Johnny ? Why should he play a part ? "

Vallon shrugged. " He has to, because everyone of these personalities concerned with the theft of the necklace is suspected of the theft or suspected of knowing something about it. Immediately he appears they all do something

121

different—something different to the normal routine of their lives. If they are guilty they think they might be being watched. If they're innocent they think they might be suspected. Everyone of them begins to play a part and all the detective can do is to watch them and play his part, or play a dozen parts, casting himself like an actor in the character necessary for each personality with whom he comes in contact. See what I mean ? "

She nodded. " I think I see. . . ."

Vallon went on : " Sometimes he has facts to go on, or a series of events which show him something. Sometimes he has nothing but merely uses his instinct, and that can be quite a thing ! You know it was with you."

" How, Johnny ? What do you mean ? "

" This instinct of yours," said Vallon, " about Allard, when he telephoned you and said that he thought he'd found your daughter. Well, the obvious thing for you to have done would have been to be delighted. You have been worrying about this girl for years ; wondering where she was ; what had happened to her. This business of not knowing was doing something to you. And here was somebody—someone you trusted—who was actually going to produce her. Yet your instinct told you not to believe this. Your instinct told you that this wasn't your daughter." He drank some whisky ; replaced the glass on the side table.

He said : " I suppose you couldn't explain to me why you left like that ? You couldn't give me any definite reason ? "

She thought for a moment. " Yes . . . I think I can. When this investigation started ; when I saw Allard the first time, I had the impression that this would be a long investigation ; that my daughter might never be found or that if she were it would take at least a year. I don't know why I thought like that, but I did."

Vallon said : " I understand that. I'd probably have felt the same thing myself."

" And then," she went on, " almost before I had got used to the idea that she might be found, Allard telephoned me and told me he thought he'd found her. My first reaction was one of delight ; then almost simultaneously I wondered. I suspected."

Vallon nodded. " I'm still with you. As you know now,

Allard wasn't so hot. He hadn't much money. The obvious thing for him to do was to extend that search as long as possible. So that, supposing your instinct was right ; supposing this girl he'd found was not your daughter, I wonder why he'd want to produce a fake. Surely he'd be cutting off his own nose to spite his face. I wonder why he'd do that."

She said in a low voice : " I've been thinking about that too . . . and I had a horrible idea."

Vallon raised his eyebrows. " Yes ? Tell me what it was."

She said : " The easiest thing to find out quickly, Johnny, would be that she was dead. Do you see what I mean ? When people die it becomes an official business, doesn't it ? There's a doctor, a death certificate, a burial. The undertaker has to have a certificate from the doctor. Supposing Allard did the obvious thing immediately he started this investigation ? That would be to wire, cable or telephone the officials—a registrar somewhere in South America, where my daughter was last heard of. Supposing they had information about her ; that they had known that she was dead ; where she was buried ? "

Vallon said : " I've got it. I see what you mean now. I think I understand Allard's point of view. You mean to say that he had some very definite information about your daughter—the information being that she was dead."

" That is what I think. That is the terrible thought that came to my mind," she said.

Vallon drank some more whisky. " And that explains Allard's attitude. If the girl were dead and he reported that, the job was finished ; there was no money for him, anyway. So the clever thing for him to do was to find a fake. If he found a fake girl who was in the job with him ; if he could pass her off on you as your missing daughter, that girl would have money, and Allard was going to take his cut. I think the idea's a very sound one, Paula. I wonder why *I* didn't think of it."

She said : " With me, as I have told you, it was merely an instinct. But one doesn't necessarily believe in one's instinct, except at the moment. I could be wrong."

" Maybe. . . . But your idea's a good one. Your idea would explain Allard's conduct, except for one thing——"

She moved a little. " What thing ? "

" If Allard was going to produce this girl—and let's imagine,

123

for the sake of argument, that she *was* a fake ; let's imagine that there was an arrangement between her and Allard that if the job came off she was to pay him money ; supposing all this were true, Allard would have to have *some* sort of documentary evidence about the girl, wouldn't he ? He couldn't just produce her and say : ' This is your missing daughter,' and to the girl : ' This is your mother. Why don't you two kiss each other ? ' He couldn't get away with that, could he ? He had to have some sort of substantiation."

She said : " Yes, Johnny. You would think that he must have found that. Mr. Dyce would want to know all about the girl. After all, he's a solicitor." She smiled. " You know what they're like."

" And there's another angle," said Vallon. He finished the whisky. She came over to him ; took the glass ; mixed another drink ; brought it back to him.

He said : " The funny thing was that Allard wanted to see me. Do you see what I mean ? Consider the situation. Your late husband's first idea was that I should handle this investigation. Remember ? "

" Yes, I do." She had gone back to her place by the fireplace. " I wish to God you had ! "

" And the next thing," said Vallon, " the job was given to Allard because your friends had recommended him. But you must remember that Allard didn't like me. He had no cause to like me. I'd been on his tail some time before. I got him kicked out from one of the commercial firms who used to employ him. He had no reason to like me at all—no reason to come to me except for one thing."

She asked : " What thing, Johnny ? What's in your mind ? "

Vallon said : " Let's try and guess. He telephones you and tells you he's found your daughter. He expects you to be delighted, instead of which you sound a little dubious. He probably senses this, and then, for some reason best known to himself, he sits down and writes me a note asking me to meet him in some remote place in the country. He wants to talk to me urgently. I wonder why. I can think of only one reason."

" Yes ? What reason ? "

" Allard was scared. He thought maybe he was going to be accused of producing a fake daughter. Possibly he wanted to

cover himself. Possibly he wanted to meet me and say to me :
' Look, you were the person who was supposed to handle this
job in the first place, but you didn't because I got it instead.
Now I think I've found this girl, and I have an idea Mrs.
Clavering doubts what I say. I have an idea she doesn't
believe this is her daughter. Maybe somebody is going to
accuse me of producing a fake. This is what I've done. This is
how I've handled it. Don't you think I've been justified in
doing what I did ? ' Maybe," Vallon went on, " this is what he
wanted to say to me."

She nodded. " I see what you mean. He wanted to get you
on his side. He wanted you as confirmation that he'd worked
properly ; that even if he *had* produced a fake girl it wasn't *his*
fault ? "

Vallon said : " That's what I think. Because there's no
doubt in my mind that he was producing a fake girl."

She raised her eyebrows. " So you think that too ? " She
smiled sadly. " Is this a case of instinct with you, Johnny ? "

He shook his head. " This is a case of evidence. Remember
the night I saw you at Montreuil and talked to you in the
garden ? You told me that Allard had said he'd got his information
about the girl originally from a man named Rene Bizard."

She said : " I remember."

" You had gone to Montreuil," said Vallon, " because you'd
heard that this Bizard was to be found at Le Touquet. You
wanted to see him, naturally. You wanted to check up on
Allard. But you couldn't find Bizard. He'd left for some
unknown destination."

She said : " Yes. I think that was a great pity."

" It didn't matter," said Vallon. " Because I found him, and
in the easiest way in the world. I went over to Le Touquet for
the purpose of trying to make some inquiries as to where he
had gone and to find out when he was coming back. I was
lucky. I found him drinking brandy in the Chatham. It was
as easy as that."

She sighed. It sounded like a sigh of relief. She said :
" But this is exciting, Johnny. What did he have to say ? "

" He confirmed in effect what your instinct told you. It
seems that Allard went over there ; saw him at Le Touquet ;
asked him to produce this girl. Bizard was a theatrical
producer running touring companies in France and other

countries. This girl was in one of his companies. Allard told Bizard that he had a very definite idea that the girl was the missing daughter of a rich Englishwoman and that he wanted to talk to her. Bizard was amused and intrigued at the idea of having an heiress playing on one of his companies. He seems a romantic sort of person, and the idea intrigued him. So he agreed, and Allard saw the girl. But Bizard told me that instead of questioning her in an analytical and dispassionate manner about her background, her memories and her antecedents, Allard asked her a series of leading questions, all the time suggesting the answers to her."

She said : " You mean that Allard was telling her in effect what her background, her memories, her antecedents were ? "

Vallon nodded. " That's the idea."

There was a pause ; then she said : " But even so, Johnny, if this was Allard's first meeting with the girl ; if she knew nothing about the position except what the man Bizard told her before Allard arrived, surely she wouldn't accept the situation immediately. If she thought she was being given the information to enable her to pose as my daughter, surely she'd want to see Allard privately first and know what she was going to get out of it."

Vallon said : " Exactly. That's what I thought. Then something else suggested itself to me. I've spoken to you about an individual called Julius Friday—the stage manager at the local theatre here—someone who doesn't like you very much. Remember ? Julius Friday was associated with Rene Bizard and the girl before Allard saw her. Bizard told me that it was through Friday that the girl originally joined the company. I have an idea that Friday had been here in Valasey Bay some time before this and he knew about you ; that he knew you had a missing daughter. Valasey Bay, as he himself told me, is a very small place. Nobody can do anything that isn't known within a few days. Friday could have got that information a dozen ways—through a clerk in Dyce's office, for instance. Why shouldn't Friday, with the idea of making a little money for himself—have talked to this girl ; told her the story ; told her that Allard was coming over ; that Allard would suggest to her the story she was to tell." He smiled at her. " Friday doesn't like you very much. Maybe I can give you a reason for it."

" What reason, Johnny ? "

" Supposing that my guess is right," said Vallon. " Supposing Friday, knowing that Allard had been deputed to find your daughter, first of all had a talk with this girl ; then got into touch with Allard and told him to meet her, tell her what to say and then produce her as the missing daughter, but he, Friday, wanted to be cut in on the financial side of the matter."

She said : " My God, Johnny . . . I believe you've put your finger on it."

Vallon went on : " If I have put my finger on it ; if what I've told you is true, maybe this would explain the sudden death of Allard."

She moved from the fireplace. She came closer to him. She asked : " What do you mean ? "

" Listen . . . supposing that what I have said is true ; that Julius Friday, the girl and Allard were in this thing together. Friday finds the girl. Allard sees her in France, gives her a broad outline of what to say. Then he gets in touch with you and tells you that he has found the girl. He realises that you doubt it. He gets scared. After all, he's been playing it pretty close to the knuckle for the last year or so. He thinks if he's discovered at this game it means he'll see the inside of a prison, so he gets the breeze up. He wonders who the devil he can go to, to cover him in this or advise him. He thinks of me. So he writes me a letter asking me to meet him.

" Then he begins to worry about Friday. What's Friday going to say ? Friday could be very angry if the little plot doesn't come off. So Allard tells Friday what he's going to do. He tells him he's going to see me about this business ask me for the best way out. I think," Vallon continued, " that maybe that's the reason why Friday also loathed Allard. He doesn't seem to like anybody very much. Friday was away from the theatre on the night that Allard was killed The truck that ran into Allard's car was the truck used for moving the scenery from the station to the theatre. See what I mean ? "

She said in a low voice : " I see. . . ."

" I've talked to Friday," Vallon went on. " I have had a heart-to-heart talk with him. I told him the story." He smiled again.

" Johnny, what did he say when you told him ? "

Vallon shrugged. " He was merely a little ruder than usual. He was careful to tell me he had a cast-iron alibi. He was also very careful *not* to tell me what it was. That's how things are at the moment."

She asked : " What are you going to do ? Whatever it is, please hurry."

He got up. " I'll do my best. I expect you're having a pretty bad time, aren't you ? "

" Yes . . . it's not good. In a way I feel I was wrong to have shown Allard what I felt. I should have controlled my feelings. I should have let him produce this girl. It might have done some good. He might have had some sort of proof. In any event, he wouldn't be dead."

Vallon said : " There's a funny little thing about this business—another thing—a thing that ties up Allard with Friday. On the day he made his appointment to meet me he was down here in Valasey Bay. Maybe he'd come down to explain the situation to Friday. Maybe he told him just where he was going to meet me that evening. Don't you see how it adds up ? "

" Yes . . . I see. . . ."

Vallon said : " You're unhappy because you're uncertain. You're unhappy because you believe in some way or other your attitude towards Allard might have been the innocent cause of his death. It's no use your thinking like that. It won't get you anywhere. I'll work as quickly as I can. It's tough, but life isn't all happiness, you know—not for any of us."

She asked : " Not for you, Johnny ? "

He shrugged his shoulders. " Like everyone else I make my mistakes. I do things that I wish I hadn't done."

She said : " I wonder what you mean. Tell me, Johnny. . . ." She came a little closer towards him.

Vallon said : " I'll tell you. I'm going to be married soon. You see . . . just that ? . . . But I don't feel like it."

" Johnny . . . how do you feel ? "

He said : " Like this, my dear. . . ."

She came into his arms quickly. He felt her arms about his neck ; then the softness of her mouth on his. She disengaged herself.

She said : " That was a wicked thing to do, Johnny. For

128

me, I mean. Go away. Get this business cleared up. Then come and talk to me again, and I'll tell you what I think."

He asked : " What do you think, my sweet ? "

She said : " I think you're the only man I've ever loved in my life. I too, have made mistakes, but——" She smiled suddenly. He saw her white teeth flash. " Neither of us have made irrevocable mistakes, Johnny. There's still the future."

He grinned at her. " You're telling me, Paula ! Maybe we'll take it up together."

He went away.

    .   .   .   .   .

When Vallon went up to his room at the Crown Hotel he looked at his strap-watch. It was half-past ten. He went over to the chest of drawers ; took out a clean handkerchief. He wiped his mouth. The mark of Paula Clavering's lipstick showed clearly—a raspberry stain on the white fabric.

Vallon opened his document case ; took out an envelope ; tore the top off. He took out the handkerchief he had picked up from the floor of Inskip's office. He put the two handkerchiefs together.

He sighed. He went to the cupboard ; took out the whisky bottle ; put the neck in his mouth ; took a long swig.

So that was that ! He felt vaguely relieved.

He went to bed.

CHAPTER SEVEN

VIEUX ROSE

VALLON WENT into his office by the private door leading from the corridor. Marvin was at the desk, sorting the morning mail. He got up; walked round the desk; said: "Good morning, Mr. Vallon."

Vallon sat down. He asked: "Anything from Chauvet?"

Marvin grinned. "Plenty! . . . Does he work! Vowles came through to me at my rooms late last night. He said the telephone and cable bills were going to be something! Chauvet put twelve operatives to work within an hour of your ringing him."

Vallon lighted a cigarette. He asked: "Well, what does it look like?"

Marvin produced two or three sheets of flimsy typing paper from his pocket. "This is a rough outline. Chauvet says he can fill in particulars if you want them later, but he'd like to get your reactions to this. He said he's been helped a great deal because this del Erest was in the papers once or twice. He made a big story, expecially the story of his death."

"Start at the beginning," said Vallon.

"Well, here it is. Del Erest married over twenty years ago. His wife was very young, very beautiful. There was one child. Apparently, about two years after the marriage del Erest deserted his wife. He went off. Nobody heard of him. He took the child with him. After he'd gone his wife had a job or two in Santiago. Then she left there and, as you know, she came to England.

"Apparently, del Erest wandered about for a bit. But Chauvet managed to get a line on him, and he finished up at Valparaiso. He was running an entertainment business. Apparently he'd got on in the world and he had some sort of association with a South American lawyer named Miguel Salvador. Some time after he'd met Salvador—and Chauvet said this would be about twenty years ago—he died. He was burned to death in an hotel fire, and that was that!"

Vallon said: "And he left some money?"

" That's right. Salvador handled his estate. There wasn't very much cash, but del Erest had a major interest in this entertainment business, which Salvador was trying to sell."

Vallon interrupted. " Does anybody know where this Salvador is now ? "

Marvin grinned. " He's in the clink. He's doing five years for fraudulent conversion—that and one or two phony insurance claims."

Vallon nodded. " I see. . . . Go on."

Marvin continued : " Anyway, Salvador was trying to sell del Erest's interests in the entertainment business and this looked a not very good proposition until there came along an individual by the name of Rene Bizard. This Bizard was also in the theatrical business. He had money because he'd just married a rich wife—a woman younger than he was who was crazy about him. She put up the money for Bizard to buy the del Erest interests, which he thought might be useful to him. There was an interest in some small theatre in or near Valparaiso. There was scenery, and effects and dresses—you known the sort of thing. Anyhow, Bizard thought these things would be useful to him and he bought them. And paid with his new wife's money. This accounts for the money that was sent to Mrs. del Erest as she was then—now Mrs. Clavering. Because, apparently, del Erest and Salvador were very friendly, and it seems that del Erest had a bit of a conscience about the young wife he had deserted. It seems he had told Salvador to get what he could for the del Erest theatre and send some of it to his wife."

Vallon said : " That's all plain enough. What happened to the del Erest child—the girl ? "

" When del Erest went to Valparaiso he boarded the child with an old nurse of his. He arranged with Salvador that in the event of his death she should be sent to a convent school when she was old enough. She was there for about eleven years ; then she went to some other school, but Chauvet couldn't check on that. He doesn't know where she was or where she went to."

" I see,' said Vallon. " Anything else ? "

" Nothing of importance," said Marvin. " The only thing was that Rene Bizard's rich wife died. She died of heart trouble and she wasn't quite so rich when she died because it seemed that Bizard had been helping himself to her money in a big way. Bizard is a theatrical producer who seems to have a flair for losing money. After his wife died Bizard concentrated his attention on France. He ran companies there up to the time the war started; then cleared out and went somewhere. It's thought he went to Equador but he wanted to get back to France because he had the lease of two or three small theatres there. Directly the war was over he went back to France and restarted his business."

Vallon said : " It was tough about del Erest dying in that fire. I'd liked to have talked to him. What happened ? "

" It was a big story," said Marvin. " It was in all the newspapers. Apparently fifty or sixty people were burned to death. It was a place called the Hotel Bolivar at Valparaiso. The fire started on the ground floor and was sucked up the lift shaft. Miguel Salvador the lawyer and del Erest were staying there. They'd gone there to complete a contract about a cabaret show. When Salvador saw that the lower part of the hotel was on fire ; that there was no chance of getting out, he realised that the only thing to do was to try and get down a drain pipe arrangement at the back—a pretty frightening job because it was a very high hotel. They were on the eighth floor. He pointed this way out to del Erest, but del Erest wasn't playing. As Salvador opened the window to get out and shinned down the drain pipe, the floor on the other side of the room collapsed and del Erest went down with it. They found just a bit of him two days later. Salvador was able to identify him by a ring."

Vallon nodded. " That's that," he said. " So the only person who can tell us about del Erest is Bizard ? "

Marvin said : " Vowles rang me through with this stuff last night. Chauvet thought it might be of some use. He wants instructions as to any particular line he's to go on after this."

Vallon said : " Well, I'm not fearfully interested, but it might be a good thing if he tries to find out what happened to the daughter after she left the convent school. Try and get a line on where she went to. She must have been quite young. Maybe she went to a finishing school somewhere."

Marvin said : " I had that idea myself. I asked Vowles about that. He said he thinks that Chauvet believed that after the first school the girl was sent out of the country some-where ; probably abroad to finish her education."

Vallon said : " Del Erest was a damned bad hat but he must have been pretty keen on that daughter to have arranged that she should be looked after so well after his death. Does anyone know why he took her away from her mother. What was the idea in that ? "

Marvin shrugged his shoulders. " Nobody knows. As you say, he was a bad hat. Maybe he did it to try and get back on his wife."

" Maybe," said Vallon. " You'd better get through to Vowles and tell him just to keep on that angle ; to try and find where the daughter went to."

" Is there anything else ? " asked Marvin.

" Yes, I went into the Glynn Laboratories this morning. Get through to them—the Warwick-road office. I left two handkerchiefs there for a report on the lipstick on them. Ask them if they've made the check yet. You can do it from here."

Marvin said : " O.K." He crossed to the desk ; began to search for the number ; then dialled it on the private telephone.

Vallon walked about the office. He was thinking about del Erest ; wondering what sort of person he was. He thought that maybe he could guess the answer to that one. A young, good-looking, irresponsible South American, he thought, with an eye for a pretty girl, interested in the " entertainment " business. Well, entertainment in South America meant all sorts of things.

And del Erest had fallen for the beautiful young girl who had come across his path and he had married her, and two years afterwards taken a run-out powder. Maybe he had found a wife too expensive to keep. Perhps they had quarrelled. All sorts of things could have happened. But del Erest had gone off and taken the child with him. After which he seemed to have done his best to see that the girl should be educated in due course.

Vallon thought it was a pity about the lawyer—Miguel Salvador—who had been tied up with some rather peculiar deals with del Erest ; who had been his friend ; who had seen him die in the fire.

Then there was Rene Bizard—the plump, smiling Rene Bizard—the Frenchman who took such a joy in life, who liked his theatrical companies in spite of the fact that he seemed to make not very much money out of them ; who had bought out del Erest's interests years before on the money he obtained from a rich wife who was now dead.

Vallon shrugged his shoulders. He thought some of the pieces in the jig-saw puzzle were beginning to fit in, but there were still too many blanks for his liking. He went to the desk ; opened the bottom drawer ; took out the bottle and the glass ; poured himself two fingers of whisky. The spirit warmed his stomach. He felt better.

Marvin stopped speaking on the telephone. He put his hand over the mouthpiece. He said : " They've made the check. You left two handkerchiefs there. They were both stained with the same lipstick. It's called Vieux Rose. It's made by a very good firm in France."

Vallon asked : " Can you buy it here ? "

" Yes . . . an agency has been opened here during the last four or five months, they tell me. It's a very popular lipstick in the theatrical profession—a peculiarly deep and attractive shade of raspberry. Do you want anything else ? "

Vallon shook his head. " That's good enough."

When Marvin had left the room, Vallon got up. He began to walk about the office, smoking a cigarette. He thought Chauvet had done a good job in the time at his disposal and, even if there were blanks, a coherent story was beginning to evolve. Vallon grinned. Life was often a matter of guessing, he thought, and his guesses so far had not been so bad.

He began to think about " 136a." This was the number he had found written on the piece of paper which had been pushed under the leather corner of Allards' blotting paper in his bed-sitting-room. The second time the number appeared was on the back of the stamp in Inskip's pocket-case. For a moment he wondered why Allard and Inskip were both interested in that number. Then he guessed. He had not been the only person to look under the leather corner of the blotting-pad. When Inskip had gone round to Allard's room on the night of the accident he had probably managed to get rid of the woman of the house for a few minutes. He had gone over whatever papers there were on Allard's writing-table, and being a good searcher had naturally looked under the corner of the blotter. He had left the piece of paper there. He had made a note of the number, and later had written it on the back of a stamp, first of all because a stamp is a very easy thing to carry, and secondly because no one is going to be interested in a postage stamp. Inskip, it seemed, had been curious about that number as he, Vallon, was.

He began to think about Allard. There was one important point in connection with Allard. Allard had found the missing daughter. That was his story and, having found her, he wouldn't be very pleased that Mrs. Clavering, during their telephone conversation, had shown that she already had some sort of suspicion that the girl was not her real daughter. Allard wouldn't like that. But he must have had some sort of substantiation of his claim. Allard was no fool. He would know perfectly well that Clavering's lawyers would want to know all about the girl. Somewhere Allard must have had documents of some sort—fake, forged or otherwise—which would go some distance to prove that the girl was the real girl. He must have these.

Vallon threw his cigarette stub into the fireplace. He walked over to the window and stood, looking out on to Regent Street.

Then he got it ! He whistled softly to himself ; went to the telephone. He said to the girl on the switchboard : " Put me through to the Safe Deposit in Chancery Lane." He hung up. Then while he waited for the call to come through he wondered if he had guessed rightly. Chancery Lane was the nearest Safe Deposit to Allard's bed-sitting-room and his office. If he had anything about the girl—fake or forged documents or anything else—he had put them in a safe place.

The telephone bell rang. The girl said : " You're through to Chancery Lane Safe Deposit, Mr. Vallon."

Vallon asked for the manager. When he came on the line Vallon said : " This is Domes, Peeke & Domes—Solicitors. We're trying to clear up the estate of Mr. Vine Allard. You may not know it but he died some days ago as a result of an accident. We're acting for the executors under his will. We have reasons to believe that Mr. Allard had a Safe Deposit box in your building. Would you confirm that ? "

The manager said : " Will you hold on a minute ? " Then : " You're perfectly right. Mr. Vine Allard has a box here—No. 136a. But of course you know, sir, we should require an authority from the executors or a Court order before we allowed the contents of the box to be handed over."

Vallon said : " I see. So Mr. Allard didn't leave any instructions with you as to the course you should adopt in the event of his death ? "

" Nothing at all," said the manager.

" Very well. We'll get the necessary authority and send someone to see you in due course." Vallon hung up. He was smiling. The last guess had been a good one. He wondered if Inskip had guessed what the number meant. If he had, it wouldn't have done him any good.

The telephone rang. The girl said : " Mr. Vallon, a gentleman to see you. He says he hasn't an appointment. His name is Detective-Inspector MacIlroy."

Vallon said : " Send him in."

He got up ; walked over to the window. The door opened. Marvin said : " Detective-Inspector MacIlroy." He went out of the office ; closed the door behind him.

MacIlroy stood just in front of the door looking at Vallon. He was a tall, slim man with a long, bony face. His hair, combed straight back from his forehead, was streaked with grey. His eyes were set wide apart. They were quick, alert eyes, Vallon thought. He was dressed in a double-breasted suit of a dark-blue material with a faint pattern. The suit was well made, the trousers perfectly creased. His shoes were made of good leather and the black Homburg hat Vallon could see had come from a good maker.

Vallon said : " I'm very glad to meet you, Mr. MacIlroy. Won't you sit down ? "

MacIlroy said : " Thanks." His voice was quiet. He sat down in the big chair opposite Vallon's desk.

" Now who's going to begin to talk—you or I ? " asked Vallon. " Whichever of us starts, I think, it's going to be interesting."

" I don't see why it shouldn't be, Mr. Vallon."

" Neither do I." Vallon's smile broadened. " By the way, Maple, to whom I spoke about this business, who put me on to you, told me you didn't like private detectives. I hope you will be able to change your opinion before this business is through."

MacIlroy said : " Maple was perfectly right, Mr. Vallon. I don't like private detectives. Actually, except in divorce cases—and I understand you don't handle divorce cases—I've never seen what use they serve."

Vallon shrugged his shoulders. "Why should you? But there are all sorts of things that happen to people—the weirdest things—and they can't all go rushing to the police, you know. There are all sorts of things outside the normal line of police work which necessitate the services of a private detective. This is one of them'.'

MacIlroy said: "That's very interesting, Mr. Vallon. But supposing I tell you what my point of view is. Shall I?"

Vallon nodded. "I'm listening . . . I'm very interested."

MacIlroy said: "So far as I'm concerned this is a very simple business. As you probably know, Detective-Sergeant Maple is concerned mainly with stolen cars, so the report about this truck and the accident near the cafe called the Sierra Madre came through to him. It had nothing to do with me. It seems that this truck came out of a side road and ran into a private car that was travelling at speed towards the apex of the cross-roads. The driver of the car—a person named Vine Allard—was seriously injured and taken to hospital at Dudleigh, where he died some hours later. Maple told me the driver of the truck was not found. He had abandoned the truck immediately after the accident and disappeared. The truck had been picked up or stolen from a theatre courtyard at a place called Valasey Bay. It was carrying two trade plates which had been fixed on with wire, and these trade plates were, it seems, stolen from the Excelsior Garage at Valasey Bay.

"All this is very interesting but all of it is Maple's concern, except that he tells me that your suggestion is that this accident wasn't an accident, so that what might have been an ordinary manslaughter had now, because the man Allard is dead, turned itself into premeditated murder." He smiled thinly. "Well, that's my job. You understand, Mr. Vallon? And the reason I came here was this: I expect you know quite a little bit about the law, and I expect you know that if you believed that this accident was no accident but an attempt at murder, which eventually succeeded, it was your business to come to the police and tell them so. You know, you might have found yourself in a difficult position as a result of not having done that."

Vallon said: "Maybe."

MacIlroy went on: "In those circumstances I thought it

would be better for all of us if I came down here to see you and had a little unofficial chat. If you'd come up to the Yard your visit there would have been an official one, and I should have asked you to make a statement—something to start this case, because there has to be a start to everything as you know."

Vallon said: " I know all that. I'm very glad you've come here for a different reason, because actually, I think we might have even more than one murder to deal with. We might have two. There again I'm only guessing, you understand ? You were good enough to point out to me just now that if I'd withheld specific information as to an attempted murder from the police I should be committing an offence." He smiled at the police officer. " But it isn't, as far as my knowledge is concerned, an offence to withhold guesses from the police. You see, I'm just guessing. I can't tell you that Johnny Brown attempted to kill Vine Allard, because I've no reason to believe that Johnny Brown or ' X ' did that. I have just got some ideas. I thought you might like to have them, and I thought if I went out of my way to give you those ideas you might like to go out of your way and do something for me."

" Are you asking me to make a deal, Mr. Vallon ? I don't like that. The idea doesn't appeal to me."

Vallon said: " Lots of things don't appeal to people, MacIlroy. But that's how it is. When I ask you to make a deal I am asking you to make a deal in the investigation you're going to have on your hands, because you can take it from me you *are* going to." He went to the chair behind his desk ; sat down. " Lets' smoke a cigarette, MacIlroy. And let's have a drink. I'm going to tell you just what I want to tell you, and I'm going to ask if you'll do what I want. Actually, I think you're going to say yes. You're going to say yes because you've got to do what I want. Eventually, you're going to do it and I want to be in on it."

He opened the bottom drawer ; took out the bottle. He went to the wall cupboard ; produced a siphon and two glasses. He poured out the drinks. He put one and a cigarette in front of MacIlroy. Then he sat down in his chair.

MacIlroy said: " I think you're a very refreshing person. I'm not going to say anything at the moment. I'd like to hear the story—or as much of it as you want to tell me."

Vallon drank a little whisky. He said: " Let's start with

138

Vine Allard. A few days before he died as a result of the accident, he wrote me a note to ask me to meet him at the Sierra Madre—the roadside café near the scene of the accident. He didn't tell me what he wanted to see me about. But I guessed that he was in a spot; that he was scared of something, and in spite of the fact that he disliked me he wanted to see me because he wanted to ask my advice. That's my belief.

"I arrived. When I was approaching the apex of the cross-roads near the Sierra Madre I thought I saw a man standing right at the apex waving a car on. I was probably right. It was probably some ordinary pedestrian who, seeing that the other road which Allard couldn't see was clear, was signalling the car coming towards him to come on. This man of course didn't think that a truck would be waiting in the side road. So Allard, I imagine, stepped on it. He approached the cross-roads much more quickly than he would normally have done. You understand?"

MacIlroy said: "I understand."

"Then," said Vallon, "the truck came out of the side road and hit him. And that was that! So Allard never kept his appointment with me. I became more curious than ever about the business he wished to discuss with me."

Vallon got up; began to walk about the office. He went on: "Allard had been employed by a rich husband and wife who lived in the country to endeavour to trace the wife's daughter by a previous marriage. The mother hadn't seen the girl since she was a small child. After a few weeks Allard apparently had the most extraordinary luck. He managed to make a contact with an individual who was able to put him on to this girl. But there seems to have been an idea—especially on the part of the mother—that Allard had produced a fake. The mother apparently told him this on the telephone. As a result of this, for some reason which I don't know at the moment, because when he went to Valasey Bay he did not go to see the mother, Allard decided to go down there, and he decided to make an appointment to see me on the same evening at the Sierra Madre, which is about half-way back to London. There's no question in my mind that Allard wanted to discuss with me this business about the girl being a fake, because he'd also arranged for her to be at the Sierra Madre. So I think I am guessing right, don't you?"

MacIlroy said : " It looks like it. Go on. . . ."

" Somebody in Valasey Bay," Vallon continued, " knew that Allard was going to meet me. After he left there somebody knew that truck was standing in the courtyard behind the theatre, and this somebody had evidently made up his mind that it would not be good for Allard to meet me. So he drove down near the cross-roads ; found the side road conveniently situated for his purpose, and adequately stopped Allard from seeing me. Are you with me ? "

MacIlroy nodded.

" Now," said Vallon, " I began to stick my nose into this business. I began to make inquiries. I talked to all sorts of people and I did a certain amount of thinking. I had an idea in my head that immediately Allard was taken to the Dudleigh hospital the authorities there, who knew he would probably not recover from his injuries, telephoned to his partner—a man called Inskip—to endeavour to find out who Allard's next-of-kin was. It's my belief that Inskip immediately drove down to the hospital, managed somehow to go through Allard's effects and abstracted from his pocket-book a letter or some document which he intended to show me if and when he'd met me.

" Now this document obviously had some bearing on the girl Allard was going to produce. It was something to do with this girl. Whatever information was in that letter or document went into Inskip's possession. I spoke to Inskip. I told him what I've just told you. I told him that unless he talked to me and talked plenty, and produced anything he had, I was going to make some trouble for him. I told him that I thought Allard had been murdered ; that if I went to the police and told them my ideas about his visit to the hospital he'd probably find himself implicated in a murder charge somehow or other. Naturally he didn't like that."

MacIlroy grinned. " I can understand that. What did he do ? Did he talk ? "

Vallon shook his head. " He was supposed to come to my office the next morning at eleven o'clock. He didn't come. He telephoned me from Valasey Bay."

MacIlroy raised his eyebrows. He interrupted. " This Valasey Bay seems to be the centre of things, doesn't it ? It must be an interesting place."

" It is an interesting place, I promise you. However, when

Inskip came through on the telephone to apologise for not keeping his appointment with me, he said he wished to talk to me at Valasey Bay. He made an appointment to meet me at a house there at half-past ten. He said that if I kept that appointment he'd tell me all about it."

MacIlroy asked : " Did you keep the appointment ? Did you meet him ? "

" I kept the appointment," said Vallon, " but I didn't meet him for a very good reason. He'd been killed."

MacIlroy's eyebrows went up again. " This is becoming very interesting ! "

Vallon said shortly : " That's what I thought. I waited in the hall-way of this empty house—it's called Valencia House— a big place standing in its own grounds behind the town—and then I searched the house. I had an idea that something might have happened to Inskip just in the same way as it had happened to Allard. Do you see my point ? "

MacIlroy said : " I see."

" I went all over the house," said Vallon, " and found nothing. Then I suddenly remembered there were probably tanks in the attics. So I got up through a trap-door. There were two tanks all right, and Inskip was in one with a broken neck."

MacIlroy drank a little whisky and soda. He said : " And you didn't report this murder to the police ? "

" Yes, I did," said Vallon. " I've just reported it. What you mean is you wonder why I didn't report it before. I'll tell you. I don't think it would have done the police any good if I'd reported that murder. I don't think they'd ever have got their hands on the murderer, but I think my way they might get him much more quickly ; much more easily. That's why I spoke to Maple at the Yard. Because now is the time for them to come into it."

MacIlroy said : " Go on. . . ."

" Thanks," said Vallon. He went on : " I searched the bed-sitting-room where Allard used to live. I found under a leather corner of the blotter a piece of paper with a number on it— ' 136a.' When I looked at Inskip's body I found nothing in his pocket-book except a little money, which I left there, and a stamp. And written on the back of the postage stamp was the same number—'136a.' There isn't any doubt in my mind that when Inskip went to Allard's room, after he'd come back from the hospital—ostensibly to search Allard's clothes and find the name of his next-of-kin—he found that piece of paper in the corner of the blotter and that he made a note of the number.

"Now Inskip was interested in the letter he found in Allard's case. It's my belief that that letter had something to do with this fake daughter, and it's my belief that Inskip thought that somehow or another he could do a little blackmailing. That's why he went down to Valasey Bay. This morning," he went on, "I thought this about Allard: Nobody could produce a girl as somebody's daughter without having some sort of evidence no matter how slim—even if it was forged or fake. That's common sense, isn't it?"

MacIlroy nodded.

"It suddenly occurred to me," said Vallon, "that this number might be the number of a safe deposit box in a Depository where Allard had that evidence." He grinned at MacIlroy. "My guess was right. I got through to the Chancery Lane Safe Deposit this morning. They informed me that Vine Allard had a box there; only they're not going to allow that box to be opened and any contents taken away without authority. But *you* could have that box opened, MacIlroy, couldn't you? You've got to have it opened when you're investigating these murders. What I want you to do is to let me accompany you when you go round to the safe deposit: to allow me to examine the documents. Do that and I'll make a full and complete statement in two or three days' time. I say in two or three days' time because there are some things I have yet to do. And when you have that statement I think you'll have the person you want."

He finished the whisky and soda. "That's a pretty decent sort of deal. I'm not asking a lot, am I?"

MacIlroy said: "Whatever information you have, Mr. Vallon, should be available for the police without any conditions, but as in this case I think you may be very useful to the police, and as you have already pointed out we have to look in this Safe Deposit now I've heard what you've said—all right."

Vallon said: "Good. . . . When can we go and look at that box?"

MacIlroy looked at his watch. "I'm going back to the Yard. I'll get an order from the Chief Commissioner this afternoon. I'll be waiting for you at the entrance to the Chancery Lane Safe Deposit at four o'clock. Will that suit you?"

Vallon said: "It will suit me very well."

"And then," MacIlroy went on: "perhaps you and I can have another little talk—a longer talk—with a lot more details."

Vallon nodded. "You can have that. But not for a day or so."

MacIlroy got up. "All right. I'll see you at four o'clock this afternoon." He got up; moved towards the door.

"Just a minute . . ." said Vallon.

MacIlroy turned.

Vallon said: "Do me a favour. Inskip . . . his body is still in the tank. I take it he's been there for a couple of days, so it won't do any harm if he stays there a few days longer. You see what I mean?"

MacIlroy nodded. "You're trying to tell me that if we advise Valasey Bay and ask them to go and get the body, it's going to start something down there?"

"That's exactly what I mean," said Vallon.

MacIlroy said: "Well, we wont' worry about Mr. Inskip for a day or two. Then maybe we'll go and look at him." He grinned. "It would be too bad for you if he wasn't there."

Vallon said: "Don't worry. He'll be there."

"I hope . . ." said MacIlroy. He closed the door behind him.

.   .   .   .

At four o'clock Vallon turned into Chancery Lane. Just down the street, parked on the left-hand side of the road, he could see the police car. MacIlroy was standing on the pavement talking to the driver.

Vallon came as near as he ever did to feeling a tinge of excitement. He thought this was something. At the back of his head was the idea that in Allard's Safe Deposit box he would find the first definite indication of what was what in the Clavering case.

MacIlroy came to meet him. He said: "Well, I didn't waste any time, Mr. Vallon. And I hope it's going to be worth the trouble."

" I think it will be," said Vallon. " Let's go and find out, shall we ? "

The preliminaries took five minutes ; then the manager led them downstairs to the vaults, along the corridors with their rows of steel drawers. He stopped before a box with the number " 136a " painted on it in white. He opened it.

MacIlroy grinned at Vallon. " You look. Maybe you'll find another dead body in there." For once he smiled almost happily. He seemed pleased with his joke.

Vallon leaned over the long, open steel drawer. He began to take out the papers ; to examine them. The birth certificate, a neatly docketed file of Convent bills at the Convent of Our Lady at Mazaras ; bills from a French boarding school ; letters ; a letter from Miguel Salvador, and then the death certificate. Vallon whistled between his teeth. The certificate was in Spanish, but it was obvious enough for anyone to see that Lolita del Erest had died of pneumonia at the age of seventeen.

The manager said to MacIlroy : " If you want to take any of these documents away, Inspector, we'd like a formal receipt for them."

MacIlroy said : " Are you satisfied, Mr. Vallon, or do you want to take them away ? "

" We want the lot," said Vallon. He took the documents out of the box ; handed them to the manager.

They went upstairs. The receipt was made out and MacIlroy signed it.

Outside, Vallon said : " There are some documents there that can be checked—the birth certificate and the death certificate. The letters are interesting—especially the one from Miguel Salvador. He's a Chilean lawyer serving a sentence in jail at the moment for phony insurance claims."

MacIlroy said : " I see. Where do we go from here ? "

" I think you could get a pretty quick check on the official documents, couldn't you ? " asked Vallon.

" Yes, I suppose we could. It'd be a certain amount of trouble, but the Consulates here and abroad would work quickly if we asked them to. Is it all that important ? "

Vallon said : " You'd be surprised. . . ." They began to walk towards the police car.

MacIlroy said : " I think I ought to tell you that we've got to take some sort of action on this business pretty soon. When I went for that order on the Safe Deposit Company this afternoon the Assistant Commissioner was very curious. That's natural. I said I'd give him a rough report on the whole thing within twenty-four hours.''

Vallon asked : " Could you get the check in that time ? "

" On the official documents, yes," said MacIlroy. " After all, the world's a small place these days, and the telephone's a very handy instrument, especially when you can get priorities as we can. I think I could get the check on the official documents in twelve to fifteen hours.''

" That's all I want," said Vallon. " I'm thinking of taking a trip this evening to Valasey Bay. I'll probably be back in my office to-morrow. If you want me, ring through and if I'm not there they'll tell you where I am. But I think in two days from now I'm going to be able to talk. And I think you'll agree that I haven't wasted your time.''

MacIlroy said : " You wouldn't like to talk now—just a little bit ? "

" No. . . . I don't want to make a fool of myself, and I know you don't either. Up to the moment we've done nothing at all except open a Safe Deposit box.''

MacIlroy grinned cynically. " So that's all we've done, is it ? According to you we have two deliberate cases of murder and a body parked somewhere in a tank in Dorsetshire which will be getting high in a minute, and you say we haven't done anything much.''

Vallon said : " I was speaking metaphorically.

" That's what I thought." MacIlroy got into the car. He said : " Good hunting ! You can have the two days ; you can even have three. But we want results then or I'm going to move on my own.''

" Don't be silly," said Vallon. " You have a bundle of papers under your arm that don't mean a great deal to you. It would take you a hell of a time to find out what they do mean. But they mean plenty to me, except that before I tell you my story I want to do a little checking.''

MacIlroy said : "All right. I'll be seeing you." The car drove off.

Vallon walked slowly back to his office.

· · · · · ·

It was five o'clock when the desk telephone rang.

The girl said : " A long distance call, Mr. Vallon—a Mrs. Clavering from Valasey Bay."

" O.K. Put her through."

She came on the line. " Johnny . . . I expect you're awfully busy, and I expect you'll be annoyed with me for ringing you up just now."

" No," said Vallon. " Why should I be ? I like it."

" I'm glad. I haven't anything of importance to say to you, but I want you to know how different I feel since I saw you last. The world isn't quite such a lonely, heavy place. I don't mean that I'm happy, but I'm not so unhappy. Do you understand ? "

Vallon said : " I know. What you mean is that having a friend is a good thing at a time like this."

" That's what I meant, except that you're something more than a friend to me, Johnny."

He said : " I'm glad about that."

She asked : " When am I going to see you again ? "

" I'm not certain," said Vallon ; " but there's a chance that I'll be in Valasey Bay soon. If I am and I get an opportunity I'll call you through."

She said : " I'd love to see you, Johnny. Thanks for everything you've done and been." He heard the receiver click.

He got up ; lighted a cigarette ; began to walk around the office. One to two things about the documents he had looked at in Allard's Safe Deposit box were amusing, even exciting. There had been a letter addressed to the Señora Paula del Erest at Valasey Bay—a letter signed by Miguel Salvador. Vallon thought he could guess what that was. This was the letter which she had received informing her that del Erest was dead ; that he had left her some money. And it was easy enough to guess how that letter had got into Allard's Safe Deposit box. When she had had her original meeting with Allard ; when the search for the missing daughter was begun, she had handed him every document she had connected with the matter—amongst them the letter from Miguel Salvador ; possibly some of the other documents.

Vallon realised that the Clavering case wasn't really so difficult as it had seemed in the first place. As he had told Paula Clavering it was a case consisting of the conflict of

146

personalities—the personalities being Allard, Inskip, Rene Bizard, Julius Friday, del Erest and possibly the Señor Miguel Salvador. And the last personality who seemed to have conflict with everybody was Paula Clavering. He thought the time had come to begin a process of elimination.

He wondered what MacIlroy's report would be. He wondered which of the documents were fake, if any of them were. He thought it would be most amusing if none of them was fake. He thought that would throw an amusing side-light on what was a very interesting situation. Supposing all of the documents were O.K. ; none of them was fake. Yet one of them *had* to be. He thought for a moment. Then he whistled softly to himself. He thought that might be a very good base line to work from. Why not ? Somewhere or other he would find out if he were mistaken. He went to the office telephone ; spoke to Marvin.

" Believe it or not I'm going away again. I'm going to Valasey Bay. Ring through and get me a room and a bath at the Crown Hotel. I'll be down there some time this evening."

Marvin asked : " Do you know when you'll be back ? "

" To-morrow I hope. But if I'm not, and Detective-Inspector MacIlroy comes through, tell him where I am."

He hung up.

. . . .

Vallon waited beneath the tree opposite the stage door of the Valasey Bay theatre. The performance was over and the audience had departed one by one. Members of the company came out of the stage door entrance ; turned in different directions towards their respective homes.

Vallon waited five minutes ; then he walked across the road towards the stage entrance. He was almost there when Friday appeared in the doorway. He grinned cynically. " So it's you again ? "

Vallon said : " That's right. It's me. Let's have a little talk, shall we ? "

" I'm rather sick of you and your talks, Vallon. Perhaps one day I'll do something about it."

" Why not ? " said Vallon. " Why don't you go to the police as I have ? "

147

Friday asked: "Is that supposed to scare me?" But he looked a little scared.

"I don't care whether it scares you or not," said Vallon. "As a matter of fact I think you are a fairly imperturbable person." He grinned. "I have a certain respect for you, Friday—not too much but a little. Let's go into the theatre and talk."

"Why not?" said Friday. "Let's go on to the stage. There's a nice back-drop there. It'll probably make an excellent pastoral setting for one of your dramatic acts." He led the way along the dark passage, snapping on a light here and there. They went through a pass door on to the stage.

Friday said: "You'd better stay here; otherwise you'll fall into the orchestra pit. I'll put a light on."

Vallon heard his steps crossing the stage; then the lights in one solitary batton were put up. Friday came out of the prompt corner.

He said: "See what I mean?" He indicated the back-drop—a pastroal scene with a cottage in the distance. "I hope you like that."

Vallon said: "I'ts fine. I like it a lot." He went on: "I don't intent to waste any words or time on you, Friday, but I think this about you. I think you have an idea in your head that whatever happens to anybody else in this business you're safe. You feel that nobody can do anything to you."

"You're perfectly right," said Friday, "that's how I feel, annoying as it may be for you."

Vallon said: "Wait a minute. That's how you feel, but it doesn't necessarily mean that you're right. You realise as well as I do that it's no good your lying. You may lie to me, but anything you tell me now is going to be incorporated in a statement I shall have to make some time. You can say what you like because you're not on oath, but unless you're very careful you will be before many more days are past."

"That's as maybe." Friday produced a cigarette case; lighted a cigarette. His movements were quick and impatient.

"I went to the police this morning," said Vallon. "I told them that I considered Allard was killed; that the motor smash was deliberately planned. I've also told them that his partner Inskip is reposing in a tank at Valencia House with a broken neck. Naturally, they are not disinterested."

Friday sneered. " The usual, charming and thoroughly English understatement."

Vallon shrugged his shoulders. " It's no use your getting annoyed. I want to ask you a few questions. If you answer them truthfully, you're going to save yourself a lot of trouble. If you don't you'll probably get into a lot of trouble. So you can do what you like. If you don't answer the questions, I'm going to put the police on to you. That's going to be very annoying for you."

Friday asked : " What are the questions."

" I'm interested," said Vallon, " in two days. One is the day on which Allard came down here before leaving for the Sierra Madre, where he met you before leaving to be smashed up and die a few hours later. I want you to tell me this : When Allard came down to Valasey Bay did he see you ? "

Friday nodded. " He came to see me. He was in a hell of a rage."

Vallon asked : " Do you know what he was angry about ? "

" He was very angry with our beautiful Mrs. Paula Clavering—the delightful widow whom we now have once again in our midst."

" Why ? " asked Vallon.

Friday shrugged his shoulders. " It seems that having been deputed to find Mrs. Clavering's missing daughter he thought he'd succeeded in doing that, and before seeing the girl or hearing anything about it Mrs. Clavering came to the conclusion that the girl was a fake."

Vallon said : " I see. And did Allard come down here to tell you that ? "

" No . . . he didn't come down to see me at all. He came down because he thought he was going to see Mrs. Clavering, but she wasn't here, so he came to see me. I suppose he felt he had to talk to somebody."

" So he knew you had some connection with this business ? "

" Of course he did," said Friday. " Even you ought to have enough sense to see that. You know that I was Rene Bizard's stage manager. You know that Allard went to see Bizard because he thought that Leila Mannering in Bizard's company was the missing daughter. Why shouldn't he come to see me ? "

Vallon said : " All right. So he was very angry. Did he tell you what he was going to do ? "

"No. He said he was pretty well fed up with the whole situation ; that he didn't know where Mrs. Clavering was ; that he'd had a rotten raw deal from everybody. He said he had an appointment that evening. He was going to do something very drastic."

Vallon nodded. "That would be his appointment with me and Miss Mannering at the Sierra Madre. What happened after that ?"

Friday said : "Nothing as far as I was concerned. He went off."

"And what did you do ?" asked Vallon.

Friday grinned. "Actually, the situation rather amused me. I went to a little trouble. I put a fake telephone call through to Ellerdine Court. I found out where Mrs. Clavering was staying. I telephoned her and I told her that Allard the detective had been down to see me and that he was furious ; that he was going to throw his hand in ; that he was threatening to do all sorts of things."

Vallon asked : "Why did you do that ?"

"Because I hate her guts, and I hoped it'd annoy her."

Vallon asked : "Did you say who you were ?"

"No. I merely said what I had to say and hung up. I hoped it would give her a sleepless night."

"I see," said Vallon. "Now let's come to the other day—or rather the other night—the night on which Inskip was killed." He interrupted himself. "Oh, just a minute . . . after Allard had left, what did you do for the rest of the day ?"

Friday said sardonically : "You mean what was I doing at the time Allard had his accident."

"All right. Put it that way. What were you doing ?"

Friday said : "You remember I gave the Mannering girl the day off because she asked for it. I gave myself a day off because I wanted to give my assistant stage manager a try out with the new show. I wanted to see how he'd handle it. But I stayed here in Valasey Bay. I just didn't go to the theatre, that's all. I went down to the Crown Hotel, and I was there until closing time. You'll find at least half a dozen people who know me well saw me there."

"All right," said Vallon. "Now let's come to the night Inskip died. What were you doing on that evening ?"

"I think that's very easy. At what time was this man supposed to be killed ?"

Vallon said : " He was killed somewhere between half-past nine and half-past ten."

Friday shrugged his shoulders. " That's easy. I've never had a night off from the theatre, except the one I told you about, so everybody will tell you that on that night I was in the theatre until the show was over. So I think that let's me out."

Vallon said : " That let's you out. I'm going to take it that what you say is true, because if there's any doubt about it we'll have the police check on those alibis."

" I don't give a damn what you or the police do," said Friday.

Vallon asked : " Have you ever heard of a man called del Erest ? I mean Mrs. Clavering's first husband ? "

Friday nodded. " Oh, yes. You know I used to work for Rene Bizard. Bizard bought some of del Erest's theatrical effects after he died. I acted for Bizard in that deal."

Vallon asked : " You don't know anything else ? "

" No . . . I don't know anything else."

Vallon said : " You're a damned liar. It might interest you to know that the police and I had Allard's private box at the Chancery Lane Safe Deposit opened this afternooon. It might interest you to know that there were one or two letters signed by you making payments to a Convent School in Mazaras, and to a finishing school in France on behalf of a certain Lolita del Erest."

Friday was caught off guard, but only for a minute. He said : " Oh, that ! . . . That's soon explained. Miguel Salvador, who was the Chilean lawyer who was del Erest's executor, asked me to make payments in France in respect of the del Erest girl. She was at school there. I did it on one or two occasions."

Vallon said : " I see. . . . It's all very interesting, isn't it ? "

" You seem to find it so. I find it a bloody nuisance."

Vallon said : " I hope you won't find it any worse nuisance than you do now, but you might easily do that. But I don't think I'll have to worry you any more."

" That'll be a marvellous relief," said Friday. " Don't think I haven't liked meeting you because I haven't. Shall I see you to the stage door exit. I'd hate you to trip over in the dark."

Vallon said : " That's all right. I expect I can find my own way. You go back to your corner and turn the lights off when I've gone."

He walked off the stage.

151

Vallon drove back to the Crown Hotel. He went up to his room. He poured himself out a stiff whisky and soda; sat on the chair. Now he understood why Julius Friday's attitude was bitter, but unafraid. Vallon saw that there was little for Friday to be afraid of. Whatever Friday had done he had never actually constituted himself an accessory before or after anything. But he couldn't go all the way. He couldn't tell all the truth; otherwise he would be working against his own interests and maybe he still hoped to pull something out of the fire.

Vallon finished his drink; picked up the telephone; asked reception to find Dyce's private number and get him on the telephone.

When the call came through Vallon said: " Good evening, Mr. Dyce . . . this is John Vallon. I'm sorry to worry you so late at night, but I wonder if it would be possible for you to meet me at your office ? "

Dyce said: " Of course, if it's necessary. Has something happened ? Have you found out some more about this extra-ordinary business ? "

" I think I've found out *all* about this extraordinary business, more or less. What I don't know I can guess. But I don't think this is the time to talk about that. What I want is to see Clavering's will. Do you mind ? "

" Not at all," said Dyce. " I'll drive round to my office now. I'll meet you there in a quarter of an hour."

Vallon said: " All right. I'll be there."

He mixed himself another drink. He thought that he was intrigued to see the wording of Clavering's will. It would be funny if he had guessed right about that too.

Dyce was waiting on the office steps, the open door behind him. He said: " All this is very exciting, Mr. Vallon. What does it mean ? Is there going to be trouble for somebody ? "

" I should think so. But just how much trouble, I don't know, or where it's going to start. Now, if I may, I'd like to see that will, and in two or three days' time I think I shall be able to talk to you at length." He grinned. " I think you're the one who's going to have the trouble, Mr. Dyce. I think you're going to have a marvellous situation to sort out." He followed Dyce into the building.

In his room, Dyce unlocked the safe. He handed the will to Vallon.

Vallon said : " I want the bit that instructs Mrs. Clavering to hand over four thousand a year of the money she was to receive after Clavering's death to her missing daughter if and when she was found."

Dyce came over. He took the will from Vallon's hand ; opened it. He pointed to a paragraph. Vallon read :

" And I direct if after my death the daughter born to Manuel del Erest and his wife, for whom agents are now searching, shall be found, that my executors, having established that she is the proper and legal child of this marriage, shall transfer to her from the monies which I have left the sum of four thousand pounds per annum tax free for the rest of her life."

Vallon re-folded the will. He gave it back to Dyce.

He said : " Thanks a lot."

" I'm very intrigued, Mr. Vallon," said Dyce. " Especially when you tell me that I'm going to have a lot of trouble to sort out. I hope as soon as possible you will let me know exactly what the position is."

" You'll know everything within two or three days I should say." Vallon took out his cigarette case ; lighted a cigarette. He said casually : " The more I see of this case the more sorry I am for old Clavering. Perhaps it's a good thing for him that he died."

Dyce asked : " Why do you think that ? After all, he'd reached a ripe age. He'd got what he wanted. He'd had an adventurous life and to a man of his type death would be rather like a fresh adventure."

Vallon shrugged his shoulders' " He must have been a brave man to marry a woman like Mrs. Clavering. He was an old man and she was comparatively young and certainly strikingly beautiful. The sort of woman that an old man might have trouble with—if you know what I mean."

Dyce nodded. " I know what you mean. But I think you're wrong. First of all it's my belief that Mrs. Clavering was really very fond of him in the nicest possible way. He worshipped the ground she walked on. But he wasn't a fool about her. I had plenty of opportunities to talk to him and always he brought a great deal of common sense to bear on his marriage to Mrs. Clavering."

Vallon said : " I see what you mean."

" He told me one day," Dyce continued, " that even if Mrs. Clavering had been a not-so-good type—someone who was merely after his money—he would still have wanted to look after her and marry her. That was the effect she had on him."

Vallon nodded. " I see why you don't want her name brought into any unpleasant business that might come along. You mean that Augustus Clavering wouldn't like that— if he were alive."

Dyce smiled. " I don't think he'd like it now he's dead. I think he'd loathe it. And, as he's your client—because even if he *is* dead he's going to pay your bill—I hope you'll remember it."

Vallon said : " I'll remember it."

" You must realise, Mr. Vallon, that Mrs. Clavering isn't an ordinary type. She's amazingly sensitive. She is very easily hurt, and in her life she has had a great deal of trouble, in spite of which she has always presented a very brave face to a world that has been terribly unkind to her. I believe I once told you that if *I* had had an opportunity of doing what Clavering did and of marrying her myself I should have taken it."

Vallon grinned. " Well, you never know your luck. Perhaps you'll have a chance now."

Dyce smiled again. " There's many a true word spoken in jest. And if I get a chance I'll take it."

Vallon went to the door. He said smilingly : " Well . . . ask me to the wedding."

He went out.

Ten minutes later he was back in his bedroom at the Crown. He wondered where the Allard letter was. But he thought that even without it the situation was fairly obvious. At the same time he realised that the discovery of that letter would finish off what was after all a complete chain of evidence. He wondered where Inskip—too clever to take the letter with him on his visit to Valasey Bay—would put it. Inskip would not have a box in the Safe Deposit. Vallon thought that the probability was that the letter was hidden somewhere in Inskip's office—in some very safe place. He thought some time he would get round to that.

He went to bed.

CHAPTER EIGHT

LOVE SCENE

IT WAS four o'clock in the afternoon when Vallon went into the office. He rang for Marvin. When Marvin came in Vallon asked : " Any calls ? "

Marvin nodded. " Detective-Inspector MacIlroy came through about half an hour ago. I said I expected you back some time before the office closed. He'll come through again."

Vallon said : " Get them to ring Scotland Yard and see if he's there. If he is I'll talk to him now."

Three minutes later the switch-board girl came through and said Mr. MacIlroy ws on the line.

Vallon said : " Well, MacIlroy . . . what does it look like ? "

MacIlroy said : " We've had a check on the important documents—the ones we *could* check. Of course there are no means of checking on the correspondence or the bills, and what I call the odd documents. But the birth certificate is perfectly in order."

" And the death certificate ? " asked Vallon. " What about that ? "

" It's phony—a very good imitation but not quite good enough."

Vallon said : " I see. . . ."

MacIlroy went on : " Any news for me ? "

" No, not yet. But I think the day after to-morrow you'll know all the answers."

MacIlroy said : " All right. But if you can make it sooner I'd like that."

" When I've got it, you shall have it," said Vallon, " and I don't think it'll be long now. So long, MacIlroy—and thanks for your help."

He hung up. Then he put on his hat ; took a bunch of skeleton keys from a drawer in his desk ; went out of the office. He began to walk towards Long Acre. As he made his way across the street, crowded with fruit and vegetable carts, Vallon thought that the chances of anyone having been in Inskip's office were remote. The place had looked as if it were only cleaned about once a month, and there wasn't very much business. Probably no one was sufficiently interested in Inskip to have missed him.

He went up the stairs. When he arrived at the office the door was locked. There was on one in the corridor. Vallon tried two or three keys until he found the one he wanted. The door opened easily. He went in ; locked it behind him.

He thought with a grin that he'd been right about the cleaning. The place was dirtier than ever. A thin film of dust was over everything. Vallon stood in the doorway between the outer office and Inskip's room looking around him. There were not many articles of furniture—a big desk ; a chair or two ; two wooden filing cabinets, the drawers of which were mostly open. Vallon wondered where Inskip would hide the letter, if he had hidden it there. And Inskip would not worry too much about the hiding-place. He would have no reason to believe that anyone would search his office.

Vallon sat down at the desk ; systematically went through the drawers. There was nothing. He got up ; lighted a cigarette ; went and stood in front of the fireplace, looking around the room. He realised that the wooden floor board on which he was standing in front of the fireplace was insecure. He stepped to one side and looked at it. He put his penknife in the crack between the boards. The piece of floor-board, which had been sawn off six inches under the oilcloth, came up easily. Vallon put his hand in the hole. He brought up a stout foolscap envelope. He took it over to the window ; opened it. He took out the letter inside. He began to grin. It was Allard's letter.

Vallon crossed to the desk and sat down. He threw the letter on to the desk ; sat looking at it. He thought that without seeing it he could guess the contents. He picked it up ; read it. It was dated the day before Allard's car smash. It was addressed to John Dyce, Esquire, of Dyce, Grant & Dyce, Valasey Bay. Vallon read :

" *Dear Mr. Dyce,*
    " *I feel that I'm in a rather peculiar position and that I ought to see you about it. There are some things which I think as solicitor and executor to the late Augustus Jones Clavering you should know.*

" *First of all, as you know, I was commissioned by Mrs. Clavering to institute a search for her missing daughter Lolita del Erest, whom no one had seen for years. Mrs. Clavering told me as much as she could, which was very little, about the girl, and I began work on what looked like an extremely difficult case. Luckily I was given some information which led me to a conversation with an individual in France, and as a result of this conversation I contacted a young woman whom I honestly and sincerely believe to be the missing daughter Lolita del Erest.*

" *It will be quite obvious to you that I should want some substantiation—some evidence that this girl was the right girl and I managed to secure it. This evidence is in a safe place, and although some of it may be doubtful it will be hard to contradict the rest of it. I have no reason to believe that the girl I have found is a fraud.*

" *Naturally, I was very pleased at having achieved success in so short a time, and the first thing I did was to telephone Mrs. Clavering and tell her of what I thought was my good luck. I was amazed at her attitude. Without giving me time to give her any information at all about the manner in which this girl had come to light, without asking me whether I had any evidence to support my claim, she suggested that the girl was a fraud - that she was not the real Lolita del Erest. She suggested that for my own reasons I had produced an impostor.*

" *It will be quite obvious to you that had I wished to make money out of this assignment I should be prolonging the search as long as possible - as you know, I was being very generously paid and allowed a large sum for expenses. Surely the fact that I produced this girl in such a short time should be a point in my favour.*

" *Now I come to the crux of this matter. I think it is absolutely essential that I should see you and discuss this matter with you frankly and fully, and it has occurred to me that after all the facts are at your disposal you might be inclined to think that I have acted in an irregular way in this matter or that I might at some time have committed an act which a lawyer might consider to be an illegal act.*

" *I would like, therefore, before seeing you, an assurance from you in writing that, in consideration of the fact that I am disclosing all I know about this business to you, you will send me a written confirmation that in no circumstances will any proceedings be brought against me.*

" I think it only right to tell you that before despatching this letter to you, I propose to meet and talk with John Vallon of Chennault Investigations. I do this because his was the firm it was originally intended should carry out the work. Chennault Investigations is a first-class investigation agency with an extremely good reputation, and as I think you will probably require the services of John Vallon in this matter after I'm through with it, I ought in fairness to myself to explain certain angles of this case to him and take his advice. When I have done this—if he agrees—I will immediately post this letter to you.

" Faithfully yours,

" Vine Allard."

Vallon folded the letter. He put it in his pocket. He went out of the office ; locked the door behind him. He began to walk back to Regent Street.

He thought that life could sometimes be very cynical. It had certainly played jokes on Inskip. Inskip, who had tried to be so clever and failed so utterly. Vallon visualised him, safely back in his office after the hurried journey to the hospital at Dudleigh, opening the envelope, reading the Allard letter, believing that the contents would put him in a position in which he could make lots of money ; then finding that the letter said in effect nothing—at least, nothing that he could understand. Because its contents boiled down to an attempt to make a deal with the lawyer Dyce—a deal by which, if Allard said this or that or the other, and in saying it implicated himself in some way, no action would be brought against him.

Inskip must have been very disappointed. But he was not finished. He reasoned that Allard must have known something very important, very urgent and very dangerous to have written that letter. Inskip reasoned that if he pretended that he was in Allard's confidence and knew the whole story, there might still be a chance for him. It was a bluff. He had tried it and it just hadn't come off. Instead of getting money Inskip had merely won for himself a broken neck.

When Vallon arrived at the office he called the switch-board ; told them to ring the theatre at Valasey Bay to ask if Mr. Friday was there. Three or four minutes later the call came through. Vallon grinned as he heard Friday's high-pitched voice on the telephone.

He said: "Good afternoon, Friday. This is Vallon speaking. Do you know where Bizard is?"

Friday asked: "Why?"

Vallon said: "You mind your own damned business You tell me where Bizard is or I'll come down to Valasey Bay and fix you. You understand me? I'm not standing any more. nonsense from you. And if you'd like a good reason for my not standing any more nonsense I'll give it to you. I've found Allard's letter."

There was a pause; then Friday said: "I see. . . . Well, I can't be certain, but I think Bizard is still at Le Touquet. I expect you'll find him there. It's a small place, you know."

" I'll find him," said Vallon. "So long, Friday."

Friday said sarcastically: "So long. You'll take *lots* of care of yourself, won't you?"

Vallon said: "You bet I will."

He hung up the receiver.

.   .   .   .

At ten o'clock Vallon stood in front of the fireplace in his sitting-room, smoking a cigarette. He was trying to visualise the different angles from which he might approach Bizard. He realised that the conversation with Bizard was going to be important—very important.

The telephone jangled. Vallon crossed the room; took up the receiver. It was Paula Clavering.

She said: "Johnny, I'm in London. I felt I wanted to talk to you very badly. I rang your office at six o'clock. The telephone operator said you'd left, but after a while she consented to give me your private number. I've rung four times this evening. I'm so glad to have caught you now."

Vallon said: "I'm sorry you had such trouble. I've been out most of the evening. What's happened?"

" I can't talk on the telephone, Johnny. Do you think you could come and see me? I'm at the Savoy."

" All right," said Vallon. "I'll be with you in a quarter of an hour."

He went to his bedroom; took off his dressing-gown; put on a jacket. He thought that life was beginning to be very interesting. He went downstairs to the car.

When he was shown into her sitting-room, he felt the same extraordinary feeling which came to him whenever he saw Paula Clavering—something that was more than a touch of excitement or a mere thrill—something that was not at all unpleasant—but still indefinable.

He said : " You look quite lovely, Paula."

" Do I ? " She was wearing a close-fitting dinner-frock of plum-coloured sequins, with matching high-heeled satin sandals. The high neck and long sleeves of the frock set off her perfect figure. She wore a large emerald brooch at her throat, an exquisite emerald ring on her finger.

She shrugged her shoulders. " It's nice of you to say that, Johnny, but sometimes I think I've got to the state of mind when I don't even care how I look."

" That's too bad. You ought not to feel like that. There's a great deal of life in front of you, Paula. You might find it very interesting."

She asked : " Johnny . . . aren't you going to kiss me ? "

Vallon grinned. "If you like . . . but I'd rather have a drink."

She flushed. " That doesn't sound like you, Johnny. Will you have whisky ? "

He nodded.

She said : " You'll find a bottle . . . everything you want . . . in the cabinet in the corner."

She stood in front of the fireplace in her usual position, with one slim arm resting on the mantelpiece, watching him as he crossed the room to the cabinet.

She said : " So you don't want to kiss me, Johnny. That isn't very gallant, is it ? You wanted to before."

Vallon was busy at the cabinet mixing his drink. He looked at her over his shoulder. " Did I—— ? " He was smiling.

She raised her eyebrows. " *Didn't* you want to ? Then why did you do it ? "

" I'll tell you," said Vallon. " You remember the night we met at Montreuil ? You told me that you were going back to England the next day. I think you were very intrigued and unhappy because by that time you knew the story of Allard's death, and you were very interested in his partner Inskip, weren't you ? "

She asked : " What do you mean, Johnny ? Why should I have been interested in Inskip ? "

160

Vallon shrugged his shoulders. "If you don't know, I don't. But I can think of one or two very good reasons."

She said : "What are the reasons ? "

"I think one's good enough," said Vallon. "After all, Inskip was Allard's partner. Allard was dead. Allard had died without having an opportunity to talk to Dyce the lawyer—or anybody else for that matter—about this report he wanted to make, so there was nobody who knew what he knew—with one possible exception. That was his partner Inskip. It was possible, you thought, that Allard might have said *something* to Inskip ; might at some time have given him an inkling of what was in his mind. He might even have confided to Inskip facts about the case he was handling for you. I think you wanted to find out. So you flew back from Montreuil the next morning or afternoon. You waited till it was dark and then you went round to see Inskip. That's why I kissed you."

She said in a low voice : "What had *that* to do with it ? "

Vallon grinned. "By a peculiar chance I went to see Inskip that night. After your meeting he'd gone off drinking and then returned to his office. He'd been having a little celebration because he thought he was on to a good thing. During our conversation he wiped his mouth on a handkerchief and drunkenly let it fall to the floor. I picked it up. There was lipstick on it. That's why I kissed you—understand ? "

She said : "I understand. You wanted a sample of my lipstick so that you could check on the handkerchief ? "

"That's right," said Vallon. "It was the same—a lipstick called *Vieux Rose.* I believe you can only get it in France, or at one or two places over here."

"I suppose it never occurred to you, Johnny, that some other woman might use this lipstick ? "

Vallon said : "Why not ? But I don't know of any other woman who was in such a hurry on that day to see Inskip as you were, and I can't imagine any woman who is as beautiful, as well turned-out as *chic* as you are, who would condescend to kiss a half-drunken rough-neck like Inskip unless she was after something."

She said in a hard voice : "I'm beginning to understand. Don't you think you're being rather unkind, Johnny ? Aren't you taking an awful lot for granted ? "

Vallon went back to the settee in the middle of the room,

161

carrying his whisky and soda in his hand. He said : " Paula, I very seldom take anything for granted." He went on : " I'm very, very sorry about Inskip, because your guess was only *half* right. Inskip didn't know a thing—not a goddam thing, even although he'd stolen a letter from Allard's pocket-case after he was injured. He had that letter all right."

Vallon grinned cynically. " But the letter didn't tell him anything. You could have broadcast it from a house-top and it wouldn't have done anybody any harm—not until Allard *explained* what it meant. But Inskip was no fool—well, not so much of a fool. He knew you wanted to know what he knew, and he wasn't going to tell you that he didn't know a thing except that Allard had written a not very obvious letter to Dyce. That's why he made the deal with you that he did make —the deal that cost him such a lot."

She moved a little. " What do you mean, Johnny ? Why should it have cost him a lot ? "

" I'll tell you. As I've said I went to see him on that night. I did a little bluffing myself and I smacked a little sobriety into Inskip. I told him that unless he came to my office the next morning at eleven o'clock and gave me the whole story—the truth, the whole truth and nothing but the truth—I was going to the police and I was going to implicate him in the Allard business—the smash that wasn't a smash. He agreed to come. He didn't turn up, but he rang me soon after eleven from Valasey Bay. You were back there by that time, weren't you ? "

She said in a dull voice : " Yes . . . I was back there by then."

" Inskip told me on the telephone that if I agreed to meet him in Valasey Bay that night he'd give me the story—the whole book ! He made an appointment to meet me at half-past ten. He'd had a telephone conversation with you before he rang me, because Inskip had told you the night before that if you found him a sum of money by the next day, he'd hand over Allard's letter to you. My guess is that he made an appointment with you to meet him at ten o'clock that night at Valencia House—that old mansion that used to belong to your husband. I was to arrive at ten-thirty, so that if Inskip was not satisfied with your reaction to his demand for money he intended to tell me what he knew, and to hand the letter Allard had written over to me some time or other. And he asked me to meet him down there in case the ten o'clock interview became a little troublesome."

She said : " I don't know what you mean, Johnny. I never went anywhere near Valencia House at ten o'clock."

" Of course you didn't, but somebody did. That's what I meant when I said that it cost Inskip a great deal."

" You mean—— ? " she queried.

" I mean that, unless someone has moved him already—and I don't think they have—Inskip is still in one of the big empty water tanks in the roof. I found him there with a broken neck."

She said in a hoarse voice : " Oh, my God . . . my God ! "

Vallon finished his drink ; got up ; carried the glass back to the cocktail cabinet. He said : " You may well say that. It looks rather as if there's going to be a lot of trouble before this lark is over."

She asked : " Have you been to the police, Johnny ? "

He nodded. " I have and I haven't. In other words, I gave them an outline of this business, without too many particulars, in order to get at Allard's Safe Deposit box in the Chancery Lane Safe Deposit. The contents were very interesting. The police have them. They're expecting me to make some sort of statement within the next couple of days. I've got to do it. I'm going to do it."

She moved from the fireplace. She came towards him. She put her hand on his arm. He thought the perfume she was wearing was delightful.

She asked : " Johnny, what are you going to tell them ? . . . *What* are you going to tell them ? "

Vallon said : " I don't know. What I tell them depends on circumstances."

" What circumstances, Johnny ? "

He smiled at her. " I can't answer that question either . . . not yet. I'll be able to soon. But I know all about it, my sweet. You're in too deep to get right out. It's too late for anyone to say to you, ' Lady, behave ! . . .' Much too late." He began to walk about the room. Her eyes followed him as he paced up and down.

He said : " When I think about you—and I think about you as little as possible—I believe you are the most heartless bitch

163

I've ever met in my life. You'd do anything to get your own way, wouldn't you, Paula? You'd make love to me—to anyone—even Inskip—to get what you want."

She said nothing.

"It took me a long time," Vallon went on, "to work out the first angles in this case. I got it eventually, but only after a great deal of thought—a great deal of searching. When you married Clavering you did so on the condition that he made every endeavour to find your missing daughter and, when he'd found her, make her an adequate allowance. He told you what he proposed to do. He told you he'd set aside a sum of money for the search for the girl; that when she was found she was to have four thousand a year, and that you, during his lifetime and after his death, would also have four thousand a year. And so you wanted your daughter found. You wanted your daughter found because you knew perfectly well in the circumstances which you'd create you would have the handling of her money as well as your own, and you wanted it, didn't you, Paula? You'd do anything for money.

"So the first thing to do was to stop Clavering coming to Chennault Investigations to find the girl, because you knew I wouldn't play it the way you wanted it. So you told him a half-true story about Allard, and you came up to London and you saw Allard. Because you knew he was a crook and that he needed money badly and would do anything to get it. You told him the story. You told him that he was to search for your missing daughter and when he asked you whether it would be a good thing to begin the search, you said he needn't really bother because you knew your daughter was dead. You knew she was dead because you had received a letter to that effect from Miguel Salvador saying that she had died from double pneumonia at the age of seventeen. So you were able to assure Allard that there was no fear of your real daughter turning up. Therefore, it would be easy for him to find a fake one. Well——?"

She said: "It seems as if you're rather a mind-reader." She was smiling—a hard, brilliant smile.

"So," continued Vallon, "you said it would be easy for Allard to find some other girl with whom he could make a proper financial arrangement, who would be produced as your daughter Lolita del Erest, with some sort of documentary

substantiation which would be verified by your recognition of
—shall we say—some birth-mark on the girl by which you
would be certain it was your daughter."

Vallon paused.

She asked : " What then, Johnny ? "

Vallon said : " You went back to Valasey Bay very satisfied
with the position. I imagine you promised Allard a possible
thousand a year out of Lolita's money for the pair of them,
and decided that you would stick to the remaining three
thousand. But when you got back to Valasey Bay you received
a shock, because in the meantime your husband had been to
see Dyce, the lawyer, and Dyce had advised against Clavering's
original idea about the money.

" He'd pointed out to Clavering that it was stupid to tie up
the capital necessary to produce four thousand a year before
the girl was actually found. He told Clavering that when the
girl was found it would be quite easy for him to allow her four
thousand a year out of his current income, but that in case of
his death he should make a will under which you would receive
eight thousand a year on the understanding that in the event of
the girl being found you would transfer four thousand of that
amount to her.

" Now you were in a spot, weren't you, and now you didn't
want this fake daughter found. What good would it serve you
having a fake daughter to whom Dyce, as your husband's
executor, had transferred four thousand a year for life, and
you dare not even try to blackmail her into giving you some of
it ; otherwise she'd have told them the truth. You had to do
something about it, hadn't you, my sweet ? "

" Yes, Johnny . . . I had to do something about it. . . . What
did I do ? "

Vallon said : " You got into touch with Allard. You told
him that the situation had changed ; that you did not want a
daughter produced—not even a fake one. You told him that it
would be no good to anybody if she were produced ; that the
way things were you wouldn't be able to get at the money."

Vallon stubbed out his cigarette end in an ash-tray ; lighted
another one. He asked : " May I have another whisky and
soda ? "

She nodded. " Johnny, I think you're a very interesting
man. You're a hell of a detective."

On his way to the cabinet, he said over his shoulder : " I think so too." He mixed himself a fresh drink ; went back to the settee. He said : " You can bet your life Allard wasn't very pleased with this news because in the meantime he'd received a tip-off from someone who doesn't like you very much—an individual called Julius Friday—that if he, Allard, contacted a certain Rene Bizard he might be able to find the very girl you were looking for. Allard had acted on that hint. He'd been over to France. He'd met Bizard. He'd seen this supposed Lolita del Erest, and he was quite satisfied with the job. In fact," Vallon went on, " he was sitting back and congratulating himself on a very nice situation. He'd found the girl and, although the search hadn't taken him quite so long as he would have liked, he was on a good thing for the rest of his life. He was going to receive a thousand a year from you less what he paid to the girl. And he'd have had you where he wanted you, because if you hadn't paid up at any time he could have blackmailed you. In other words, Allard wasn't prepared to stop when he was told to stop.

" So he told you this was perfectly O.K. by him, so long as he was paid a sum of money. And he told you that if he did not receive that sum of money by a certain date he was going to Dyce. He was going to tell Dyce the whole story even if it implicated him—as a crook. Well, you didn't pay the money. You hadn't got it. Allard came down to Valasey Bay after making an appointment to meet me that evening because he was scared and wanted my advice. He went down to Valasey Bay to see you and you weren't there. So he saw Friday. He told Friday what he proposed to do. He told him that he'd written a letter to Dyce ; that unless he got what he wanted he was going to send the letter to Dyce.

" That was in the afternoon. In the late afternoon he drove to the Sierra Madre to meet me, and he had arranged also that the fake Lolita del Erest should meet him there. But he never got there. He was smashed up instead." Vallon grinned. " The strangest things happen to your private detectives, you know, Paula." He got up.

She asked once again : " Johnny, what are you going to do ? " Her voice was hard.

Vallon said : " I'm not certain, but I'll give you half a dozen guesses." He picked up his hat. " I had a talk with

Dyce not very long ago. He told me something. He told me about old Clavering and you. He said that Clavering was crazy about you ; that he was really a fine old boy ; that you represented to him everything in life that he'd missed," He grinned at her. " Dyce is awfully struck on you himself, you know. It's amazing—the effect you have on men, Paula."

She said : " Thank you for nothing, Johnny."

Vallon continued : " He told me that Clavering had said that even if you were bad ; if you'd only married him for his money, he'd still be for you. Well . . . I'm working for Clavering. Originally, he intended to be my client. I consider him to be my client now. Also he's paying my bills, so what I'm going to do is what I think he'd ask me to do if he were here now."

She said urgently : " Tell me, Johnny . . . tell me what you think he'd ask you to do ? "

Vallon said : " Nuts ! Why should I satisfy your curiosity ? Good night to you, Paula. If I were you I'd go back to Valasey Bay and stay put."

He went out.

CHAPTER NINE

VALLON FINISHED writing the letter at half-past twelve. He read it through; then called on the office telephone for Marvin. When Marvin arrived Vallon sealed the envelope. He addressed the letter to Detective-Inspector MacIlroy at Scotland Yard. He gave it to Marvin.

He said: " Don't lose or mislay that. Just keep it with you. Don't let anyone else handle it."

Marvin said: " All right. And what do I do with it eventually ? "

Vallon leaned back in his chair. " I'm going over to France this evening. I shall be at Le Touquet, but there won't be any need for you to try and get in touch with me. I propose to come back to-morrow. I should be here in the office by mid-day, but if I don't arrive, wait until four o'clock in the afternoon and then take that letter round to Scotland Yard and give it to Detective-Inspector MacIlroy. You know what he looks like. You've seen him here."

Marvin said: " I understand." He went out.

Vallon got up; lighted a cigarette; began to walk about the office. He thought the interview in front of him might be very amusing. It might be. . . .

He went over to the desk; opened the bottom drawer; took out the nearly empty bottle of whisky. He poured three fingers—the remains of the bottle—into the glass. He held it up. He said, with a grin :

" Well, here's to you, Johnny. . . ."

He drank the whisky.

.　　.　　.　　.　　.　　.　　.

The breeze from the sea came up over the deserted Plage and through the main street at Le Touquet. It was eleven-thirty and all the shops were illuminated attractively. The long, narrow street presented an air of gaiety.

Vallon came out of the English bar and began to walk down the street towards the Chatham. He looked at his strap-watch.

It was a quarter to twelve. He grinned to himself. He thought there was nothing like giving the other fellow a chance.

Not that Bizard wanted one. Vallon thought that he had a certain respect for Bizard. As much respect as one could have for such a man. But he was brave and ruthless and entirely sincere in what he was trying to do. And he was filled with hatred which he dissembled under an air of quiet joviality and *bonhomie*. Vallon wondered what Bizard would do now. There were two things he could do. It would be interesting to see which way out he selected.

Vallon went into the Chatham. He sat down at a table by the bar ; ordered a glass of brandy. When the waiter brought it, Vallon said : " Has Mr. Bizard been in to-night ? He usually comes in here, doesn't he ? "

The waiter said : " But, yes, M'sieu. Usually, but not always. I don' think he ees coming to-night because when he does come it ees earlier than now. There ees a fren' of his in the corner. You see ? . . . The gentleman drinking Dubonnet— the one with the béret. He would probably know eef M'sieu Bizard ees coming."

Vallon said : " Thanks." He crossed over to the table in the corner. The occupant was a well-set-up looking man of about sixty-five. He wore his béret with a jaunty air and the dead stub of a Caporal cigarette hung on the corner of his lower lip.

He looked up at Vallon. He smiled. He said : " M'sieu Vallon?"

Vallon said : " Yes. I wanted to talk to M'sieu Bizard. The waiter isn't certain whether he is coming here or not. He said you might know."

The other man nodded. " But, yes. M'sieu Bizard thought possibly you might be looking for him to-night."

Vallon grinned. " I wonder why he thought that."

The other shrugged his shoulders. " I don't know, M'sieu. I have known Bizard for a long time but he never tells me what he thinks. However, he asked me to tell you if I saw you here that he would be very glad to talk to you. He has a villa about a mile outside the town on the Montreuil road. You remember the woods on the left and right of the road ? "

Vallon nodded. " I know. . . ."

" It is the third turning on the right after you get out of the town. You can't mistake it. There is a notice on the side of the lane which warns motorists to drive carefully."

169

Vallon said : " I am much obliged to you. How far is this place ? "

" If you feel like walking," said the man, " it is half an hour, but of course you can always get a cab."

Vallon said : " Thank you." He went back to his table ; finished his drink ; paid for it. He went out of the Chatham ; began to walk through the brilliantly lit street towards the woods outside Le Touquet.

.   .   .   .

The villa was set deep in the wood, a good half a mile from the road. The path which Vallon had followed led directly towards it and the villa turned it into a cul-de-sac. It was an attractive place—white-walled, with a red, tiled roof. It almost gleamed in the moonlight.

Vallon pushed open the gate ; walked up the well-kept path. There was a bell handle beside the painted door. He pulled it. He stood there waiting, his hands by his side, the half-smoked cigarette hanging in his mouth.

The door opened. Bizard stood framed in the doorway. He said : " Ah, M'sieu Vallon. I thought we should meet again, and I had an idea you would wish to see me, so I asked a fren' of mine to let you know where I was in case you went to the Chatham. Pliz come in. Make yourself at home."

Vallon went into the hall. Bizard closed the door.

Vallon said, with a grin : " I wonder why you expected me to-night, especially. Perhaps some little bird's been talking to you on the telephone, hey ? "

Bizard laughed. " Well, you know, M'sieu Vallon, birds do talk."

Vallon said : " I wonder what sort of bird it was. Was it a very beautiful bird or a funny little bird with a rather high-pitched squeak ? "

Bizard said : " Have a drink, M'sieu Vallon. I can see that you have a sense of humour." His round face was pleasant, smiling.

Vallon followed him into the dressing-room. Bizard indicated the table filled with bottles and glasses.

He said : " I have an idea that you and I are going to have a long and interesting talk. Let us enliven our conversation with

170

a drink. I recommend some cognac that I have. I tell you that it ees the best in France."

Vallon said : " Thanks. I'd like some." He sat down in the chair his host had indicated.

Bizard went over to the drinks table ; began to pour the drinks. He said : " About these birds . . . which bird do you think it was ? "

" I hope I'm wrong," said Vallon, " but I think it was a rather beautiful bird—a most alluring bird."

Bizard said : " You are wrong, my fren'. It was not. It was the cockatoo with the high-pitched voice."

Vallon said : " Julius Friday ? "

Bizard nodded. " No other . . . my good, my faithful, my very dear fren' Julius, who ees so kind and often ver' clever." He brought the tumbler half-filled with cognac to Vallon.

Vallon said : " You're telling me, he's clever ! He's pretty good, that one. I don't think he even lets his left hand know what his right hand's doing...."

Bizard said : " I think he is a ver' wise man." He raised his glass. " M'sieu Vallon, I would not like you to think that I underestimate you. I would like to drink your health."

Vallon grinned. " That's kind of you. I don't think it's very much good my drinking yours."

Bizard raised his eyebrows in mock display. " No ? What do you think ees going to happen to me, M'sieu Vallon ? Something interesting ? "

" I should think it'd be damned interesting," said Vallon. " I should think they are going to give you a six-foot drop, Bizard. I think they'll have you extradited from France and I think they are going to hang you."

Bizard made a mimic noise of dismay. He clicked his teeth. " How terrible . . . but this ees shocking ! . . . What an impossible end for Rene Bizard. Did you come all thees way to tell me that ? "

Vallon said : " No. Actually, I'm not very interested in you, I'm interested in Mrs. Clavering."

Bizard walked over to the table ; refilled his glass. He sat down in the arm-chair opposite Vallon. He said : " So you are interested in Mrs. Clavering. I do not wonder at that. Such a lovely and delightful woman would interest any man."

171

"Believe it or not," said Vallon, "I'm not particularly interested in her as a woman. My interest is almost impersonal. I'm interested in her because she was the wife of my client Augustus Clavering."

Bizard nodded. "I see. . . . You are one of those serious detectives that one reads about in books. Who, whatever the situation ees, never fail to do what their client wants—even if he ees dead. I wonder what you theenk he would have wanted."

Vallon said : "I think that, in spite of the fact that Mrs. Clavering is a bitch, he'd want to keep her out of as much trouble as possible. That can be done if you'd like to help do it."

Bizard said : "And why should I want to help you ? "

"I'm not quite certain," said Vallon. "But we'll come to the point later. Maybe I can persuade——"

Bizard grunted. He said : "Maybe you could persuade the pig to fly ! Ees not that your English proverb ? "

Vallon said : "We'll see. . . . The point is this : If I were to suggest that Paula Clavering was implicated in the two murders that you've committed—the murder of Vine Allard and the later murder of his partner Inskip—every bit of evidence in this case points to her being associated with those crimes. In any event, the other things she's done in this business would rather make any jury believe that she was in it up to the neck ; that she ought to be hanged. I think if they had the story as I know it, they'd not only hang you but they'd hang her too—even if she was in fact innocent because the circumstantial evidence would be too strong for her."

Bizard made another clucking noise. "How terrible . . . for our lovely Paula to have that white column of a neck stretched by an extremely vulgar rope. And what about my fren' Julius ? Do you think they would want to hang him too ? "

Vallon shook his head. "Julius has been much too clever, and none of these things was really his fault, you know. Actually, I think Julius has been rather nice in his own odd, peculiar way. He's certainly been damned nice to you. But there's nothing to tie onto Julius. He's made a few telephone calls of course, such as the phone call to you to tell you that it was a stone certainty I'd be coming over to-night ; to tell you that I was coming to see you. Incidentally "—Vallon grinned —" he told me to take great care of myself."

" No ? " said Bizard. " That was wicked of him. Do you mean that Julius suggested I might try and do something to you ? "

" Why not ? You weren't very sympathetic with Allard or Inskip."

" I think it ees time you had another drink," said Bizard. " Let me refill your glass."

He refilled it ; brought it back to Vallon. He said : " Tell me how you knew about Allard."

" It's simple enough," said Vallon. " Mrs. Clavering saw Allard and asked him to go and find a daughter—a fake daughter—so that this girl could get the money that was supposed to be coming to Lolita del Erest and which she, Paula Clavering, could control. A week or so afterwards she discovered that the financial arrangements had been altered ; that it wouldn't do her any good to have a fake daughter, or any daughter. Also, she believed that the real Lolita del Erest was dead. So she told Allard to lay off. But Allard wasn't laying off. He'd been over here and he'd seen you. He'd got the fake daughter. She was all ready for production, together with the documents you gave him to substantiate his claim that she was Mrs. Clavering's daughter. Allard, who expected to make a lot of money out of this case, wasn't going to take that lying down. So first of all he made an appointment to meet me to ask my advice. Then he wrote a letter to Dyce, Grant & Dyce, the lawyers, trying to make a deal with them ; telling them that if they'd guarantee not to take proceedings against him he'd tell them a story that would interest them."

Bizard said : " And how it would have interested them ! These lawyers, their ears would have flapped . . . hey ? "

" It would have knocked them for a boundary. Allard could have told them enough to fix Paula Clavering once and for all, and he intended to do it unless she paid him off."

" My poor, poor Paula," said Bizard sardonically ; " Sometimes my 'eart bleeds for her . . . like hell it does ! "

He sipped his cognac with a sigh of enjoyment.

Vallon continued : " Allard didn't say what the story was in the letter. He put it in his pocket and, early in the afternoon of the day on which you killed him, he went down to Valasey Bay and he saw Julius Friday. He told Friday that he was going to make one hell of a stink ; that he was going to tell

Dyce the truth and that he was going to blow Mrs. Clavering sky high. Julius rather liked that. You know how much he loves, Mrs. Clavering, don't you?"

Bizard nodded. "I've never known a man 'ate a woman so much in my as Julius does our *delightful* Paula."

Vallon went on: "So Julius rang her up and told her. She wasn't in Valasey Bay, but Julius, who knows everything, knew where she was, and *she* telephoned *you*. You were in London, weren't you? And you went hot foot to Valasey Bay. You wanted to get hold of Allard and stop him by some means or another, but you arrived and couldn't find him. But you saw Friday, and Friday told you exactly what Allard intended to do later in the day. He told you that he was going to meet me at the Sierra Madre; that he was producing the girl; that he was going to ask my advice and, if it matched up with what he thought he should do, he was going to post that letter to Dyce. I think," Vallon continued, "that you had your meeting with Friday at the theatre. It would be empty at that time. And I imagine you left the place with him. Then you got rid of him because you'd noticed the scenery truck standing in the courtyard behind the theatre. You knew the form about the truck and the scenery; you ought to, because it was *your* theatre.

"So, having got rid of Friday, you looked in the truck. I think you found the two trade plates under the driver's seat, which is the place where a driver who drives new trucks under trade plates usually keeps them. You took off the truck's number plates and wired the trade plates on. You knew perfectly well there was only one road that Allard would take to get to the Sierra Madre and you drove there like hell. Well, you know what happened. You meant to kill Allard and you killed him."

Bizard said definitely: "But no ... that is *not* true. It ees perfectly true of course that I was forced to kill Allard, but I did not *mean* to kill him then. I hoped he would leesten to reason. Would you like to know exactly what happened?"

Vallon nodded.

Bizard said: "I will explain. Figure to yourself. Nobody of any importance knew that I was in England. Nobody of any importance had seen me at Valasey Bay. As you have said, my interview with Julius was at the theatre, which was empty. No one saw me take the truck. I was careful not to drive through the town, but round behind it on to the main road. When I arrived near the Sierra Madre I parked the truck in the side road that runs at an angle on to the main road. Then I walked down the road ; went through the path towards the Sierra Madre café, but when I got there I knew Allard had not arrived. There was no car outside. So I went back, and I drove the truck along the side road till it was almost on the main road.

" Then I saw Allard's car approaching. I thought he would slow down when he was driving towards the apex of the roads, but he did not. He accelerated. My original idea was to drive the truck out on to the road and make him stop so that I could talk reason to him before he kept his appointment with you. Well, it was unfortunate. He was travelling very fast, and the truck was heavy. I drove out of the side road a little too late." Bizard spread his hands in mock dismay. " And I hit him. It was too bad. He was doing about sixty miles an hour. I knocked him into the ditch. I got out of the truck and looked at him. It was obvious to me that he was badly smashed up, and it was quite obvious to me that he would not be interested in talking to you or anybody else for some time. So I jus' walked away. Jus' like that ! I walked feefteen miles and caught a train back to London."

Vallon said : " And that was that !. . ."

" *Mais oui !* . . . That was that ! But you understand theese Vine Allard was a fool—what the Americans call a piker. I theenk he ees better off where he ees."

Vallon said : " You make it sound as if you'd done him a favour, don't you ? "

" Well . . ." Bizard's round face broke into a pleasant smile. " When things are necessary I make up my mind and I think very quickly."

" That's as maybe," said Vallon ; " but under English law you committed a murder. What's the good of you saying you never intended to kill him ? I suppose you're going to tell me that you never intended to kill Inskip ? "

" No," said Bizard decisively. " I will not tell you that. In this case I am telling you the truth. I definitely intended to kill Inskip, but I wonder if anybody would be able to prove it."

" And why shouldn't they ? " said Vallon. " You know

175

what happened, don't you ? Hear the evidence and work it out for yourself. I came over here to Montreuil to see Mrs. Clavering. She was staying at the Château at Montreuil. She told me that she believed Allard had produced a fake daughter ; that her instinct told her that. I asked her some questions and she told me that in his search for his daughter he had been over here to Le Touquet to see you ; that he'd found a girl through you. But Mrs. Clavering couldn't find you. You'd gone away. Then a funny thing happened. I came over to Le Touquet the same night and I found you very easily. I should think anybody looking for anyone in Le Touquet would go to the Chatham or the Casino. It occurred to me that it was very funny that I should have found you so easily when Mrs. Clavering had had such difficulty. Then it occurred to me that she might have seen you ; that she might have seen you and concocted the little story you told me. Well, I was right. That stuff you told me about Vine Allard seeing you, meeting the girl, asking her leading questions, giving her all the information he was supposed to be finding out, was a lot of nonsense, wasn't it ? That was to support her in her theory that the girl was a fake so that she could get rid of Allard ; so that under Clavering's will she'd have all the money and no fake daughter."

Bizard nodded his head. " Very good . . . very, very good. . . . Tell me some more."

Vallon went on : " She went back to London the next day. I had put another idea into her head. I'd put the idea into her head that Allard might have told her partner Inskip about this business. So she had to see Inskip. She went to see him that night. Inskip had the letter Allard had written to Dyce and, although the letter told him nothing, he thought here was a good chance for blackmail." Vallon grinned. " You can't imagine how Paula worked on Inskip. I arrived at his office to see him the same night after she'd gone. He was half-drunk and his handkerchief was covered with lipstick—*her* lipstick." He grinned at Bizard. " She's pretty thorough, isn't she ? She was even prepared to make a pass at Inskip to get what she wanted."

Bizard said : " But how right you are. But apparently she did *not* get what she wanted."

" No," said Vallon. " Inskip went down to talk to her at Valasey Bay the next day. She promised at the interview in his office that if he came down to Valasey Bay and handed her the letter she'd give him the money he wanted. She made an appointment at ten o'clock at Valencia House. She made the appointment late in order to give you time to get there. My guess is she telephoned you here from London the morning after she'd seen him in his office. She told you that Inskip had Allard's letter ; that he was prepared to sell it, and that she'd made the appointment at Valencia House. And you told her you'd handle it.

"You flew over. You went to Valasey Bay that night. You waited for Inskip. Well, it's my guess that if he'd had the letter on him he might have got away with it, but he hadn't. He told you that the letter was in a safe place ; that nobody knew where it was except him. This was all you wanted. You broke his neck."

Bizard said : "That ees not exactly true. I broke his neck with a ver', ver' nice little ju-jitsu neck lock. It ees almost painless. He never knew what had hit him."

"Perhaps that was as well for you," said Vallon. "You took him upstairs and you pushed him over the top of the empty water tank. I found him there."

Bizard said : "I see. . . . You found him there. And you 'ave the letter ? "

Vallon nodded. "I have the letter. So what are you going to do about it ? "

Bizard said : "I am going to give you another drink." He went on : "If I were a logical man I should kill you of course. One murder more or less would not make very much difference. I would have lots of time to clear out. That ees what I ought to do."

"But that's what you're not going to do. You're not going to do that because if you did you'd ruin the thing you've been trying to do all your life, wouldn't you ? If you killed me there's no hope for you or anyone else. Do you see what I mean ? "

Bizard said slowly : "No, I do not see what you mean."

"Supposing I help you a little. You remember that Allard came to see you at Le Touquet and that you produced Leila Mannering as the missing Lolita del Erest ? "

Bizard said : "I remember ver' well."

Vallon went on : "Allard was afraid of one thing, wasn't

he ? He said to you : ' It's all right about this girl, but supposing the real girl turns up ? That's not going to be so good for anybody, is it ? ' You were prepared for that. You produced the forged death certificate showing that Lolita del Erest had died at the age of seventeen with double pneumonia. That was a fake, but the other document you gave him wasn't."

Bizard said : " You mean the birth certificate of Lolita ? "

Vallon nodded. " That's what I mean. Now listen to me, Bizard. You say you're bored. I think you are. I think life has caught up with you, but I'm going to tell you something that might be of great use to you. I think you've led a funny sort of life. I think you've been chasing moonbeams. I think that the worst thing that ever happened to you was having anything to do with Paula Clavering."

Bizard said smilingly : " My fren', I theenk you are ver' clever."

" I just follow my nose, that's all," said Vallon. " And in the process I went to see the lawyer Dyce a day or so ago. I asked him to show me Augustus Clavering's last Will and Testament. He showed it to me. The will laid down that if the daughter of del Erest and his wife is produced, and if she is found to be the legal daughter of these two, born in wedlock, then the estate shall pay her the sum of four thousand a year tax free. You see what I mean ? The will says nothing else—just that."

There was a silence ; then Bizard said : " *Mon dieu* . . . now I am beginning to see what you are driving at, M'sieu Vallon. *Now* I am beginning to see."

Vallon said : " You hate Paula Clavering. You'd do anything in the world you could to get back at her. Well, can you imagine any better way than this ? Just think for a minute and realise what her position is now. Although maybe she was innocent of any actual connection with your two murders she could easily be brought into it. But my dead client wouldn't want that. It's my business to keep her out of it, but she'd still have a hell of a punishment, especially if somebody like myself and the lawyer Dyce, who is a very straight lawyer, saw that the terms of Clavering's will were carried out in the spirit and the letter."

Bizard got up suddenly. He asked : " What ees your first name, M'sieu Vallon ? "

" My name's John. They call me Johnny."

Bizard said : " Finish your drink. I want to give you a toast."

Vallon drained his glass. Bizard refilled the two glasses ; gave one to Vallon.

He said : " Johnny, I think you are straight. I am going to put my shirt on you. You are right when you say that I hate Paula Clavering. How right you are. You are right when you say that you know what I want. Will you give me your word that you will do what your dead client and I would like you to do ? "

Vallon said : " Of course I will. I give you my word."

Bizard raised his glass. " Here ees your good health, Johnny. And here ees good-bye. I have done a lot of mad things. I was silly to do that to Allard. But that ees how it ees sometimes. I act before I think. And all the time I had this idea in my head. Inskip was a dirty blackmailer. I did not like him. I do not mind having killed him. Now there remains for me only one last murder—almost what you call a judicial one. Here's to you, Johnny." He drained his glass ; watched Vallon finish his. Then he said : " It ees late and I expect you have a lot to do. I give you my good wishes. Good night, Johnny."

Vallon picked up his hat. He went to the door ; opened it. He walked away from the villa and looking over his shoulder saw Bizard framed in the open doorway. Then the door shut.

Vallon began to walk towards the main road. He had walked fifty paces when he heard the shot.

He turned ; began to walk slowly towards the villa.

CHAPTER TEN

ACCOUNT RENDERED

VALLON ARRIVED at his office at three o'clock in the afternoon. He stood, looking out of the window at the busy street below, smoking a cigarette, thinking about Madeleine. He wondered where she was ; what she was doing.

Vallon thought that Madeleine was pretty good value. She had everything. She was beautiful and she behaved herself as a beautiful woman should. She did not chase moonbeams and she did not expect a man to turn into Sir Galahad merely because she loved him. A process which attacks most women in love.

The telephone on his desk rang. It was MacIlroy.

Vallon said cheerfully : " I thought you'd be on my tail."

" I've had to move, Vallon," said the Detective-Inspector. " I couldn't hold out any longer. I've got in touch with the Valasey Bay police. They've moved Inskip from the tank, and he's at the local mortuary now. Incidentally, your time's nearly up, isn't it ? "

" Yes . . . but it's all right. I can do all the talking you want now. Perhaps you'd like to meet me later to-day. I'll call you on the telephone."

MacIlroy said : " All right. I'll be here until about eight o'clock to-night. And don't leave it later. The Assistant Commissioner is raising hell. He thinks I've behaved in an unofficial manner. He's not a bit happy."

" Too bad," said Vallon. " But I understand. If I were an Assistant Commissioner at Scotland Yard I wouldn't be happy either. Wasn't it Gilbert or Sullivan or both of them who said a policeman's lot is not a happy one. But don't worry, I'll be seeing you."

MacIlroy said sarcastically : " Thanks a lot ! "

He had hardly replaced the receiver when the bell jangled again. The girl on the switch-board said : " Mr. Dyce—long distance from Valasey Bay."

Vallon said : " Put him through. . . . Good afternoon, Mr. Dyce."

Dyce said : " I'd like to see you as soon as possible, Mr. Vallon. I think there is some sort of explanation due from you. As you know, I've left the conduct of this case entirely in your hands, but there are all sorts of things happening which I don't like at all."

Vallon asked : " What things ? "

" I understand that the man Julius Friday has started one or two rather appalling rumours. You know what sort of place this is. The town's buzzing with talk."

" Who are they talking about ? " asked Vallon.

" They're talking about Mrs. Clavering. And I don't like it.

Vallon said : " I bet you don't. But keep your hair on. It's no good getting excited, you know. And if it will interest you, she isn't Mrs. Clavering, anyway."

" What do you mean ? " asked Dyce. " I——"

Vallon said : " Look . . . why don't you take it easy ? I don't propose to talk on the telephone. I want to see Mrs. Clavering myself. I'll probably be down some time this evening."

" She isn't here," said Dyce. " She telephoned me this morning from the Savoy and, having regard to the situation here, I thought it much better that she should stay there."

" I think that was wise of you. Anyhow, don't worry your head. There's nothing you can do—not at the moment. You'll get a full report within the next few days—and our account. Maybe I'll bring it down myself. Good afternoon."

" Just a moment, Mr. Vallon," said Dyce angrily. " I don't think you're taking the right attitude about this situation. Mrs. Clavering is my client—a valued client—and her reputation must be protected. You will remember I told you that the other day and you agreed with me."

Vallon said : " I'm doing plenty for Mrs. Clavering at the moment. If her reputation is getting a little part-worn in Valasey Bay that isn't my fault, and all you can do at the moment is to sit still and wait until the rumours die down—or some fresh ones start. So long."

He hung up the telephone. He thought that even lawyers could be human. He grinned. He thought it was tough that Dyce should be so keen on Mrs. Clavering. He wondered if there was anyone she had ever met, with the possible exception of himself and Julius Friday, who *hadn't* been crazy about her.

He picked up his hat ; went downstairs ; hailed a passing taxicab ; told the driver to drive him to the Savoy.

Ten minutes afterwards he was shown into her sitting-room. She was reading a book. She wore a black wool afternoon frock with one or two pieces of exquisite jewellery. Her face was white and there were deep circles under her eyes.

She got up. She said : " Well Johnny—— ? "

He said : " I don't know whether it's well or not, but I think you've been fairly lucky, Paula—as lucky as you can be."

She asked : " What do you mean ? "

" I suppose you couldn't guess, Mrs. del Erest ? "

She sighed. Her shoulders drooped. " So you know all about it, Johnny ? "

" You bet I do," said Vallon. He took out his cigarette case ; lighted a cigarette. He stood looking at her. " Del Erest always hated your guts. I should think during those two years of marriage you must have given him hell. He was probably very much in love with you, but even then I suppose you were the same, Paula—out for what you could get—men and money. Falling for people all over the place, searching always for money and more money, and another man. So he walked out on you, and he took your child with him. Personally, I think he was wise. I wonder if you ever think of those days."

She said in a low voice : " I spend too much time thinking of those days. I've been a fool, Johnny. I know I've been a fool."

Vallon grinned. " I think you flatter yourself. You're no *fool*, Paula. But let's get on with the story. Two or three years went by. Del Erest went all over the place, getting himself mixed up with all sorts of shady business. He'd parked the child somewhere and she was being looked after. One thing del Erest always did, whatever his faults may have been, was to try to look after his daughter. He meant to try and educate her ; to try and do the best he could for her. Things got pretty bad for him, I should imagine, and he was tied up in one or two near-the-knuckle enterprises with a lawyer named Miguel Salvador. This Salvador is in jail at the moment. He was sentenced for fraudulent insurance claims. So it was easy to see what they did. Salvador and del Erest came to the conclusion that it was time that del Erest died. They probably took out a policy in Salvador's favour. Then soon afterwards they had what they thought was a bit of luck. The hotel they were staying in caught fire. Here was the chance they were looking for. Del Erest cleared out quickly, but Salvador swore he'd seen him die in the fire, and the next morning identified a burned body by a ring of del Erest's. Well, it's easy to put a ring on an unrecognisable corpse's finger, isnt' it? Anyhow, they got away with it. I suppose the Insurance Company paid up and this enabled del Erest to go to France, calling himself Rene Bizard—a Frenchman. And to start his theatrical business in France.

" Soon afterwards, del Erest—now Rene Bizard—met a rich woman who wanted to marry him. So he married her. In order to make his death look good, Miguel Salvador wrote you a letter. He told you that del Erest was dead and he sent you some money which del Erest was supposed to have left you. I think that was rather nice of him," said Vallon. " So that was that ! You believed the letter. They knew you'd believe it if some money arrived. So you wrote off del Erest in your mind.

" The years rolled by, and then Salvador wrote you again and told you that your child was dead ; that she'd died of double pneumonia. He did this at the instigation of Rene Bizard who had been looking after the girl, seeing that she was properly educated. He didn't want any contact between her and you at any time . . . at least he didn't then.

" Then an interesting thing happened—one of those things ! Julius Friday, scouting around England to find a cheap repertory theatre in the country where a company could be started, found the place he was looking for—Valasey Bay. And he saw you and recognised you. He also found that you had married Clavering and he heard that you were going to institute a world-wide search for your missing daughter ; that Clavering was going to finance that, and when the girl was found to settle money on her. So he did the obvious thing. He got into touch with Rene Bizard—your real husband—who was very much alive, whose new wife had died, who hated you and who was hard up.

" He told Bizard who, chuckling to himself at the situation, came over and saw you. You were in a spot, weren't you, Paula ? Bizard could have ruined you at any moment by going to Clavering and telling him that he was your husband and still very much alive, but he didn't do that. He told you

183

he was going back to France. He suggested to you that you employ the services of Allard whom he knew to be a crook, and said that he would find a fake girl. He told you that your daughter Lolita was dead, and you believed that because of the letter you had had from Salvador.

" In the meantime Clavering had been talking about employing me to find the girl. Well, you talked him out of that. You saw Allard. You told him to start the search for this girl and you told him he'd have to produce a fake girl because the real girl was dead. Allard agreed. Friday suggested to him that a Mr. Rene Bizard in France might be able to give him some information about the girl. Allard went to France, saw Bizard, met the girl whom he thought was the fake girl. Bizard gave him some documents and told him they were fake. One was the birth certificate, which was in fact the proper birth certificate of Lolita del Erest. He also gave him a letter written by his friend Miguel Salvador before he went to prison, telling him of the death of Lolita del Erest. So Allard thought he was safe and on a good thing.

" But when he came back to England, you didn't want the girl because under the new arrangement you'd get the money anyway. Now you were scared stiff. You knew that your marriage to Augustus Clavering was null and void ; that you'd committed bigamy. So you had to do what you were told. You made a vain attempt to stop Allard producing the fake girl, but he wasn't inclined to stop. He wanted money. But one thing you didn't know, Paula, and Allard didn't know. Only two people knew—Bizard and Friday. The supposedly fake girl who was produced by Bizard wasn't a fake at all. *She was the real girl*—Lolita del Erest. She had not died. She'd been brought up and educated by Bizard, through the agency of Friday, as Leila Mannering—an English girl—and with a cynical sense of humour Bizard had sent her to the theatre at Valasey Bay to play in his company. I think she's a very nice girl.

" When Allard began to make trouble, what could you do ? You were in a spot, but Bizard got you out of that. He killed Allard—he says accidentally—but whether it was accidental or not, he killed him, and his reason for doing that was obvious. Allard believed that the girl was fake. If Allard had told his story to Dyce, the whole business would have been washed up and over. You'd have been finished. Everybody would have been finished. There would have been no money for anybody, and Bizard wanted money for the girl because, believe it or not, he was very fond of her ; she was about the only thing in the world he cared about. And the situation amused him. If his plan had succeeded his real daughter would be looked after and financed by Dyce, and all the time you would be believing she was a fake. I think this idea must have amused Bizard quite a lot. D'you see why, Paula ? "

" Why ? " she asked dully. Her eyes never left his face.

Vallon said : " Here was Bizard's chance to get back at you and make you suffer hell. He was prepared to allow Allard to think the girl was a fake, and he wanted you to think she was a fake. Allard thought he'd be able to make a deal with the girl and get some of the money but Bizard would never have allowed that. He intended the girl to keep her own money and he intended to blackmail you and make you pay his and Allard's cut out of your own inheritance. Rather a nice idea, don't you think ? "

She shrugged her shoulders.

Vallon went on : " Well, you weren't feeling quite so bad, because now Augustus Clavering was dead. You believed that Bizard would keep quiet for his own sake. You went over to Montreuil to see him, and you did see him. You told him I'd been appointed to go on with the investigation. You told him that I'd probably find him somehow. So Bizard agreed to play ball with you. He agreed to suggest to me, when I did find him, that the girl was a fake. Bizard intended to implicate you right up to the neck if you made any trouble, so you daren't do it.

" Then, as a result of what I told you, you thought Inskip knew something. So you went to see Inskip, and when you found he had Allard's letter you agreed to meet him the next night at Valencia House, knowing that you could get in touch with Bizard in the meantime, and hoping that he would pay off Inskip. Well, he paid him off. But not in the way Inskip had suggested."

Vallon stubbed out his cigarette end. " It's a nice story, isn't it, Paula ? This is where the bill comes in."

She asked : " What is going to happen now ? "

Vallon shrugged his shoulders. " I don't know, but I can make a pretty good guess. Dyce was on the telephone to me this morning. He's a nice old boy and he's very fond of you. He thinks you're marvellous. I wonder what he'll think when he hears the truth." He grinned. "He was very angry with me because, apparently, Friday's been talking out of turn about you. And he can do it too, because nobody's got anything on Friday—not anything they could prove, anyway."

"What does my husband—my real husband—propose to do now?" She smiled suddenly—a hard smile. "If he tells the truth he'll implicate himself just as much as me, or anyone else. He's a murderer."

Vallon nodded. "He *was* a murderer. I went to see him last night and after I'd told him one or two rather interesting things he took the easy way out. He shot himself. He's dead. So you haven't got a husband at all now, Paula. It must be quite a change for you."

She said: "You say he shot himself because of something you said to him?"

"Yes . . . I told you that he was very fond of the girl. I was able to tell him something that pleased him immensely. I had a look at Clavering's will the other day, and in the paragraph relating to the money that was to go to your daughter when she was found it lays down that four thousand a year is to be produced from his estate for this girl providing she is the proper and legal daughter of Manuel del Erest and you, Paula del Erest. So, as Leila Mannering *is* the proper and legal daughter of Manuel del Erest and yourself, she gets the money. But nothing in Clavering's will regarding yourself is legally effective, because at the time he made that will, and at the time he died, you weren't his wife at all. I think that's funny, don't you?"

She said in a harsh voice: "So that girl will have the money?"

"That's right. She'll have four thousand a year tax free for the rest of her life, and you'll get nothing—not a penny—unless——"

She said: "Unless what?"

Vallon said: "I think, when I've seen Dyce and told him all about it, he'll be prepared to make some sort of a deal with you. Apparently, there are monies connected with Clavering's estate, the bestowal of which is left to the discretion of his executor. I'm going to suggest to Dyce that if you like to get out of England and stay out, he might make you some payment—something like five hundred a year."

She laughed. " Do you think I could live on five hundred a year ? "

Vallon shook his head. " I don't think *you* could, but you'll probably find a means of making some more. Anyway, you'll take that sum and like it."

She said bitterly : " Why should I ? "

" If you don't," said Vallon, " I'm going to tie you in with the Inskip murder. I'm going to suggest that when Inskip told you he was coming down to Valasey Bay for the purpose of blackmailing you for the Allard letter, you got in touch with Bizard. Only *you* could have told him where the appointment was. I'm going to suggest that you instigated Inskip's murder."

She got up. " But that's a lie. I never did. I hoped that my husband would buy him off."

Vallon said : " I believe you, but who else will ? If all the evidence in this case was put before a jury I know what they'd do, don't you ? They'd find you an accessory before and after Inskip's murder. So you'll be a good girl. You'll take the five hundred, and you won't worry that nice girl who's your daughter. You'll stay in this country until I've got this business settled up with Dyce and then you'll clear out. You can go to France ; anywhere you like, so long as you don't come back here. Dyce asked me to look after your reputation and whatever happens I'm going to do that—my way ! "

He picked up his hat. He said : " So long, Paula. You'd better stay here until you hear from Dyce. I think you'll find he'll do what I tell him to do."

She said : " Just a minute. . . . Why can't we be friends, Johnny ? If you only understood. . . ." She came towards him. She put her hand on his arm.

Vallon said : " Look, why don't you stop trying, Paula ? It's all over. You've had it. So long." He went out of the room.

She stood in the middle of the floor, her arms hanging by her sides, looking at the door. Then she said a very rude word. Then she picked up the vase from the table ; flung it at the mirror over the fireplace. Then she flopped on the settee ; began to sob bitterly.

.   .   .   .   .   .

At nine o'clock Vallon and MacIlroy came out of the saloon bar of the Five Stars public house in Long Acre. They began to walk towards Piccadilly.

MacIlroy said : " You wonder why I don't like private detectives. You bring me in on this case. You give me two murders. You use me to get that Safe Deposit box opened because you have to have that evidence before you can go any further. Having done all that, all I have to do then is to collect a dead body from a tank in Valasey Bay. And I don't get any murderer because he's shot himself. I think you're a hell of a guy."

Vallon shrugged his shoulders. He grinned at the Detective-Inspector. " Well, MacIlroy, if you'd been me, what would you have done ? "

The other said : " What's the good of going into that now ? I'm me ... not you. And I've got to go back and talk to the Assistant Commissioner. He's going to kick me from here to Hades for not having taken the proper legal steps days ago."

Vallon said : " What could you have done ? Anyway, you've got a very interesting story to tell him."

MacIlroy put up his hand ; stopped a passing cab. He said : " Good night, Vallon. The next time you get in touch with me at the Yard and ask for something, just see what happens."

Vallon smiled cheerfully. " I know what'll happen. You'll be just as helpful as you were this time. Good night."

The taxi disappeared in the traffic.

Vallon walked back to his office in Regent Street. He went along the corridor into his own room. The night girl on the switch-board rang through.

She said : " Mr. Vallon, Miss Thorne's here. She's in the waiting-room. She's been here for an hour. I told her you'd be coming back to-night."

Vallon smiled into the telephone. " Ask her to come in." He went to the door ; opened it.

Madeleine came in. She said : " Well, here I am, Johnny. Have you been good ? Has it been an interesting case ? "

He said : " I've been very good and it's been a very interesting case. But it's all over now. Supposing we go and have dinner together. Would you like that ? "

" I'd love it. You know, Johnny, I'm so fearfully sorry we missed each other when you came to Montreuil."

188

Vallon said : " Are you . . . for any particular reason ? "

She said : " Yes. First of all I wanted very much to see you, but, apart from that, there was a most lovely woman staying at the hotel—a Mrs. Clavering. I've never seen anybody quite so beautiful." She looked at him sideways. " I think she was your type too." She sighed. " I did want you to see her."

Vallon said : " Well, life's like that. Anyhow, the only woman I want to look at is you." He put his arm round her waist. " Let's go and have dinner, sweet. And you can tell me all about the lovely lady at Montreuil."

THE END